The Treasure in the East

By

Tony Myers

The Treasure in the East

Copyright 2023 by Tony Myers

All rights reserved. No part of this book may be reproduced or transmitted in any form without permission from the author. The only exception is in the case of brief quotations.

www.tonymyers.net

A note to the readers:

Thank you for picking up this novel. When I wrote my first book, *Singleton*, it seemed crazy to think of people actually reading my book. I thought if I could get a hundred people to read it, then that would be mind-blowing. Now, here as I sit and write this note, it seems incredible to think this is my seventh full-length novel, and I have a small fan base that is constantly sending their encouragement. I must say you guys are great, and these novels are for you. I can't thank you enough.

This book is an adventure featuring the explorer Marc-Claude and his companion, Cobra. I originally introduced these characters in my novel, *The War of the Kings*, but this book is written as a stand-alone. My hope is that it can picked up independently of the other novel(s), if desired.

Also, the last six chapters of this book contains a short story about Marc-Claude and Cobra called "The Journey of a Lifetime." Timewise, it occurs prior to the story of *The Treasure in the East* and *The War of the Kings*. I debated with myself whether it should be placed before the actual novel (serving as a prequel), or be placed it at the end of the book (serving as a supplemental story). In the end, I chose the latter, feeling that was a better fit for both stories. BUT, if you are one who would prefer to read in chronological order, then feel free to read the supplemental story first.

Overall, however you choose to read it, I hope this book brings you great enjoyment. Once again, from the bottom of my heart, thank you for picking it up and purposing to read it. You guys are great.

Acknowledgments

A big "thank you" to the fans! Their encouragement is both motivating and inspiring. I never want to take them for granted.

To the editors, Charity and Stephen, I appreciate your work and your patience. *Your grate peoples, ain't nothin' gettin' past u.*

I want to thank my kids for the excitement and fun they bring to my life. Each day is an adventure with them. As they get older, I hope these books will encourage them to live life to the fullest and have courage.

Again, I want to thank my wife Charity for being by my side through the ups and downs of life. Who knows what will happen next... but we will face it together.

Above all, glory to God. He created the mind and the will. He is the very inventor of the idea of a story. In all my ways I want to acknowledge Him because He makes my path straight. I'm thankful for the new life I have in His Son.

To my kids,

Love God, help others, and enjoy the journey.

The Treasure in the East

Prologue

The wealthy merchant Von Dechauer sat in his dark room in the middle of the night. A large coat with a hood covered his head. The sleeves stretched down past his hands in an attempt to keep warm. The only light was the glow of a nearby candle. He preferred this setting. It helped him to think and plan, especially when he had a headache. He rubbed the bridge of his nose as he thought about what to do next.

His business was far and wide, and his wealth was extensive. With this great wealth, power had been achieved. Other merchants submitted to his demands and rulers of smaller kingdoms often cowered in fear of him. In his possession were no less than thirty shipping vessels and many storehouses for goods. Many of these houses lay in secret, scattered among the kingdoms of the world. They had to be in secret since a large portion of his goods had been stolen or at least ripped off from an unexpectant client. He didn't mind trading and doing business in a civilized fashion, but if he knew he could get his goods for a discounted price, then why not take advantage of it. Laws and regulations were only a minor nuisance for him.

Von Dechauer was stationed in the Northern Empire, situated to the north of Mendolon and the Northern Territory. This was the only place where his reputation didn't overshadow his production. Though the citizens knew of his exploitations and corruption, he did provide for them the necessary resources of tools, wood, metal, medicines, and a variety of foods, among other items. Also, the Emperor and the other authorities weren't intimidated by him, because their kingdom was much more powerful than any others in the world.

The merchant reached forward and poured himself a glass of wine. He took a sip before leaning back in his chair and closing his eyes. He wished he could sleep, but this headache was too strong. Many worries plagued his mind and, as of late, his worries were getting worse. His reputation was falling apart, and as a consequence, he was losing income. Many people weren't intimidated by him anymore and even two of his vessels had been robbed in the last couple of months. All of this would have been completely unheard of a year ago. And at the moment this all seemed too much for him. A part of him wished he could ignore it all and continue to grow his wealth. That was what he had done in the past, but he knew this time was different.

He could trace the start of his problems to nine months ago. That was when a small-time thief named Marc-Claude eluded him and thwarted his plans. And though this was a frustration and an inconvenience, the rumors about it were far worse than what actually happened. The latest gossip was that a simple pirate courageously intercepted a shipment of prized weapons from Dechauer and cleverly stole them in plain sight. And now, this pirate Marc-Claude was living a life of luxury in a hidden mansion on an island. It was a story of triumph, and other thieves thought that if a simple pirate acting alone could rob from Von Dechauer, then why couldn't they do the same?

Even thinking about all this brought greater pain in his head, especially since the real story of this thief was actually much simpler. Von Dechauer simply hired Marc-Claude to steal something for him, and he didn't follow through with his agreement. Though this was unacceptable, it was nowhere near the story of triumph that was reported. He knew all of this had to be stopped. He would have to find Marc-Claude, capture him, and punish him severely. Only then could the rumors stop, and new tales could begin of Von Dechauer punishing those who stood in his way.

There was a knock on his door. "Come in," Von Dechauer responded.

One of his assistants walked into the room. "Sorry for the intrusion."

"This better be good," Von responded, leaning forward in his chair.

The assistant couldn't see his boss' face because of the hood, but this didn't bother him. He knew he'd been struggling with headaches. The assistant spoke urgently. "There have been sightings of Marc-Claude in the east."

He immediately leaned forward, "What? ... Tell me more."

The assistant took a step closer. "Yes, supposedly he's gathering information, trying to find The Lost Treasure of Sophia."

Von Dechauer shook his head. "Foolishness!" he exclaimed. The Lost Treasure of Sophia was supposedly a vast amount of gold and jewels hidden on an island in the east. Many had attempted to locate it during the last hundred years, only to fall short. The story had now evolved into that of a legend. Few knew about it and even less talked about it. There was also always a sense of mystery to the treasure as if there were more to it than simple wealth. Within the treasure supposedly was a door of possibilities and new opportunities that were beyond this world. And if the promise of gold wasn't enough, this added mystery made the legend of the treasure more intriguing.

Dechauer continued. "He thinks he can find what so many others have given up on.... such nonsense."

The assistant stepped closer. "I agree, my lord, but it may help to detect where he's going."

Von Dechauer rubbed his chin and thought deeply. He liked where this was heading. He'd been chasing Marc-

Claude for too long without getting close. Six months ago, he learned that Marc-Claude was hiding in plain sight in Grimdolon. He had immediately ordered a team of hunters to infiltrate the kingdom and find him. But by that time, he found out that it was far too late. Marc-Claude was already out to sea and sailing away before his forces could enter Grimdolon. Von Dechauer tried to inquire from others out at sea as to where he went, but information was scarce. This new information concerning Marc-Claude's hunt for the treasure was his best clue in a long time.

His train of thought was broken by the assistant. "Do you want me to send out some of your men to hunt him down?"

Von Dechauer opened his mouth to shout out an affirmative, but quickly stopped himself. He didn't want to be too hasty. This may be his best chance to catch Marc-Claude, and he didn't want this opportunity to slip out of his hands. He cleared his throat and spoke under control. "Why don't we go a different route? Let's hire the most skilled explorer we can to track him down."

"Yes sir, how much money should we spend?"

Von Dechauer snickered as he sat back in his chair. "There's no price I won't pay. Simply find someone to track down this thief they call Marc-Claude."

Chapter 1

Marc-Claude was out to sea. He was steering his ship across the water. The skies were clear, and he was looking for another boat on the horizon. A bandana was tied around his head and a well-groomed goatee donned his face. He was wearing a white shirt, and a gold chain hung around his neck. It was the last of the gold on the ship. His money had run out long ago, and now he was looking for another boat he could steal from.

But even though he was out of resources, his confidence had never been higher. Various stories and rumors were spreading about him far and wide. Though some were exaggerations, he didn't care. Rarely did he come across a boat where there was no one who had not heard of the triumphs of the infamous explorer and seafarer, Marc-

Claude. It was the fame he'd always dreamed of. And now, in his mid-thirties, each day he woke up with a smile, ready for a new adventure. Now, if only he could have the wealth to go with his prestige.

His large companion Cobra was on the deck lifting a steel bar, working his muscles. Cobra wasn't lacking for strength, but rather wanted to enlarge his arms. He'd recently drawn a tattoo of a sun on his bicep, and he thought it might look better if his muscles were slightly larger. At one time he was known as a skilled tattoo artist, but those days were long gone. Now, he simply doodled on himself from time to time, nothing more. Currently he was a man of the sea, and first mate to his best friend.

Marc-Claude looked down at Cobra, straining as he lifted the weight. Marc-Claude could see the skin on the top of Cobra's balding head starting to turn red. The sun was high in the sky and very few clouds were in sight. It was near perfect conditions for a sunburn. "Hey mate, don't you want to put on a hat? At this rate you're going to feel miserable by the evening."

Cobra put down the weight and took a breath. He was wearing a shirt without sleeves. Flexing his bicep he stared at his tattoo, hoping it was larger. He then looked up at his friend. "Yeah, maybe I should. I, um, wanted to get in a good workout while I was feeling strong."

Marc-Claude kept looking out to sea. "It's not your muscles I'm worried about. It's so hot out here, within minutes you're going to fry your skin." Marc-Claud raised his eyebrows, "...and maybe your brains."

"What's that supposed to mean?" Cobra said defensively.

Marc-Claude squinted with a painful expression. His last statement about brains touched a soft spot in Cobra's mind. Cobra was very sensitive about any joking concerning his intelligence, or lack thereof. Ever since he was a kid, Cobra was often ridiculed by others. His large stature and awkward smile made him an easy target. Knowing this, Marc-Claude had been working hard on holding his tongue, but often he would let a witty comment or a sly insult slip. Marc-Claude recognized this and tried hard not to criticize his best friend, even if it was just in jest. He knew it was something he'd need to work on.

"Oh sorry, mate," he said with a smile. "Trying hard to tame the tongue."

"I understand." Cobra said with a hint of sadness in his voice.

Marc-Claude felt disappointed in himself. "I'll keep at it," he said, trying to reassure his friend.

Cobra nodded before speaking. "Thank you... As the saying goes, 'If you can tame the tongue, you can be a perfect man.'" Marc-Claude rolled his eyes. He'd heard this statement a number of times over the last few months. Cobra read it in a book and never forgot it. He'd been quoting it ever since.

"Just grab a hat, will you? Before you get burned."

"Ok," Cobra said, walking into the small cabin and grabbing a hat. Marc-Claude was constantly encouraging him to put on a hat or a bandana ever since the time Cobra's head was burned so badly, it made him irritable for days.

And for someone as big and strong as Cobra, a bad temper out of control could crush others at a moment's notice. It made him thankful that Cobra usually displayed a spirit of gentleness.

Eventually, Cobra exited the cabin, wearing a large captain's hat. "What is that?" Marc-Claude exclaimed, in a humorous tone.

"Well, I thought it'd protect my nose as well." He paused to adjust it and looked up at Marc-Claude. "You sure you won't be needing it?"

Marc-Claude forgot he owned such a hat. "No, you know it takes a lot for me to get burned." It was true. Marc-Claude's skin was very tan and rarely, if ever, did he burn. "But don't you think it's a little much, mate?"

"I kind of like it!"

Marc-Claude smiled big. A clever insult came to mind. He knew he shouldn't say it, but he couldn't resist. "It kind of reminds me of the time when we were on that snowy beach and you hit your head on that sandbar. I imagine you couldn't think straight after that as you..." He stopped mid-sentence, caught off guard by another ship on the horizon. The insult would have to wait.

He pointed out to sea. "Cobra, do you see that boat?"

Cobra peered out and saw what Marc-Claude was referring to. It looked close to two miles away. "I do."

"Haha!" Marc-Claude's joy couldn't be contained. "That looks like a boat to me. I think we're looking to increase our wealth substantially. A boat this big will help to grow my reputation as well. Oh, the joy of being me!"

"Are you sure this is a good idea, Marc-Claude?"

"Absolutely!" he responded, turning the wheel. "You know we're out of money and supplies." It was true they had spent all their money journeying to the east, looking for a mysterious treasure. After assisting the king and queen of Grimdolon in the War of the Kings, they received a large payment that now had been spent. At first Marc-Claude was wise and bought supplies and various needed resources, but then he had gotten lax in spending his money and purchased various luxuries and the finest food. Cobra, on the other hand, bought something he'd always wanted—teeth. For many years he had been missing many of his teeth, and upon finding a doctor who could put fillers in, he jumped at the first opportunity he had. A silver smile now was displayed with every grin.

The boat was now within a mile. "Here's the plan," Marc-Claude said, talking quickly. "We jump on board before they realize we're enemies. We'll pull our swords quickly and hold them out to threaten the first person we see. You be sure to look big and intimidating. Try hard not to smile, and flex as much as you can."

"But what if there's a lot of them?"

"Ha," Marc-Claude laughed in a dismissing manner. "Their vessel doesn't look like a war ship. No more than ten common men, probably only a few fighters in the group. We can take them."

A sad look formed on Cobra's face. "But... but what if they're nice people?"

"They're out to sea, mate. Chances are they're pirates."

"Like us?"

"No... no, not pirates. Not us. We have morals. A greater mission."

Cobra took a deep breath. He knew his friend couldn't be deterred. "Well, it sure seems like we're pirates," he said under his breath. Marc-Claude chose to ignore this statement.

The boat was now just a few yards away. This vessel was about three times the size of theirs. They caught a glimpse of one man on board moving some crates, but they knew there had to be more. This boat was too big to be manned by only a few individuals, especially seeing that this was most likely used as some type of shipping vessel.

It looked as if they had just now been noticed. A man stood at the helm with his hand over his eyes. He had been distracted by those working onboard, but now was trying to get a grasp on the boat coming toward him. He then turned and shouted to others on board that a boat was beside them.

"This is it, Cobra." Marc-Claude said, with great focus. "Remember these first few moments are crucial."

"Ok," he responded, somewhat passively.

Their boat rammed into the side of the larger boat. Marc-Claude threw a grappling hook on the boat's railing to secure his boat. The two men then quickly jumped up and grabbed the side of the boat and pulled themselves up. They landed on the deck and saw three men approaching them.

They appeared to be guards, but didn't look too concerned, simply curious.

One of the guards started to speak, but Marc-Claude didn't wait. Without warning he pulled his sword and held it to the throat of one of the men. "Whoa!" said the guard with eyes opened wide.

Cobra, upon landing on the deck, threw his shoulder and forearm into the chest of one of the men, who stumbled backwards. As he was falling, Cobra grabbed the guard's sword and held it out. This made the third approaching guard stop right in his tracks and hold up his hands.

"On your knees!" Marc-Claud shouted to the men. They quickly responded, even voluntarily pulling their swords and throwing them to the side. "Good!" he said, pleased with their response.

He continued, trying to sound calm, yet intimidating. "Now, if you men would be so kind, we are two weary travelers, looking for a little assistance. We don't want any trouble, simply a portion of your goods and then we will be on our way." None of the men answered, but simply looked at one another.

Marc-Claude cleared his throat. "Gentlemen, I'm not feeling overly patient and would like an answer."

One of the men spoke, trembling. "Umm, we were given an abundance of figs at our last stop. We're more than happy to let you have some."

Another man spoke up, "Yes, we have two types of figs. In a region to the southeast there's a variety whose harvest is later, and it gives them a sweeter taste. I would think you'd like ..."

"I don't want figs!" Marc-Claude shouted. "We're particularly looking for gold and any currency you may have."

"But I like figs," Cobra responded.

"Quiet, Cobra!"

One of the guards continued. "Please sir, we don't have much as this is..."

"Hello!" another man said, interrupting them. All turned to see the man approaching them from the right. He was dressed in an impressive fashion wearing a long robe. He looked to be in his mid-forties with long golden curls running down his back. His beautiful wife stood by his side, dressed royally as well. Her long blondish-white hair radiated in the sun's light. They stepped close to their guards.

"Don't come any closer!" Marc-Claude spoke out. "We don't desire harm to come to you, only payment."

"We mean no harm to you as well," said the robed man. He appeared relaxed. "My name is Corleone, and this is my wife, Gabriella." She bowed slightly.

"How do you do?" Cobra smiled, bowing in return.

"Well!" Marc-Claude spoke loudly, still trying to sound intimidating and trying to take a hold of the conversation. "I'm sorry to say your vessel has been apprehended by me, the most famous thief Marc-Claude, and now I will demand a portion of your goods for..."

"Oh, Marc-Claude!" said Gabriella with excitement. "We've heard reports of how you foiled the efforts of Von Dechauer. How wonderful! Word has spread of your good in the West. Is it true you've saved captives and assisted in the War of the Kings?"

Cobra nodded. "Oh, yes, everything is true... or most of at least. Some of the reports are clear exaggerations. Like for example, he didn't wrestle any tigers, or fight a knight in hand-to-hand combat." He paused to chuckle. "Marc-Claude couldn't do those things, and also there's the one about how..."

"Can we stay focused here?" Marc-Claude interrupted. "To put it bluntly, we're robbing you."

Corleone laughed slightly. "Oh sorry, my friend, what do you need?"

Before Marc-Claude could answer, the couple's three kids came running toward them from the cabin. "Papa, what's happening? We saw the other boat and we were hoping we had visitors."

"We do, my loves," Corleone said, giving them each a big hug. "This is the famous Marc-Claude, who came to visit with his friend... uh... sorry, I didn't catch your name."

"Cobra."

"Oh, thank you. Cobra is his name."

"Wow," all the kids responded in joy. "This is exciting."

Marc-Claude stuck his sword into the deck in frustration. "Excuse me! But we're getting distracted. WE

ARE STEALING from you! Please give us some gold or money, or jewels, or whatever you have... anything but figs."

"But I like figs!"

"Quiet, Cobra!"

Corleone continued, "Certainly, sir, anything you desire."

"But Papa!" his oldest boy spoke out. "If they steal our money and food, what will we give to the orphans?"

"The boy's right," one of the guards added, still on his knees. "You know the orphans' resources are scarce. Very little can be spared."

Corleone smile and shook his head. "Oh, it's ok. Remember the mantra we say each day, 'Do not worry saying 'what shall we eat' or 'what shall we wear.' Each day has enough trouble of its own. Tomorrow will worry about itself.'"

Cobra lowered his sword and turned to his companion. He spoke in a whisper. "Marc-Claude, we can't steal from these people. They're working with orphans."

Gabriella spoke up. "It's true. We help run a home for orphans in a kingdom west of here. We help gather and deliver resources for them." She paused a moment as she stepped closer to the men. "But surely, we can spare some resources."

Corleone stepped forward to join his wife. "Yes, we're definitely happy to help. We can even help with your haggard clothing and find you men some new outfits." He faced Marc-Claude. "Is it true your feet are irregular? Oddly enough we heard a passing story of how a certain shoemaker made you a special pair of boots."

Marc-Claude didn't know how to respond. He was still trying to think of a way to turn this back into a robbery. Looking for the right words to say, he slowly opened his mouth, but he couldn't find the correct wording. Before he could speak, Cobra interjected, "Yes, that story is true. Marc-Claude has developed large bunions on his feet."

"Cobra! You didn't have to add that."

Corleone laughed. "Come, let us put down our swords. Won't you men join us for some refreshment?"

"Oh, most certainly," Cobra said, handing his sword back to the guard, still on the ground. "Sorry, friend. No hard feelings." The guard smiled nervously in response.

Corleone started to lead Cobra toward the deck cabin. "So, what are you two fellows doing this far out?"

Cobra grinned. "We're actually on a mission, looking for the Lost Treasure of Sophia."

"How exciting!" Gabriella added.

"Cobra!" Marc-Claude yelled out, frustrated that he had revealed to them their mission. He closed his eyes and smacked his forehead as he now stood there all alone.

Everyone stopped and turned to look at him. A few moments of silence passed before Corleone spoke. "Won't you be joining us, Marc-Claude? We truly do have the most exquisite figs."

Marc-Claude looked out at the sea and shook his head. He took a deep breath before speaking in a defeated tone. "Fine... lead on."

Chapter 2

Marc-Claude and Cobra sat at a table close to the shore line. They were at an outdoor eatery enjoying a plate of seafood and a little bit of wine. Once again, the sun shone brightly as they enjoyed themselves. They talked casually as boats came to dock and sailors would disembark for a quick meal. People from various parts of the world would stop by as this spot was well-known among seafarers.

A full day had passed since they shared a meal with Corleone and his family on their boat. Marc-Claude and Cobra had had a hard time leaving as the family was so generous with their food. During the time with the family, it had taken Marc-Claude a long time to relax and start enjoying himself, but eventually he settled down and forced himself to forget about the supposed robbery. Even before they left, he told their kids a few sea stories and gave them some trinkets from their ship. Currently the men were enjoying this meal, courtesy of the money given to them by Corleone.

The two men continued to sip their wine. The restaurant where they sat was a small oasis on a tiny island, no larger than a half mile long and a mile wide. There were only a few structures on this island, one of which was a covered outdoor eating area and a kitchen building. A few dozen yards away stood a storage building along with a large cottage that housed the owner and her workers.

The owner was named Roselin. She was a fiery red-haired woman with freckles. Her business was well-ordered and well-run. She demanded excellence from her employees, so in consequence she paid them generously. Like Marc-Claude, she was in her mid-thirties, and to any observer she was a woman of the sea. Her clothing reminded one of a pirate, and her brown hat almost always sat on top of her head. She was gifted at remembering names, and though one wouldn't describe her as 'warm,' generally she gave each person their due respect. Marc-Claude had sought her out for information regarding the treasure. In speaking briefly with her earlier, she said she would engage with them, but it would have to wait, for now she was busy with customers.

Cobra swallowed a bite of fish. "This has to be some of the best fish I've ever had."

"I agree, mate, truly a treat." Marc-Claude picked up another filet. "In all our travels, I do believe we've never had fish quite like this."

"Should we order more?"

Marc-Claude gave a side smile. "You read my mind, but maybe we should wait till we talk to the owner. It looks like the customers are slowing down, so it shouldn't be too much longer before she comes around."

"Have you ever met her?"

"No, at least not that I can remember. I've heard of her, and many others say she's good at collecting information as sailors come through."

"I see," Cobra nodded in response. Like Marc-Claude, he was hopeful this would lead to information regarding the Lost Treasure of Sophia. In the past few months they had come to many dead ends. They could only hope that this one opportunity would provide at least a clue to lead them to their next destination. He was anxious to find this treasure.

Cobra glanced to the side and could see two men staring at him. They looked like some type of military captains. They quickly turned away and snickered. An angry expression formed on his face. It was obvious they were mocking his appearance. One of the men looked back at Cobra, only to turn away again, this time with a stronger laugh. Cobra clinched his fist. A part of him wanted to jump up from the table and instantly give these guys a pounding they would never forget. But another part of him preached self-control. No matter what these guys were saying, it wasn't worth it. He would have to put it out of his mind.

His anger slipped away, and his fist relaxed. For as long as he could remember he was a target of sneers and insults. Going back to his childhood, other children would pick on him for his lack of intelligence and looks. Not only would they say he was stupid, but he looked the part as well. At times he let his anger get the best of him, and he would try to fight other kids. This just led to more insults, particularly kids describing him as a big angry ogre. The insults then tended to follow him into adulthood. He felt as if nothing he could do would change his reputation. When Marc-Claude gave the offer to join him on the seas, he jumped at the opportunity. He left home and never looked back. Though his life wasn't perfect, Cobra was thankful for this opportunity in life—an opportunity to start fresh and have a new beginning.

Cobra was interrupted from his daydream by his good friend. "Here she comes, mate. Let's hope this goes well."

Roselin confidently approached the two men and sat down at the table. Nothing about her seemed rushed or curious. She displayed an attitude of focus as this was her normal routine. Because of the amount of activity she observed and rumors she heard, she was often asked about various information from mariners and pirates. Part of this was her way of marketing her restaurant. Pirates and seafarers were constantly looking for news on the seas. Others came to her to introduce themselves in order to gain fame. They wanted their names and exploits to be mentioned and in circulation among those out to sea. In the end it proved to work and kept the customers coming back.

"Good afternoon, gentlemen. I hope you enjoyed the fish," she said, unwavering. She was still wearing her hat.

"Oh yes," Marc-Claude said as cheerfully as he could. "It was quite splendid."

"Very good, excellent," Cobra added.

Roselin smiled slightly in return. "Well, what can I do for you men?"

Marc-Claude spoke. "Oh, yes, allow me to introduce myself. My name is Marc-Claude and I..."

"I know who you are." she said with a look of offense. "Your story is spreading quickly. Maybe faster than anything I've heard. You're quite far from home."

Marc-Claude was taken aback. He was speechless. He felt pleased with himself for catching the attention of this woman. She heard new names and stories every week, and for him to be remembered like this was truly an accomplishment for him.

The conversation quickly became awkward as it fell silent. Cobra and Roselin could tell Marc-Claude was caught in a daydream. After a few more seconds passed, she cleared her throat loudly. This jolted Marc-Claude back to reality. "Ah... thank you, yes, where were we?"

"You needed something?" she said, holding out her hand.

"Of course, we've recently heard of a treasure to the east of here. We were looking to glean as much information as we can concerning its genuineness and ability to be found."

Roselin folded her hands, still unmoved by the conversation. "It depends on what treasure you're looking for. We get hundreds of pirates coming in every week, most are either fleeing authorities or looking for treasure."

Marc-Claude held up his index finger. "Yes... but let me say, that we're not pirates, simply treasure hunters. Looking for any treasure put before us."

Roselin laughed slightly in reply and gave a clear look of disbelief. She thought about challenging this point but decided to instead let it go. "So what treasure is it that you boys are looking for?"

Marc-Claude leaned forward and spoke quietly. "It's called 'The Lost Treasure of Sophia.'" He sat back in his chair. "Have you heard of it?"

"I have. It seems to be more of a legend than a reality. You may be on a fool's errand."

He shrugged. "Possibly, but me and Cobra here have heard enough that we figure it's worth the journey."

"Do you have a map or anything?"

"No, just leads."

Roselin smiled in amusement. "How have those leads turned out?"

"Well... um..." Marc-Claude stumbled over his words. "You see, it's not quite developed... you know... I think..."

Cobra shook his head. "We're stuck now. Got nothing. Almost no money. Poor, simply out of luck."

Roselin raised her eyebrows and started to stand up. She'd heard enough. This situation sounded like a dead end, and she didn't want to waste any more of her time on this conversation. "Maybe you men need a job first. Thank you coming today, but..."

Marc-Claude knew he needed to stop her. He knew she would have something to share. He would only need to find it within her. "No, please, don't leave, Madam. Surely, there's something you can think of to help us." He reached down beside him and held up what little money he had.

She laughed slightly in pity. "Cute. But you can keep your money. I'll send over two pints of our ale, on the house, but other than that..."

Marc-Claude stood up to match her. He wasn't opposed to begging. There was pity in his voice. "Please, don't leave. There's got to be something you can give us. Something to direct us further along."

Roselin paused for a moment to think. She took off her hat briefly, displaying her red hair. She rubbed her chin as she thought about anything or anyone in these parts that could help them. It was just a moment later that she spoke up. "There is one thing that comes to mind."

"Oh, and what's this?"

"There's a governor to the southwest here, in the city of Bourges. He is a collector of rare books, and he has an extensive library. There may be something there that could help you." She sat back down. "But you probably won't be able to see it. He's not very hospitable... and not well-loved by his people for that matter."

Marc-Claude smiled and nodded. He slowly took another sip of wine. Dumar Pasure was the governor's name. Marc-Claude had stolen from him twice, many years ago. One of those times Marc-Claude robbed his boat while the governor himself was on board.

"You know of whom I speak?" she said curiously.

He brought down the cup from his lips. "Oh, yes, Governor Dumar Pasure is his name, or as I like to affectionately refer to him... Dumpas."

Roselin broke out in laughter. Others in the restaurant looked over. It was a rare sight to see this stern businesswoman laugh like this. Marc-Claude and Cobra joined her. It was close to a half minute before she could speak again. "Dumpas. I'll have to remember that one," she said, rising to her feet.

"Thank you for your help," Marc-Claude said appreciatively. "You truly believe his library is extensive enough where it would contain the information we need."

"Certainly. I've heard he's spent a lot of money acquiring rare books." She placed her hat back on her head. "Thank you for the good laugh. It truly has been a while since I've laughed like that." She turned to walk away. "I'll send over a few fish filets with the ale. All are my treat."

"You are too kind," Marc-Claude said loudly. He watched her as she left. He was smitten.

❦

Von Dechauer was in his study in the dark when he heard a knock on the door. His hood was still pulled over his head and only a few candles were lit as he still had a headache. "Come in," he said loudly.

The door opened and in walked one of his servants. He seemed anxious with information. "Sir, he's here!"

He sat forward in his chair, excitedly. "Great, bring him in."

"Yes, sir," the servant left the room to achieve the task. Von Dechauer rose from his seat and rubbed his hands. He began pacing around the room. He had hired a mariner, who he thought was capable of finding Marc-Claude. Dechauer was happy that he had responded so quickly.

His mind went back to how much gold he should offer for this job. He wanted this mariner to know he was serious about this pursuit, yet, he also wanted to be sure that he didn't offer too much. As a crafty businessman, he was always looking to save as much money as he could. He had never worked with this individual before, and he was wondering how much he traditionally charged.

Close to two minutes passed before the servant returned with the mariner. His name was Riché. He was short, but well-built. One would guess he was about 180 pounds, while standing at 5'6. Most of his weight was muscle. His attire appeared to be one who was trying to dress like a pirate, but it was obvious he was not. His clothes were too well-kept, and he was well-groomed and very clean cut. His brown hair was long, pulled back into a ponytail. As he walked in, the look on his face tried to display an air of confidence.

The most astonishing thing about this individual was that he was only seventeen. He was from a very rich family. In fact, his family had funded his expeditions since the age of fourteen. As a young man he did have great talent out on the sea, but Von Dechauer mainly called on him for the resources behind him. His father seemed bent on supporting his expeditions, and even painted on the side of his boat, "Riché the Explorer." Von Dechauer detested the counterfeit aspects of this seafarer, but knew he needed his resources and his skills. Plus, he knew that Riché and his father would jump at the opportunity to increase their prestige.

The servant spoke confidently. "May I present to you, Riché the Explorer."

"Welcome, thank you for coming." Von Dechauer said. "Do you think you can the find the one I'm looking for?" He didn't want to waste any time in getting down to business. He was incredibly anxious to have Marc-Claude caught.

Riché, on the other hand, was caught off-guard. Von Dechauer's presence wasn't what he was expecting. He froze in silence. Between meeting someone famous and finding his appearance to be different from what he imagined, his mind became clouded, and this left him bewildered for a brief moment.

Dechauer grew impatient with the silence. "Well, can you do what I ask?"

The young explorer snapped back to reality, back to confidence. "Of course, there hasn't been a mission yet that I've backed down from. We've traveled far and wide, never to be outdone by anyone."

Von Dechauer despised even the way he talked. It was like he was pushing the words hard out of his mouth when he spoke. Dechauer rubbed his head, feeling like his headache was growing stronger. He walked back over to his desk and put on his glasses. He casually poured himself a glass of wine. Speaking quietly, he continued to address Riché. "How many men do you have?"

"I have ten men on my ship. We move fast. I know we can catch this thief and catch him quickly, just as you ask."

Von Dechauer finished pouring his drink. He walked closer to Riché and spoke casually. "Will a year's worth of gold suffice?"

Riché was struck again with silence. Even for a boy from a wealthy family, this was way more money than he'd ever been offered. Clearing his throat, he tried to gain his composure. He wanted to act like this was a normal occurrence for him. He had a passing thought to negotiate the price but hearing the sheer large amount caught him completely off guard. "Um, sure, that will be acceptable."

"Good. I will give you a quarter of the reward initially and the rest when you bring him back, preferably alive."

"Oh, yes, I can do that."

Von Dechauer walked back around his desk and sat down. "Very well, this one, Marc-Claude, was hiding in the east, looking for treasure. His reputation is growing steadily, so it shouldn't be difficult for you to find him."

"Oh, leave it to me. He stands no chance against my abilities and resources." He paused to smile and point toward Von Dechauer. "I can almost assure you this won't be the last time you call on my services."

Von Dechauer felt the urge to insult this young explorer. His arrogance was more than he could take. If he thought he could find someone else who could better help him, then he would have pursued that option. Nevertheless, he fought his impulses and decided to keep moving forward. "Fine, that's all I need from you. You can be on your way." He brushed the air with his hand in a backhand fashion, trying to clear the room.

Riché was not leaving just yet. There was still something on his mind. "But, hey, there's still something I've got to know."

"Yes, speak your mind," Von Dechauer said, somewhat irritated.

"What about this treasure? Is there any hope that this thief will actually get close to it?"

Von Dechauer shook his head. "It's a fool's errand. If he has any treasure, simply bring it back to me. Now, will you please leave? I'm not feeling well."

Riché didn't like this answer. A frown formed on his face. "Very well. Next time you see me I'll have your thief." He turned and left the room. His mind was still on the treasure.

Chapter 3

The small ship pulled into the port town of Bourges. After speaking with Roselin, Marc-Claude and Cobra had left immediately for this area, traveling a full day and through the night to get there. They were anxious to follow up on the lead she had given them as any news of the treasure was motivating.

The two men quickly disembarked after securing their ship. They were dressed in their best, clean attire with hats and vests. People passed by all around as imports and exports were coming in and going out. This time of year a lot of fishing boats were coming and unloading crates. They took note of those around them as they worked. Mostly everyone was working hard, very busy with various tasks. There wasn't an idle hand in sight.

The two men needed information. Marc-Claude stopped a middle-aged man carrying a crate of fish. "Excuse me, sir?"

"Not now," the man said, upset. He then went on his way.

Marc-Claude knew they would get nowhere with these people. He turned to Cobra. "Let's head into town and see what we can do."

"Good idea."

The two men walked through the crowds of people into the streets of the small port town. Most of the people looked sad. From what Marc-Claude knew of this town, these citizens were burdened with heavy taxation, and tough economic times had fallen on them. It seemed odd that this area wouldn't be more prosperous, yet on the other hand the governor, Dumar Pasure, was known for his heavy-handed regulations on the people. All new businesses and trades were met with protocols and various procedures that seemed to weigh down the town's progress.

Off in the distance Marc-Claude could see the governor's mansion standing tall on a hill. It truly did stand apart from the rest of the town. It was made of brick and looked to be at least three stories high with countless rooms spanning each floor. Judging as best as he could from this distance, Marc-Claude figured a ballroom was probably on the lower floor. A short wall stood around the outside of the mansion, creating an outdoor courtyard or greeting area. In his mind he pictured some type of fountain or statue sitting in the middle of this courtyard area.

"Nice house," Cobra commented, seeing Marc-Claude eyeing it.

"Yes... indeed."

"It makes me want to get inside, just so I can see it."

Marc-Claude snickered. They kept passing others on the street. The two men could see that their appearance and clothing made them stand out. They were given more than a casual stare from some. "One thing for certain, we'll never get in there undetected in these clothes, mate. Let's find the tailor."

They walked through town for a half hour before they found the tailor shop. It was a small shop placed between two other places of commerce. The building looked old and in need of repair. A rickety old sign hung out front, swinging slightly in the wind. Without hesitation, the two men walked in. A bell rang as they entered.

The inside of the shop was much different from the outside. It was well-kept, with beautiful coats and trousers on display. One could tell instantly that this tailor probably supplied clothing for dignitaries and other people of prestige. Being a port city, it easily lent itself for clothing to be traded and shipped far and wide. Many of the display stands in the shop seemed to be made of wood and looked hand-crafted with designs etched in the wood. This led them to think that maybe this tailor was a carpenter as well.

Toward the back of the shop, Marc-Claude could see a man working tediously on a piece of clothing. The man was wearing a leather apron. He was bald with a beard full of grey. Seeing the two men approach he looked up at them thoroughly, eyeing them up and down before looking back at the coat he was working on. He spoke softly. "I can tell you men aren't from around here."

Marc-Claude gave a half smile and laughed slightly. "Well, that's why we're here. We hope you can help us with that."

The man looked up at them again and particularly looked at what the men were wearing. He looked back at his work and spoke slowly and quietly. "I'm not sure you men know what kind of shop this is. Most of these garments are exported. Some are even sold to a monarch in the west. The prices aren't usually within the range of seafarers or pirates."

Marc-Claude cleared his throat. "I would have you know we're not pirates."

The man didn't respond at first, but rather kept working on the jacket in front of him. Marc-Claude looked over at Cobra who shrugged in return. The two casually turned and looked again at the items in the store. It was clear that this shop would be outside their price range.

Marc-Claude started walking toward the exit when the tailor spoke out again. "What do you need new clothing for anyway?"

Cobra spoke up this time as Marc-Claude was now fifteen feet away. "We were hopin' for something that would be presentable before the governor."

The tailor looked straight at Cobra. There was a slightly angry, slightly puzzled look on his face. He put down his tools. "And why would you want to see that dreadful roach? He's no friend in these parts."

Marc-Claude turned on his heels and headed back toward the tailor. This was music to his ears. He couldn't get back to the counter fast enough. "Aw, yes, my good friend. We were hoping to somehow get a meeting with the beloved, or not so beloved, governor."

The tailor shook his head. "He won't see you. He doesn't care or listen to the concerns of common people, only dignitaries. Even I, as an esteemed tailor, couldn't see the light of his face."

Smiling in return, Marc-Claude started to realize this man could be an asset in their plans. He decided to disclose it all to him. "But you see, maybe you could help us. We desire to explore his personal library, and maybe help ourselves to some of his collection… and maybe some of his money."

The tailor was intrigued. He rubbed his fingers through his beard, straightening it. "What do you men have in mind?"

"Um, mate, maybe you could help us think of something." He was going for complete honesty as he thought this man was now fully engaged in the conversation. "We didn't really have a strategy, but we were going to scope things out, maybe see what our best options were, and then execute a plan."

The tailor slowly stepped around the counter. They could tell his mind was working and the beginning of a plan was forming. Walking close to the men, he paused a moment to think through options. A half-minute passed before the tailor spoke again. This time he spoke with confidence. "I think I know of a way in, and a way I can help you."

Marc-Claude's eyes grew wide. "Aw! This sounds great. I'd love to hear it."

"In one week, governor Pasure will have a formal ball for different officials and their spouses from our kingdom and beyond. They're gathering at his mansion. I can get you men outfits that are worthy of the occasion."

"Would you know of the best way to get into the event?"

The tailor nodded. "I would suggest the most obvious."

"And what would that be?"

"Secure an invitation."

Marc-Claude liked where all of this was headed. He placed his hand on the tailor's shoulder. "Let's talk more."

The tailor looked toward Cobra. "Go lock the door and we'll come up with a plan."

◆◆◆

Cobra woke up suddenly, crying out. He was sweating from a bad dream. It was the middle of the night. He looked across the room and saw that Marc-Claude was still fast sleep. He looked unmoved. They had spent the latter part of the afternoon and evening with the tailor, learning all they could about Governor Pasure's home and his upcoming event. They made a plan to infiltrate the event and find their way to the governor's library. While inside they would need to wait for a simple distraction and then sneak into his personal library. From there they would need time to search through his resources and see if he had any possessions that would further help them. According to the tailor, Governor Pasure did have a vast collection, and it was almost certain that he would have at least some information concerning the treasure.

When evening approached, the tailor invited them to stay with him. He was pleased to work with Marc-Claude, since he knew he planned on foiling Pasure's event. Like Roselin, he found much pleasure in the governor's nickname, Dumpas. He appreciated any insult directed toward Pasure. For far too long the tailor had been a victim of the governor's harsh taxation and rules of folly. Many times he had thought about packing up shop and moving to another area in the kingdom, but then he would think twice because this city had been his longtime home. Above all, the tailor was delighted to help them if it meant disrupting the governor's plan, and possibly helping the village, even just a little.

Taking a deep breath, Cobra laid back in bed and tried to close his eyes. He quickly found it futile to try to get back to sleep. His dreams had been too vivid this time. He turned to look out the window. There was a little bit of light coming in as a new day was beginning. He slid out of bed and walked toward the window.

The house was on the edge of town, and their window looked out onto the vast rolling hills of the countryside. Truly, it was a beautiful sight to behold. It was what he needed after such nightmares. He'd been doing well for a while, going a long period without any bad dreams. It was truly unfortunate that they were back. Most of his dreams involved other people, kids and adults, shouting at him, reprimanding him. It was a little discouraging to have the dreams come back so suddenly and without warning. They were dreams of the past. Dreams of his life and of the ways he had fallen short as a person. Cobra wondered if this was an indicator of how he felt he was always on a search in his life. A search to better himself. A search to leave behind his short-comings and faults. Maybe all of these thoughts were cluttering his mind and seeping into his dreams.

    He looked back over to Marc-Claude, who was still sleeping soundly. He then looked back out the window. His mind began to drift to the treasure in the east, wondering if they'd ever find it. Usually, he was only mildly interested in the treasure itself. He often thought that he actually enjoyed the hunt and the expedition more than the wealth the treasure generated. But this was altogether different. He longed to find this treasure. With his whole heart he sought after it.

    According to legend, there once was a young woman of wealth named Sophia. She was of noble blood, high esteem, and untold riches. Yet in spite of these, her heart longed for the simpler things of life. She grew tired of her wealth and the fame it brought. Eventually she came to the conclusion that she would do anything to break free from her life of wealth and prestige. She sold her assets and traded all her possessions for gold and jewels. She searched far and wide for a place to dispense her riches. Supposedly she grew obsessive with her search for the perfect place to conceal this treasure of hers. And as time would have it, after searching far and wide, she found a mysterious island where she could hide her wealth. She then set sail, leaving hints as to where she had gone. Many would have liked to ask her about her clues and seek more information, but unfortunately, according to legend, she was never seen or heard from again. So many clues scattered, so many tales spoken, and through it all, the legend of the treasure grew. Today it seemed as if any talk of the treasure was shrouded in mystery. It was like there was a hidden secret about it that people couldn't verbalize, like there was both a veiled reward and danger to it.

All of these thoughts filled Cobra's mind. Along with Marc-Claude, he had read every report or clue brought to them. And recently he had purposed in his heart that after everything he had read, he would stop at nothing before he found the Lost Treasure of Sophia.

The sun was now in the sky as dawn was upon the world. A new day was before them.

Chapter 4

A week had passed, and it was now the day of the governor's party. Marc-Claude and Cobra were dressed in extremely fine attire made exclusively for this event. Marc-Claude wore a burgundy coat with a gold pattern on the sleeves and collar of the coat. A vest was under his coat. His pants were of the same pattern with long white socks up to his knees and white shoes. Cobra, on the other hand, was dressed in a blue coat with gold accents placed in appropriate positions on the sleeve to get one's attention. The collar of a white shirt emerged from the top of his coat. A fake pair of glasses sat on his face. To say both men felt uncomfortable would be an understatement. The tailor tried to make their clothing as comfortable as they could, but even still Marc-Claude and Cobra struggled.

This past week the tailor had gone over all the information he knew concerning the governor's mansion, and particularly where the library might be. The tailor had never been inside, but he had lived in this town long enough to hear random facts in passing. He had also instructed the two men on procedures and customs across their kingdom. They wanted to blend in with the crowd of dignitaries as best as they could. Even Marc-Claude's accent was fine-tuned to sound more like a local. Cobra was instructed simply to smile and to talk as little as possible.

Currently it was nighttime, and the two men were walking through the port arena, looking for a way to secure an invitation. Their plan was to either bargain with someone, or simply take the invitation by force. Taking one by force would be tricky as many of the officials who pulled into the port had guards with them. Bargaining would be difficult and would need to be with the right individual, a dignitary that wasn't as wealthy. The tailor said they could trade a custom outfit from him for an invitation if need be.

So far, they hadn't come close to securing an invite. Two hours had passed. They had seen officials exiting their boats by the port, but none looked like a good candidate for bargaining or apprehending. The party was set to begin in a half hour, so they would need to think of an alternate plan soon or they would be out of luck and their whole mission would fall apart.

"I don't think this is goin' to work," Cobra said, looking through the crowds of people coming to port. "I think we're in deep water with this one."

"Just a little more time," Marc-Claude said, standing on his tiptoes looking over the heads of the people.

"Why don't we just sneak in like we've done at other places?"

"You heard what the tailor said. Dumpas isn't going to let us get anywhere close to his mansion without an invitation."

"Well, I'd say, let's just get back on our boat and try something else. There may not even be a book in his library about the treasure."

Marc-Claude didn't respond to Cobra. He wasn't going to take no for an answer. He'd snuck into many different areas over the years, and this was definitely not one that would stop him. Surely, there had to be a way, an opening to get into the event. He turned and looked behind him and saw a few more boats pull into port. "Follow me, Cobra."

The two men walked back to these half-dozen boats coming in to dock. The first boat looked to be officials from a southeastern region of Bourges. Two or three guards exited the boat with them, so they knew this wasn't an opportunity. The boat beside it looked old, as if it had been through a number of repairs. Marc-Claude noticed the writing on the side, and instantly recognized that it was from the island of Plaisir, just southeast of the Northern Empire. Marc-Claude watched closely for a few moments, and then he saw an opening, a way to get into the party.

He looked over at Cobra and smiled. "Follow me, my good boy."

"Ok," he said with a shrug. As Cobra followed his friend, he realized what he was moving toward. Exiting the boat were two ladies both dressed in exquisite dresses, one blue and one pink. Four attendants waited on them as the women took in the scenes. It was evident that this was their first time in Bourges. They were smiling and talking with one another joyfully as Marc-Claude approached.

"What are you doing?" Cobra said, grabbing his arm.

"Just follow my lead," he said, pulling away from Cobra and approaching the girls.

As he got closer to them, he spoke out, "Well, hello there, ladies, welcome to Bourges." His accent was thick and sounded authentic. He was pleased with himself.

"Hello," one of the girls said. "Thank you." The girls looked to be in their twenties, maybe ten years younger than them.

"You're very welcome. My name is MaClave, and this is my friend, Coberé. We are world travelers, who've had dealings with Mendolon, the Empire, and even the Forest of Saison. Seeing the symbols on the side of your boat, we just knew had to come up and introduce ourselves," Marc-Claude reached out for the hand of one of the girls and kissed it.

The two girls giggled. "Pleased to meet you. Yes, we are from the island of Plaisir."

"We work as actresses for a theatre," the other girl said.

"Wow!" Marc-Claude interjected, trying to sound genuinely excited. "You must be here for Dumpas'... I mean, err... Governor Pasure's party."

"Exactly!"

"Well, we're just headed there ourselves, and wanted to see if you ladies would help us find the way. This is our first time here, and we tend to get lost, even with simple directions." Marc-Claude forced a laugh when he was done speaking.

The two girls looked at each other, and the younger of the two spoke. "Oh, certainly. This is our first time here too."

The older girl cleared her throat before trying to speak officially. "Yes, we are here on official business for the owner of our theatre. We're here to represent him in all business matters... and ...." The girl stopped to laugh, looking over at her sister before continuing. "Honestly, we don't know what we're doing. We're just here to see the land and enjoy ourselves."

Marc-Claude began laughing again, but now it was genuine. "Haha! Well, this makes four of us." He knew he had found the right individuals to help them out. "Why don't we all find the party together. It will be a splendid time."

"Sounds wonderful," one of the girls said with a smile. "Our assistants here can help lead the way."

"Very well, shall we then?" he held out his arm in a gentlemanly fashion for the girl to take ahold. Cobra followed suit.

"We shall," the girls said, putting their arms around the men's. They then found a carriage and made their way toward the governors' mansion. The first step in the mission was accomplished.

∽∾

Marc-Claude and Cobra approached the party at the governor's mansion. Similar to what they'd seen from afar, the mansion looked magnificent. It was four stories high and looked spacious. A large gate blocked their entrance into the courtyard. Lanterns and torches illuminated the area. Guests were greeting one another inside the courtyard area. As expected, the guests were dressed in the most exquisite attire, and it was easy to see that most were either dignitaries or servants. Joyous music could be heard coming from the courtyard. Marc-Claude was a little surprised that this governor had the ability to put together a well-organized event like this one.

The two men had been talking with the girls in-depth while they traveled to the party. Their names were Leah and Rachel. They were enamored by Marc-Claude's stories. Oddly enough, the stories were mostly true, which made them flow more naturally. A few times he had let his accent slip but was quick to correct it. The girls' responses were different from each other. The older of the two, Leah, became more and more excited about the party. Marc-Claude made it sound like this party could be an unpredictable event, where something unexpectedly exciting could occur. Leah could only hope.

Rachel, on the other hand, grew more nervous. Being the shyer of the two girls, she hoped the evening would be a fun affair, but she didn't want to be caught up in any curious and bizarre situations like what Marc-Claude described in his stories. She wished for a simple evening of conversation and enjoying the frills of the party.

As they came within a few dozen yards of the gate, Marc-Claude started telling the girls a verbose story about a formal party that was on a ship that eventually capsized. It was very engaging, which was Marc-Claude's hope. He didn't want to speak to any officials as they passed through the gates. There were two doormen taking invitations, while two guards passively stood by their sides.

When they were within feet of the doormen, Marc-Claude began laughing at a point he made, before telling more of the story. The assistants who were with the girls handed the two invitations to the doormen. The group easily passed through into the courtyard, as the guards obviously thought the two men were related or married to the two sisters. Given how Marc-Claude and Cobra were dressed and their casual behavior, no questions were asked, and they were ushered into the party.

They walked a few feet from the entrance gate, and Marc-Claude instantly relaxed. He looked around to assess his situation. A dozen guards were stationed around the courtyard area casually watching the crowd, but also enjoying conversation with other important people. Under Marc-Claude's leadership the group casually strolled toward the entrance of the mansion. It would be there that he could further form a more thorough plan as to how to get a good look at the governor's library.

The girls stopped Marc-Claude on occasion, pointing to others they knew in the crowd. Though he didn't let on, this frustrated Marc-Claude a little as he was anxious to get inside, but nevertheless he decided to stay patient. He knew that the less rushed he appeared, the less suspicious they would be of his true identity.

Eventually they made it into the mansion where the others were starting to gather. A few hundred guests were talking casually with much excitement. It was an eclectic group, filled with diplomats, various warriors from different kingdoms, counts, nobles, and even a queen from a smaller kingdom. All were dressed in the most exquisite attire, and Marc-Claude wondered what the overall net value of the clothing in this room was.

The banquet hall itself was stunning. The room was bright, lit by various lights along the walls and six large chandeliers that hung from a high ceiling. Two large fireplaces blazed from each wall. Diamonds were used in various decorations along the walls and banisters. Light reflected off the diamonds, giving the room an even brighter look. A group of musicians played beautifully on the side of the room, and three or four tables of food and drink stood at pivotal positions. By anyone's estimation, it was truly extravagant décor, an obvious product of the heavy taxation brought upon the people.

"Wow... this is beautiful," Leah said, amazed.

"Yes... yes, it truly is," Marc-Claude said. He pulled his arm away from the girl. "Well, ladies, why don't Coberé and I go and grab us a round of drinks."

"Yes, certainly," the girls responded.

"Very good, right this way," Marc-Claude pulled Cobra toward a table where drinks were served. They weaved through the crowd as the music continued through the large room. Governor Pasure could be seen in a yellow coat with long tassels. He was a short, overweight man who usually had an inquisitive look on his face. Marc-Claude wanted to be sure to stay far away from him, just in case he was noticed.

They arrived at the drink table. "Marc-Claude, what's your plan?" Cobra said urgently.

Marc-Claude picked up two glasses of wine. "I'm not sure," he said casually. He handed a glass to Cobra. I'd say we wait and see if anything develops, and maybe an opening will be put before us." He continued to scan the room, assessing the situation. He could count at least thirty guards with a casual glance. These men seemed to be more attentive, and far less distracted by the important guests at the party. "Sorry to say, I think we underestimated the governor and how difficult it would be."

"What should we tell the girls?"

"I don't know, mate. Why don't you head back with the drinks and make sure they're in good spirits. I'll have a look around."

"All right," Cobra said, hesitantly. He was beginning to think Marc-Claude was in over his head at this point.

The men went separate ways. Marc-Claude casually walked up a flight of steps that led to a balcony area. He smiled and nodded at people along the way. He was trying his best to seem casual, yet not looking anyone in the eye for too long. A few diplomats descended the steps, passing him by. Thankfully, they took no notice of him.

Reaching the top of the steps, he found a few doorways that led to various corridors of the mansion. He wondered which to take. Looking to his left and right he could see a few dozen people congregating on this balcony, along with a handful of guards. No one seemed suspicious of him, but he knew he couldn't enter one of these doors without making a scene. He sighed as he began to think that he underestimated this mission.

He was just about to admit defeat when he saw his luck start to change. In the midst of the crowd, he spotted a familiar face. Bernard, the knight from Mendolon, was in attendance. Marc-Claude almost didn't recognize him as he was dressed formally. As opposed to casual clothing or knight armor, he was dressed in a formal tailored coat and slacks. Marc-Claude knew he had to take advantage of this opportunity. A plan started to form in his mind. He clapped his hands and descended the steps, excited for this new display of fate.

As quickly as he could, he passed through the crowd, looking to catch Bernard. Before he could reach him, Cobra stopped him again. "Marc-Claude!"

"Shh... not so loud," he reprimanded him. Between the music and the immense chatter in the room, most likely no one heard him, but nevertheless Marc-Claude didn't want anyone figuring out who he was.

"Sorry, I'm just noticing some folks are starting to become suspicious of me."

He brushed his hand aside. "Ah, no bother. I've got a plan, but it's going to take some coordination."

Cobra scratched the top of his head. "Oh, will we be a sneakin' around, with one of those stealth plans of yours?"

Marc-Claude smiled. "Oh, no... I plan on causing a scene."

Cobra's eyes grew wide. He knew what his best friend was referring to.

Chapter 5

Marc-Claude moved closer to where Bernard was standing. The knight was currently talking informally with a group of a half-dozen officials from another kingdom. They were all holding glasses of wine and looked to be completely relaxed. Bernard looked different from the last time Marc-Claude had seen him. He appeared more confident as he carried himself with more esteem. This was particularly impressive, knowing that he was only in his mid-twenties and many of the officials in front of him were twice his age.

The group was laughing casually when Marc-Claude joined the group. He began laughing obnoxiously as he walked up. The laughter of the others quickly quieted as they turned to see who had approached them. Marc-Claude kept laughing as he spoke. "Oh yes, a good laugh indeed, hahaha."

The group looked at each other with suspicion as they wondered about this newcomer. A few seconds passed before one of them spoke up, holding his chin high. "And who might you be?"

"Oh..." Marc-Claude held out his hand and smiled. "My name is MaClave. I'm from the northeast."

"How do you do?" one of the officials responded, shaking his hand.

"Fine... fine." Marc-Claude said, using a fake accent. "I just saw my old acquaintance, Bernard, and I wanted to come by and give my greetings."

Bernard looked closely at the man in front of him. A puzzled look formed on his face. One of the officials turned to him. "Monsieur Bernard, do you know this man?"

The young knight looked perplexed and began scratching his chin. "Well, I can't say I do. Or at least I don't think I remember him."

Marc-Claude laughed again. "Oh, yes you do, my boy. Lots of good memories of dinners, games, social excursions... and umm... hot peppers."

Bernard felt his stomach drop and his mouth dropped open. A period of awkward silence passed as the two men looked at one another. Eventually one of the officials cleared his throat and spoke. "It sounds like you men might have a history together."

Clumsily, Marc-Claude reached up and patted Bernard on the arm. "Yes, we're old friends. There's this funny story about him where..."

"Can I have a word with you?" Bernard quickly said, interrupting him and pulling him away from the group. The two men walked to one of the food tables.

Arriving, Bernard spoke quietly, but harshly. "Marc-Claude, what are you doing here? How did you sneak in?"

"Bernard, good to see you too," he said, feeling slightly more at ease now that he'd gotten Bernard's attention. "Cobra and I are here on a mission to find the Lost Treasure of Sophia."

"You think the treasure is here?"

He rolled his eyes at the absurdity of this question. "No, but we've heard that Governor Pasure's library is full of old books and manuscripts that may have the information we need."

"Oh, well how you plan to get in there? This place is swarming with guards."

He chuckled. "Funny you should ask." Marc-Claude pulled him in closer and spoke in a whisper.

∽∽

Across the room Cobra sat in a chair next to Rachel. The stairwell to the ballroom balcony was right beside him. They weren't talking, but both were quietly observing the crowd. Rachel was holding a plate of food and nibbling at different hors d'oeuvres. As a quiet young lady, events like this made her feel more shy than usual, and this occasion proved to be no exception. Oftentimes she fed off her sister Leah's personality. But in this instance Leah wasn't much help, as she was walking around the room, seemingly bored by the party itself.

Cobra scanned the room, wondering when Marc-Claude would begin his great plan. He felt anxious with what he had been told. There were a few things that would need to fall exactly into place for the plan to come to fruition, and with the amount of people at this party there were a lot of variables that one couldn't account for. Cobra wondered if there was anything else he could do to make sure everything went as planned.

He took a sip from his glass when Rachel spoke up, breaking his concentration. "Are you enjoying yourself at this party?"

Cobra looked over at her, not completely sure what to say. He cleared his throat and tried to quickly get back into character. "Oh yes, splendid. The food is great, and I enjoy talkin' with all the government people. They're... uh... nice."

Rachel smiled and looked down at her plate, amused by Cobra's answer. She then looked up at him. She spoke honestly, "You're not a diplomat, are you?"

Cobra about choked on the food he was eating. "Oh... um... what makes you say that?"

Rachel shrugged her shoulders, still smiling. "It's kind of obvious," she responded quietly.

Cobra didn't know what to say. He thought about fighting her suggestion, but knew there wouldn't be a point to it, and besides that, he didn't want to lie to this young lady. He smiled back in return. "Yeah, I guess you're right. We don't exactly fit in among all the officials."

She shook her head. "No, but I don't think we do either. I'm not used to events like this."

The two of them fell into silence as the music continued to play. They watched as the officials and diplomats mingled and ate the hors d'oeuvres. Cobra watched Marc-Claude walk around the room, talking to various individuals and getting various items in order. He even spent several minutes explaining things to Leah. Cobra was a little worried that either they might run out of time, or someone would notice Marc-Claude's scheming. Either way he tried to stay focused, trying to remember his part in the grand plan of everything. Cobra thought of all of their past endeavors through the years. He took solace in the fact that they had encountered much in the past and lived to talk about it. Hopefully by the end of this adventure, it would simply be another story to tell.

Rachel coughed slightly, snapping him out of his mental wonderings. He looked over at her again and grinned, showing his new teeth. She chuckled slightly, before speaking pleasantly. "Is your real name even Coberé?"

He leaned over to her and spoke quietly. "My friends call me Cobra."

"Close, I guess." She was starting to find it amusing. "Is that even your real name?"

Cobra paused for a moment. Now the conversation was getting very personal. Very few people he met knew his real name, but Rachel's sincerity had opened him up and made him feel comfortable. He didn't see the harm in it. "My real name is Curtis." He spoke, almost blushing.

"Curtis, hmm... I like it. I think it sounds proper."

Cobra smiled back, thankful she approved. For just a moment, he forgot he was out on a mission with Marc-Claude.

Rachel continued, "What are you guys actually doing here?"

Biting his lip, he wondered what he should say in response. After a few moments, he figured he might as well fess up. The truth had never led him astray in the past. "We're actually here trying to get a glimpse at Governor Pasure's library. We want to see if he has a book about treasure, particularly a lost treasure in the east."

"I see... sounds interesting."

"Oh, it will be. Me and my friend have been on many adventures in the past. This is gonna be no different."

Rachel was intrigued. "What kind of adventures?"

"Oh, you name it. We've probably been there." He looked over at her and lowered his voice a little more. "Do you know the Mendolon chaos from last year?"

"Yes?"

"Well, we were in Grimdolon for a while, helping to solve it."

"Really, wow! I imagine you have some stories."

"Oh, yes, if it was a different time, I'd love to tell you more."

"I'd like that, too," she quickly countered.

Cobra quickly turned and locked eyes with her, suddenly feeling nervous. He blushed again, before rubbing the back of his neck. "Umm... yeah... maybe that would be ice... I mean nice sometime."

Rachel gave him a side smile. "Maybe when things settle down for you, we can meet up again and talk."

Cobra nodded. "Yeah. That would be great."

The couple smiled at one another for a brief moment as a mutual interest was growing. This was a new experience for both of them. They sat staring, wondering what else to say. The two didn't have to wonder long before they heard a voice ring out among the crowd. "Attention everyone... attention!" They looked and saw it was Marc-Claude, standing on one of the food tables close to the middle of the floor. Others in the crowd were caught off guard as well. The governor looked particularly in shock.

Marc-Claude continued, speaking jovially. "Why don't we add some spice to this party with a little music." He then pointed at the instrumentalist across the room. He cleared his throat and began to sing.

"There once was a man, named Marc-Claude.

He danced, and he sang, and was feared by all.

No one could ever catch this man,

But so very many tried as he ran..."

The band easily joined in as the tune was a popular sea shanty. Across the room, Bernard put his face in his hands, wishing he could be somewhere else.

The room fell into a mixture of shock and amusement. Most in the room thought this was entertainment brought in by the governor, but a few knew this was some type of unruly disturbance brought on by a vagabond. Audible gasps could be heard, along with expressions of shock. The governor's face was turning red in fury as he instantly thought this was a drunken sailor that had snuck into his party. He was so angry that he couldn't speak.

Marc-Claude continued to sing and dance in beautiful rhythm as he masterfully jumped to another table.

"I look for treasures no matter where they are,
You'll find me out to sea or by the sand bar,
Just come with me and take me by the hand,
I'll show you a good time no matter where we land."

Cobra knew this was part of the plan, but he was still shocked to see it occurring. It didn't matter what Marc-Claude did the last time; it was like he always found a way to outdo himself. At first, he found it a little odd that Marc-Claude used his name in the song, but then again, if this plan worked, then this interruption and song would only continue to increase his fame.

A small part of Cobra wished that they could've just enjoyed the party for a few more minutes. He was finding great pleasure in simply talking with Rachel, but unfortunately, everything was now in pandemonium.

Not taking her eyes off Marc-Claude, she spoke matter-of-factly, "You know... he does have a good singing voice."

Cobra nodded, "That he does. That he does." He could have stayed there and watched Marc-Claude for a long time as his best song and dance moves were on display. It was especially entertaining to watch as he performed while jumping between different tables, dodging a couple of the guards who were there for security. He would occasionally kick a piece of fruit or another type of item toward an approaching guard before jumping away. All of this was done in near-perfect rhythmic dance.

A few guards ran down the balcony steps beside Cobra. This broke his concentration and was his cue to get started with his side of the plan. He turned to the young lady beside him. "Good-bye, Rachel, I'm sorry to cut our evening short, but I do hope somehow we can meet again someday."

"Thank you. I look forward to it."

Cobra smiled one last time before casually standing to his feet and moving up the steps. Another guard ran past him, looking quite fearful and out of sorts. He stayed focused moving up the steps. Reaching the balcony, he glanced over his shoulders and saw Marc-Claude land a cartwheel off one of the tables. After this Marc-Claude ran from a guard and slid feet first under another table. He then stood to his feet and kept singing at the top of his lungs. At this point, more in the crowd were beginning to think this was a planned performance. Many of the people began clapping along to the music.

Nevertheless, Cobra knew that it was time to proceed with the plan. A set of double doors was behind him. There were still a dozen guests on the balcony and one guard, but they were watching the chaos on the lower level. Cobra casually walked toward the doors, opened them, and entered in the hallway unnoticed.

The hall was decorated beautifully with carpets and lanterns lighting the way. A few more doorways stood on each side, but he knew these wouldn't be the entrance to the library. He kept moving forward a few yards to an area where the hall opened toward another larger room. Already he could see more doors. Cobra tried to think back on what the tailor had told him about how the mansion was laid out. Time was limited, so he hoped that everything he knew would point him in the right direction. He just hoped that Marc-Claude could keep distracting everyone for as long as he could.

※

Marc-Claude continued to dance across the room. By this time, he was on his second song and many in the crowd were joining in as this one was a familiar song. He got creative to avoid the guards as he ran through the crowd, who cleared the way for him. Now, he found himself once again on top of one of the tables with food. Quickly scanning the crowd, he could see Cobra was gone. It was now time for the second phase of his plan.

Looking again at the crowd, he found a particular guard that he wanted to engage. Glancing down at the table, he saw a large knife next to a ham. Without a moment to lose he grabbed the knife and strolled toward this particular guard, all the while remembering to keep up his singing.

Marc-Claude jumped off the table and the people in the crowd parted. He smiled at the guard who was approaching him. There was an angry look on the guard's face. Marc-Claude held out the knife, and the guard pulled his sword in return. Many in the crowd responded, "Ooh" or "Ahh," still thinking this was part of an entertainment scheme by the governor. Marc-Claude went into a fencing position, still wearing a big smile. He greatly hoped this guard was not a gifted fighter.

The two locked weapons two or three times before Marc-Claude could tell that this man wasn't particularly skilled in the art of swordplay, but nevertheless he could tell the guard was at least his equal. Even though he had to stop singing at this point to remain focused, he was thankful that the crowd was singing with the band still playing.

After only a few seconds of sword fighting, the guard became frustrated. He pulled back and tried to stab forward. Marc-Claude dodged the attempt easily. Reaching out with his knife, he locked on the set of keys hanging off the belt of the guard. This was the reason he particularly wanted to engage *this* guard. Quickly he sliced through the guard's belt. His pants loosened, and the keys slid onto the floor.

The guard was unprepared for this move. He let down his sword and grabbed his pants. Marc-Claude, on the other hand, knew this was his chance. He dropped the knife and dove for the keys. He then rolled back onto his feet and quickly threw the keys to the side of the room. Many in the crowd looked at this move with confusion. Marc-Claude shrugged his shoulders and joined in again with the song.

He then ran through the crowd again as best as he could. Some were caught off guard, while others still sang along. Governor Pasure could faintly be heard shouting various instructions. As Marc-Claude moved to the center of the room, the music stopped abruptly. Now, the governor could be heard more clearly, shouting and even reprimanding the band.

Marc-Claude was almost in the middle of the room when he was suddenly met with a punch square in the nose. He fell on his back and grabbed his nose with both hands. "Ahh!" he said as rolled on the ground. Some in the crowd began to laugh.

"Sorry," Bernard said, as he raised his fists into a boxing position. The plan Marc-Claude laid out was that Bernard would challenge him to a fight when he made it to the middle of the room. Unfortunately, nerves got the better of Bernard and seeing Marc-Claude emerge from the crowd, he simply struck his friend.

Bernard was sweating a little as he continued to hold his fists up. "Can you get up?" he asked Marc-Claude who didn't respond, but rather continued to wallow in pain. Originally, they were hoping to fight in hand-to-hand combat for a few minutes in order to keep buying time for Cobra and to help Bernard win favor with the governor. But at this point, this part of the plan and the charade was over. Marc-Claude could only hope Cobra was given enough of a head's start.

Chapter 6

Cobra crept through the different hallways and rooms of the mansion. He knew he was getting close. He tried to stay casual but knew that time was limited. He could only hope that Marc-Claude's plan had worked, and no one would remember that he had come with him. If they did, then surely officials would come looking for him. So far, he had only been passed by a few servants and maids. A few paused to marvel at his size, but mostly they didn't give him much thought. His expensive clothing indicated he was someone of high esteem.

The interior of the mansion was decorated elegantly. If it was another time, he would have liked to have taken his time and admired some of the paintings and artwork on display, but for now, the mission demanded his focus. As best as he could, he tried to remember everything the tailor had said about the layout of the mansion. So far, all of his instructions had been correct. According to their best guesses, the library should be close.

Cobra arrived at two large double doors, each twelve feet in height. He grabbed the handles and pulled them open. Gladly his suspicions were correct. This was the library. But not only was it the library, but a room displaying other pieces of delicate artwork and artifacts. It appeared that Governor Pasure was indeed a collector. Stepping into the room, he found ancient weapons from faraway lands, armor from knights and warriors of various kingdoms, paintings and structures from renowned artists and relics from ancient times. This was all in addition to three large bookshelves, each standing ten feet high.

He stepped into the room and took just a moment to admire some of the relics that were on the wall and sitting on shelves. One was supposedly a jar of sand from the Undying land. It was interesting, but then again Cobra wondered if it was authentic. Another was a sword from "Albert, Chief Knight of Mendolon." He thought about grabbing it but quickly thought otherwise. He couldn't be distracted.

Cobra focused on the books on the shelf. There were many different sizes and shapes. Many looked old, while others looked as if they had never been opened before. He quickly got to work, pulling the books off one by one, and flipping through them. There were history books, cookbooks, fiction books, language manuals, and everything in between. Most of the books he tried to put back on the shelf. A few of them he couldn't put back into place, so he just tossed them on the ground. A part of him felt like he ought to be respectful of this library, but he knew he was in a hurry.

He was deep into his search when a voice called out to him. "Hey, you there! What are you doing?"

Cobra turned to see a guard with a javelin in hand. He was short and very thin. "Oh, hello," Cobra smiled back as he spoke.

"You're... you're not supposed to be here." The guard was obviously nervous. "I'm going to have to report you to the governor. He's not going to like this."

Cobra put down the book he was looking at and slowly walked toward the guard. He stopped right in front of the man, who was shaking a little. The man held the javelin a little higher. Cobra looked down at the tip of the javelin and then down at the man who was a foot shorter. The guard stared back at him. The whole world around them seemed to go silent as the two men observed one another.

It was then in a swift moment that Cobra grabbed the javelin and easily pulled it out of the guard's hands. The guard's eyes grew wide in terror. With his other hand Cobra grabbed the top of the man's shirt. Cobra cleared his throat before speaking up. "What should I do with you?" he said with great calm in his voice.

The guard shook with fear, wondering if this was the end of the line for him. Suddenly, he thought of a plan to spare his life. "You could... um... put me in the closet." He looked toward the side of the library where a small closet was located.

Cobra looked over in that direction. "Great idea." He then dragged the man over to the closet and put the javelin to the side. He opened the door to the closet and found it mostly empty, save for a bookcase with a few dozen books. He quickly shoved the man inside. As Cobra was closing the door, he noticed the binding on a few of the books. It said something about treasure. He quickly opened the door back up again. "Pardon me," he said to the frightened guest. He then began looking at some of these older books. The guard stood there awkwardly, not saying a word. Eventually, Cobra found a few books that contained information and rumors about the Lost Treasure of Sophia.

"Great," Cobra said under his breath. He then turned to the guard again. "Oh... and uh... have a nice day." The guard continued to say nothing, but simply stood quietly, thankful this intruder didn't throw him out a window. He then shut the door and slid a table in front of it.

Cobra sat down on a nearby chair and started skimming through some of these books. The information was interesting, and he knew these manuals would be helpful, but they weren't enough. He needed more. His hope was that somehow Marc-Claude had caused enough of a distraction to buy him more time.

※

Marc-Claude was led upstairs through the mansion by the guards. His hands were tied behind his back. He was to be imprisoned in the attic. Governor Pasure wanted to question him before he was turned over to the authorities. Bernard tried to convince the governor to hand him over to him, so he could deal with this intruder. Pasure was not to be persuaded. This man had ruined his party. He was not going to deal with him lightly.

Arriving upstairs, Marc-Claude stood before a large cell with another individual in it. "Charming," he said mockingly.

The governor came over and grabbed the side of his face. "Who are you and what are you doing at my party?"

Marc-Claude was slightly insulted. "Didn't you hear my song? And how can you not recognize me… Dumpas?" One of the guards chuckled under his breath. The governor remembered him instantly.

"Marc-Claude! How did you sneak into my party?"

"With great joy, my friend!"

This seemed to infuriate the governor further. "How dare you get into my mansion uninvited!"

"It was quite easy actually and you truly decorate nicely… but I found your entertainment low quality and boring. You ought to be thanking me for providing a little song and dance to bring some grandeur to this occasion."

The governor's face started to turn red as he clenched his teeth. Full of anger, he felt faint. "I ought to… ! I mean… you're gonna… ahh!" He then reached up and began choking Marc-Claude.

The guards around him quickly grabbed the governor's hands and tried to calm him. The scene became a little chaotic. "Sir, stop, your blood pressure," one guard warned. "This is against the law," another said.

Eventually they were able to separate the governor from Marc-Claude, who was gasping for air. He tried to speak. "After all I've... done for you, Dump... (cough)... (cough)."

Another guard approached the governor. "Governor, you must remember your guests. They expect your hosting and a toast."

Pasure took a deep breath and brushed off his clothing, trying to calm himself. "Fine, toss him into the cell with the drunk. If he says anything, let me know immediately."

"Yes sir," the guards said, throwing him into the large cell. He stumbled and fell to the floor. The group left the area, leaving one to stand guard.

Marc-Claude sat for a moment to catch his breath. His nose still hurt, which wasn't fun, but thankfully it didn't seem as if it was broken. He slowly rose to his feet and stretched a little, taking note of the situation. The drunken man sat to the side of the holding cell. He didn't say much, as it appeared he was sleeping or just resting. A few strands of black hair covered his face. Marc-Claude didn't pay him much mind. Rather he walked to the guard and spoke. "I guess you drew the short stick, mate." The guard didn't respond.

It was apparent that Marc-Claude would be kept there until the party was over, and then he would either be interrogated, killed, or moved to a different prison. For now, he could only bide his time and hope the rest of his plan was progressing.

∽⁕∾

Cobra knew time was of the essence. From the shelf, he picked up another book about searching for treasure, but he knew he needed something more, something big. Turning around he looked back toward the closet, recalling that he had found two books about treasure in there. He started walking back toward the closet when his eyes focused in on one of the artifacts displayed on a table.

He stood before the artifact, taking it in. The world seemed to fade away for a moment. This was one of the most beautiful pieces of art he'd ever seen. He couldn't help but pause for a moment and admire it. The grandeur of it was truly breathtaking.

It was an antique map, written uniquely in different symbols and word pictures. Its dimensions were two feet in width and a foot and a half in height. The colors were vibrant, which made it look like a piece of art more so than a map. The sea was easy to distinguish, painted with mostly light blue and white patterns and served as the background of the map. Some of the pictures were also easy to decipher, such as fruit or crops, while others were abstract shapes that littered various parts of the sea. A few of the symbols looked to be pointing toward dangers, along with written instructions on how to avoid those areas. Unfortunately for Cobra, he couldn't read most of it. The writing style and pictures were from a forgotten time of art symbols. Still, it was easy to see that this was something that he needed.

Gently he lifted it off its stand and felt the texture. It appeared to be some type of animal skin, thus helping its preservation. He glanced on the back and saw the name of the artist, but that was indistinguishable as well. Turning it back over, he wondered what the best way to carry it would be. He didn't want to roll it as it may damage it, but on the other hand, it would be noticeable if he simply carried it out. After a moment he thought of a plan. Reaching behind, he stuck it between his body and his coat. He pulled the ends of the coat tighter, making sure it stayed secure. He picked up his books again and readjusted his glasses, hoping he looked sophisticated.

Cobra walked toward the doors of the library. He took one last glance toward the closet with the guard inside. Being a gentle soul, he thought about releasing the man, but then he thought otherwise. He calmly walked out of the library and shut the door behind him.

※

Marc-Claude was leaning against the holding bars, tapping his feet. Close to fifteen minutes had passed since he was placed in here. The other prisoner had hardly moved, and the soldier had said nothing else. The time passed slowly. Marc-Claude preached to himself to stay calm. Standing here waiting was definitely the hardest part of the plan.

He was starting to get slightly nervous when another soldier arrived at the room with Leah. She was at his side, crying. "Please let me see him," she told the man guarding the cell.

The guard who brought her in took a deep breath and spoke in an exhausted tone to the other guard. "She says she's his wife. I told her he wasn't to have visitors, but she was relentless."

The other guard looked back at Marc-Claude, who simply raised his eyebrows and shrugged. The guard scratched the back of his head, wondering what to do. He looked back at the woman, who had her hands over her face. "Oh... fine... make it brief," he said with frustration in his voice. He then motioned with his head. The young woman then fell on her knees close to the cell. Marc-Claude got down on his knees to match her.

"Oh, I've missed you. I've missed you so," she said, reaching out.

Marc-Claude reached out as well, but in a very sly manner received three keys from her. She had narrowed it down to these three. "Oh, thank you so much for coming to me," he said unable to contain his joy. Earlier in the evening, when Marc-Claude noticed Leah was bored at the party he decided to bring her in on the mission. The plan was for her to be placed at a specific area of the ballroom during his song and dance. When he got close to the guard who was holding a ring of keys, he would find a way to take the keys and toss them in the general direction of Leah. She would then retrieve them and come see him in the holding cell. So far it was working well. If this didn't work, Bernard was to keep trying to persuade the governor to let him take the prisoner back to Mendolon. Thankfully, plan number one was still working.

Leah began laughing after she had passed off the keys. A part of her couldn't believe it worked. She tried to turn it into a cry, but it came out as an awkward sounding giggle. The guards just looked at one another with strange looks on their faces. Marc-Claude tried to keep talking and make the conversation sound normal. "Uh, be sure to take care of the children while I'm away, my dearest."

"Oh, yes," Leah said, playing along. "All seven of them. I don't know how we are going to make it without you."

Marc-Claude's eyes grew wide at the thought of having seven kids. The guards looked at one another with puzzled looks. Marc-Claude spoke up again, trying desperately to make it sound believable. "You must be strong, my love, you must be strong. All those little ones must be fed and cared for. You must carry on, you must."

The "couple" went back-and-forth with this banter. Leah, being a girl who loved adventure, was enjoying this short escapade. She would most definitely have a story to tell when she got back home.

Eventually the guards became anxious. "Time's up. You can wait in the ballroom after the party is done. The governor will have much to say to you, Madam."

The soldiers grabbed the girl by the arm and pulled her away. Marc-Claude called out. "Good-bye, and thank you for coming," he said, trying to sound sincere. Leah reached out her hand, trying to further sell her acting role.

When the soldiers and Leah were out of the room, Marc-Claude knew he had a matter of minutes to try the keys before one of the guards came back. He quickly got to work trying the keys in the lock. Thankfully with the second one, he heard a click and the cell door unlocked. Marc-Claude removed the key but kept the door shut. The guard then returned and resumed his post of waiting by the door. Marc-Claude stood waiting for a little while, looking for the best opportunity to escape.

Close to five minutes passed and Marc-Claude saw the guard yawn. He figured this was his opportunity. Before the guard's yawn ended, he threw open the door to the cell and sprang toward the guard. "Ahh!" the guard yelled out, surprised. Before Marc-Claude could grab him, the guard pivoted to the side and hit Marc-Claude in the nose in the same place Bernard had struck him. He stepped back a few feet and grabbed his nose. The guard then came at him with another punch, which Marc-Claude dodged. He tried to throw another punch, but Marc-Claude grabbed his fist. The men then locked arms and began wrestling. Marc-Claude tried his best to outsmart his opponent but found the guard stronger than he.

The guard got to a position where he was able to kick Marc-Claude off himself. He then was able to pull a small sword from his side. Marc-Claude backed up. He knew he was in trouble. "Back in the cell!" the guard shouted. Marc-Claude didn't move. "I said, back in the..."

He wasn't able to finish his sentence before the other prisoner in the cell came with a fierce kick on the arm of the guard. The guard dropped the sword, and before he could react, the prisoner acted quickly with a punch to the guard's head and a kick to the side of his body. He wasted no time before picking him up and tossing the guard into the holding cell. The prisoner then shut the door. He turned toward Marc-Claude, "Do you have the key?"

Marc-Claude quickly reached into his pocket. Pulling it from his pocket he showed it to the man while smiling. Not saying a word, he grabbed it from Marc-Claude and locked the door. It was easy to tell this man was from the east and was some sort of trained fighter. His hair was black, and a thin mustache donned his face. His clothes were simple but a little disheveled and dirty. The guards called him a drunk, but it was apparent that he was now sober enough to use his fighting skills.

Marc-Claude cleared his throat and spoke up. "Would you like to come with me? Escape? My name is Marc-Claude."

"Pleased to meet you, my name is Lin," he said patiently. When he finished locking the door, he looked directly at Marc-Claude. "I will come with you, but I suggest you follow me, and we'll get out of this place together."

"Deal!" he said without hesitation.

"Let's go."

Chapter 7

Marc-Claude and Lin left the room and walked into a hallway. They knew they were on the fourth floor of the mansion. They found a nearby stairwell and started descending. Lin was in front. He was only able to take a few steps when he heard a group of people coming up the steps talking casually. "Turn around, turn around," he whispered to Marc-Claude. Abruptly the two men went back up the steps and back into the hallway.

Lin went toward another door with Marc-Claude following closely behind. "Hey mate, why didn't you just fight those guys? You looked like you've been trained for it."

"One on one, yes. Two on one, maybe, but three or four, I would be overmatched," Lin responded. Marc-Claude was a little disappointed as he was hoping to see this martial artist take on a whole group of men in a stairwell.

    The two men entered what looked like an office. A desk, a bookcase, and a few chairs were stationed around the room. What Lin was most looking toward was the window on the far side of the room. He quickly strode toward it and kicked it open. The night air blew in swiftly. Lin lifted a foot out the window and grabbed onto the bricks. The men were close to forty feet from the ground. Marc-Claude wasn't so sure about this plan, but nevertheless he looked the other way out the window and saw lattice, along with vines. This looked to be a much safer option.

    Marc-Claude climbed out the window and started to grab ahold of the lattice when Lin shouted out. "No, don't go there. The light of the moon is shining right on that area. If someone comes, they will see you."

    He looked down and saw what Lin said was right, but for him it was a chance he would have to take. "Listen mate, I don't think I can climb like you. I'm going to have to take my chances."

    Lin didn't argue any further but just kept meticulously climbing down the outside of the building. Marc-Claude did the same. At times he was a little worried as he began hearing creaking sounds from the lattice. After a few more paces, he tried to grab a better hold of the vines. He didn't think he liked this any better as the vines proved to be more slippery at times. Nevertheless, all of this was motivation to keep climbing down.

Marc-Claude put his hand down on what appeared to be a normal handhold, but saw a wasp come out and head straight for his hand. "Ahh!" he yelled out as he was stung.

Lin looked over and saw what happening. Unfortunately, he looked over and saw not just one wasp, but many wasps starting to emerge from the lattice. It was apparent that Marc-Claude had disrupted a nest. Lin could hear him start to yell out with every wasp sting. There was nothing he could do for him, but he just kept moving. Marc-Claude tried to move with haste, but the sting of wasps made it even worse.

After a few more feet he felt as if he had made it past the wasps. He took just a moment to breathe a sigh of relief. He closed his eyes, feeling thankful to be past that trial. It was then that he felt something on his nose. He opened his eyes and saw another wasp. "Oh, no!" He quickly shook his head and tried to get it off, but it was too late. The dastardly fiend stung him right on the sore spot on his nose. This made him scream out even louder in pain. "Aww… great spawn of evil! You…aww!"

A dozen guests were outside standing a few feet from where they were climbing. They heard him yell out. Stopping their conversations, they looked up to see what was transpiring. They were shocked to see two men climbing down the outside of the building. Many found this entertaining, while others thought this was concerning. "What are you men doing up there?" someone called out. The two of them didn't respond, but kept climbing down. Abruptly, a few in the crowd left to go get security.

"Quick, we don't have much time," Lin said.

They tried to climb a little faster, but their speed was in vain as a few guards showed up. "Stop, immediately! ... Or rather climb down!"

A few feet above Marc-Claude was another window. He quickly climbed back up and threw a kick into the window. It took one more before the window swung open, breaking its latch. He grabbed ahold of the frame and pulled himself in. Lin saw what he had done and quickly followed.

Getting to his feet, Marc-Claude realized they were in a bedroom on the second floor. He thought about walking casually but knew there would be no way to conceal Lin, as disheveled as he was. The men walked to the door of the bedroom and peeked out. Marc-Claude could see a few guards moving about. He waited just a moment before it was clear. "Let's go," he said, walking out.

The men ran down the hallway toward the doors leading to the ballroom balcony. The men wasted no time in throwing them open and bursting into the room. They could see the party was still going strong, with music playing and guests enjoying themselves. A few in the crowd saw Marc-Claude's abrupt entrance and took notice. "There he is!" a woman shouted. This caused others to stop and take notice.

"Give us another song!" a man said joyfully. This brought a round of laughter from the crowd. The musicians slowly stopped playing, noticing that the people were distracted.

The governor turned his gaze toward the men at the top of the steps. "What! How did you escape?" he shouted.

Marc-Claude and Lin froze as they felt trapped. Marc-Claude knew he had to think of something quickly. He said the first thing that came to mind. "Ladies and gentlemen, I would suggest we have ... a toast! Yes, a toast! Who could throw such a grand party with the food, the company, the music?" There were a few in the crowd that started clapping. Marc-Claude held his hand in the air to signal that he wasn't done. "Who else in the crowd, except that beloved master of ceremonies, that man of intrigue, the agent of glamour, the one and only Governor Dumar Pasure, or as I like to refer to him as... Dumpas!"

Many in the crowd started to clap again, while others laughed hearing this nickname. Those close to the governor started patting him on the back in laughter. "Oh, yes, Governor Dumpas, that's a good one," a close official said.

This only made him more furious. "Shut up! Don't call me that!" he said, turning red. Regrettably not many in the crowd heard him, but just continued in their laughter.

A group of guards started coming up the steps toward the men. Marc-Claude thought about turning around but knew this was futile as other guards were in the hallways of the mansion. He looked around and saw his next best option, one of the large chandeliers that hung by the side of the staircase. Thinking it was worth a shot, he took a few steps back, and ran with all his might, jumped over the railing, and grabbed ahold of the chandelier. The distance to the chandelier was shorter than he anticipated, and his body hit the side of the structure, knocking off some of the glass pieces in the process. On the other side of the stairwell Lin followed suit and jumped into the chandelier that was on the other side of the balcony, except his execution and landing were much more graceful.

Marc-Claude climbed down and slid to the bottom of the chandelier and onto the floor. He knew this little stunt only bought him a few seconds. He quickly started running again toward the front door of the mansion. Lin was also making his way through the crowd, doing his best to avoid any guards.

Bernard, along with the rest of the crowd, watched the excitement transpire. He looked on with concern for his friend and as he scanned the crowd, he saw that Marc-Claude wouldn't make it. There were too many guards close to the doors that would stop them, and especially with the amount of people blocking their exit they wouldn't have a chance.

Quickly the young knight looked around, trying to think of something. Looking behind, he saw a fireplace burning steadily. A plan quickly came to mind. There was no way for him to evaluate the merits of this plan, he just knew he had to implement it. He pulled his sword, stabbed one of the burning logs, and quickly flung it onto a nearby table. Thankfully, no one noticed him as they were distracted by Marc-Claude's escape. He stabbed another log and flung it across the floor, sliding it toward another table. "Fire!" he called out as loud as he could.

Others turned to look and, indeed, saw these logs burning and starting to burn the tablecloths and other items surrounding them. A few in the crowd yelled, "Run! A fire!" This set off a panic with most of the people starting to run toward the front door. People were pushing and shoving in panic as they tried to get toward the exit. Others opened the windows and tried to climb out. The guards felt overwhelmed, not sure whether to help put out the fire, assist people in the escape, or continue to chase Marc-Claude and Lin.

From the balcony doors, Cobra quietly entered the ballroom and descended the steps. He was trying to stay calm, but also look like a person who was concerned about the fire. Above all, he was worried about the map on his back. He wanted to be sure he left with that undamaged. As quickly as he could, he joined the panicking crowd and made his way toward the exit.

Moving with the crowd, Marc-Claude and Lin were able to exit the mansion amidst the confusion. As much as they could, they stayed in the middle of the crowd and passed into the outside air. Once outside, they kept pace with others moving toward the outer gate, only a few yards away from freedom.

Just as they were about ready to step off the premises, Marc-Claude turned to see Governor Pasure standing a few feet away, looking at his mansion and shaking his head, upset that his party had been ruined.

Marc-Claude knew the wise thing to do would be to simply leave, but he knew he couldn't resist one more insult. As loud as he could, he shouted in the governor's direction. "Many apologies on the ending of your evening... Governor Dumpas!"

"Don't call me that!" He yelled back, looking through the crowd.

Marc-Claude ducked, concealing himself. He couldn't help but smile as he walked out the gate.

∽∻∾

Marc-Claude and Lin weaved through the streets of the shops, now avoiding the crowds wherever they could. Marc-Claude was moving toward his ship, which was docked on the far northeastern side of the harbor, the same place it had been for the last week. A few times he and Cobra went back to check on things and to pay the small docking fee, but other than that, the boat had stayed dormant.

Lin didn't really have a plan other than to follow his new acquaintance and hope to escape with him. Marc-Claude had told him that he had a boat and was looking to leave the land. He figured at least he could ride along with him and then leave at the first port city they came to. From there he would just continue traveling to the northeast, back toward his home country.

After moving slowly for an hour, the two men came out of an alleyway and saw the ship. "There it is, mate." The boat looked undeterred and the same as when they had left it. Marc-Claude looked both ways and saw all was clear. He then proceeded forward to the vessel with Lin close behind. No one paid them any mind as the two men made it onto the ship. Once on board the two men sat down for a moment to catch their breath. They ducked low, just in case anyone was watching.

Marc-Claude peeked over the vessel's railing and saw that all was clear. He breathed a sigh of relief.

"Hey Marc-Claude! Welcome back!" Cobra announced, startling his friend in the process. "I must say, your song tonight sounded wonderful. You know you need to sing a little more. I think you could…"

"Cobra, what are you doing here?" he said, a little upset at being scared.

Cobra looked perfectly calm and relaxed, the exact opposite of how Marc-Claude felt at the moment. "Oh, I've been doing some reading from the books I took from the governor's library. Very interesting stuff about all sorts of treasures abroad."

Marc-Claude rose to his feet. "That's fine, but we need to get going. Ole Dumpas might come after us. I'm thinking he's going to come looking for us toward the north, so we need to set a course for the southeast for few miles before we can circle back northeast."

"Ok… but who's this?" Cobra said, pointing toward Marc-Claude's new companion.

"This is Lin. He helped me escape the governor's mansion. He's going to be joining us, at least for a little while."

"Well, pleased to meet ya', Monsieur Lin."

He put his hands together and bowed in response.

Marc-Claude was at the wheel of the ship as he spoke up again. "Time to be going, Cobra. Say goodbye to the city of Bourges." He chuckled a little as he spoke. Cobra got into position to cast off to sea. Lin did what he could to help as well.

As their ship started to pull out, he spoke to Cobra again. "So, you say you got a couple of books concerning the treasure?"

"Yes, along with an ancient map that will help us, and it'll probably fetch us a big payday when we're done with it."

"Haha, that's what I like to hear... great job, Cobra... great job!"

"Thank you, Marc-Claude. I think things are starting to turn for us."

Marc-Claude now couldn't hold back his smile. "Oh yes, indeed, old boy! It's great to be us!"

Chapter 8

The sun was rising over the sea in the early morning. The men had sailed through the night without sleep, trying to put distance between them and Bourges. Marc-Claude checked often, but he never saw any other boats following or coming close. He figured that the governor may have been preoccupied with the party and the fire in the mansion. Cobra wondered if the party had continued after the ballroom was cleared or if all the guests had dispersed. If he was honest with himself, he'd have to admit that he enjoyed being accepted among the socialites, at least for an evening. It wasn't something he was used to.

Being concerned about the escape, Marc-Claude hadn't been able to assess what Cobra had taken from the library, but he was anxious to see it. Especially hearing that he had stolen a map that was of particular value. If anything, he was thankful to see it as a trophy of a successful mission into the library of Governor Dumar Pasure. He was hoping that maybe more word would leak out about the escape, and it would continue to bolster his reputation. His dreams were growing by the minute.

Now that there was some light from the sun, Cobra spent the morning looking through the books he had taken. He was still captivated with this lost treasure and being in the library only seemed to increase his fascination. He was excited to tell his friend everything he had found.

He approached Marc-Claude at the ship's wheel. "Would you like to see the map now?"

"Oh, would I ever!" he replied with great excitement.

Cobra placed it on a nearby table, while Marc-Claude stepped away from steering. He was quite amazed at what he saw. "Wow! This is incredible, mate. I wonder how old it is." He touched the edges of it, feeling the material it was written on. "Extravagant, simply wonderful." Especially in the light of the sun, the pictures and colors on the map were truly a work of art. One had to take a moment and admire it before analyzing the riddles of what the pictures and symbols meant.

"Yeah, it's good," Cobra said. "I wished you could've seen the library. There was lots of good stuff in there."

Marc-Claude turned to smile at his companion. "Maybe one day, we can go see old Dumpas again and pay another visit to his library."

"Oh, I'd love to show it to ya' sometime."

Looking at the map thoroughly, he could identify a few places for points of reference, such as a majestic crown, possibly signifying the Northern Empire, or a boat being cut into two by a sword, signifying a giant sea battle that took place over a hundred years ago. This was helpful because it helped show him a date for this map. At least he could see that it was from the last hundred to a hundred and fifty years, and most likely, even older than that. There were a few places marking spots of treasure on the map. Three of these were in the east at various locations. Marc-Claude spotted a picture of a gold coin, a treasure chest, and a jewel in various locations. There were also a few symbols from another language, one he had never seen before. He looked particularly at different points trying to decipher this riddle.

One of the most difficult things about this map was that it was not drawn in perfect scale. It appeared that the artist was more concerned with the beauty and splendid nature of the piece as opposed to the exact dimensions of the distances. But still they were thankful to have a map that depicted places past the far east. Areas that many people would label as 'uncharted.'

"Hmm," Marc-Claude rubbed his chin as he thought.

"Can you read it?" Cobra asked.

"It's difficult. I recognize a few spots. There are some places that are making it difficult to gain my bearings."

"Ok, you could look at the books as well. They've got some good stuff in there."

"Yes, I look forward to looking at them, but first I think we need to figure out a way to read this map."

"Well, what do you suggest?"

Marc-Claude took a deep breath and looked out to sea. He also felt his stomach growl. This gave him an idea. "I think we should head back to Roselin's island and see if she's seen anything like it or knows someone who can read it."

A puzzled look formed on Cobra's face. "Marc-Claude, are you just trying to get more of her delicious fish she made us?"

"No... no... well, yes, but I also think she could help us."

Cobra nodded his head and shrugged his shoulders. "Yeah, I think it would be a good plan, and the fish filets sure were tasty."

Marc-Claude gave a side smile. He then looked around Cobra and saw Lin sitting against the side railing of the boat, drinking from a bottle. He looked lost. "Pardon me," Marc-Claude said quietly as he walked around Cobra toward their stowaway.

He tried to talk upbeat. "Monsieur Lin, it has been great to have you join us, but I will let you know that we are journeying to Roselin's restaurant, wonderful wine and delicious fish. It's a very famous place."

"Yes, I've heard."

"Very well. Many travelers come through those parts, and it should be easy for you to find voyage to wherever you would like to go."

Lin shook his head and took another drink. He then spoke up with a defeated tone in his voice. "I have nowhere to go." He looked down at his bottle, and with a deep reflective tone began to tell his story. "I was a criminal mastermind who was arrested in Mendolon. I escaped during the famed attack from the Savage, and then again during the Chaos. At that time, I completely left the kingdom and forsook my band of criminals. I then journeyed to Bourges and tried to make a new life but reverted back to stealing and thievery. The night before the governor's party, I was drinking outside his mansion. Guards were sent after me, but I couldn't fight them off. They threw me into the prison, where you found me." He then paused as he looked off to the sea. "I've dishonored my family with crimes. I've lost everything, and I have nowhere to go. I am simply a lost traveler going toward the void of nothingness."

Marc-Claude just stood there in silence. He wasn't sure what to say. "Well… um… nice story, mate. I hope you figure things out. They… um… do have nice fish at Roselin's."

By this time Cobra had joined him by his side. "Marc-Claude! Get ahold of yourself." He then turned to Lin. "We'd love to have you on our journey. Especially after all you did for us back there in the mansion. You could be a real help." He put his arm around Marc-Claude and pulled him close. "Ain't that right?"

Marc-Claude took a deep breath. "Yes, he's right, mate. We'd love to you for as long as it takes for you get on your feet."

Lin smiled slightly. "Thank you. It would be an honor to travel with you men."

Cobra reached out and shook hands with him before helping him up.

"Very well," Marc-Claude announced. "Let us set sail for Roselin's."

"Great, I'll take the wheel this time," Cobra said joyfully.

"Sounds good... but the sun is out, so you need to first put on your hat!"

※

Their vessel pulled up to the dock of the small island. It was getting close to the evening meal. Roselin was cleaning a few glasses when she noticed the ship pull into the dock. She knew it was Marc-Claude, and she was anxious to know if he'd been successful in getting into Governor Pasure's library. She put down the glass she was working on and casually walked toward the ship. Thankfully it was a slow stretch, right before the evening rush. She had time to talk.

Marc-Claude, Cobra, and Lin were disembarking when she arrived. "Ah! Greetings!" Marc-Claude announced joyfully.

"Where have you been? What took you so long?" she asked curiously.

"There were challenges, but Marc-Claude is a man of his word. We were able to get a personal tour of the governor's library."

She was taken back. "No, you didn't! Impossible."

Cobra broke in. "He sang a song, and I snuck in." Marc-Claude smiled in response.

Roselin snickered as she shook her head. "This will be a tale I will want to hear." She then turned to the eastern man with them. "And who is this?"

"This is Lin," Marc-Claude said. "He helped me escape a prison and then climb down the outside of a building."

She put her hand on her forehead. "This tale is getting better by the moment. Come, I'll have some drinks prepared, and you can tell me the rest." She started walking back toward the restaurant before turning and asking one more question. "Oh, and Marc-Claude, what happened to your nose? It looks awful."

"Don't ask."

The three men were led to a back office in the restaurant. Unlike the rest of the restaurant, this area was enclosed by four walls. A window let in light. Drinks were brought in as the four of them talked casually for a few moments. The men described the account of sneaking into the mansion. Roselin took in every word with full attention. She even laughed at some of the intervals along the way. This was good for her as much of her life was focused on the business.

As the account ended, she was anxious to see firsthand the map the men described. Cobra spread it out on a table. Upon seeing it, a shocked look appeared on her face, "By the north star! What is this?" She scanned the whole map before looking up at Marc-Claude. "This is gorgeous." She took off her hat and walked over to a shelf on the side of the room. She grabbed an eyeglass. "Truly astounding... this came from the governor's library?"

"It did," Cobra responded proudly.

She held the eyeglass close to her eye and examined the same things that Marc-Claude and Cobra had observed: the beautiful colors, the intriguing symbols, the material it was written on, and all of this among the overall breathtaking picture of it as a whole. She'd seen many things in her time as the restaurant owner, but this would definitely be something that would stand out in her mind.

The men found it curious that she focused her attention on different areas than what they found interesting. Marc-Claude spoke up, "Can you read it or interpret it?"

Roselin smacked her lips as she stayed focused on the map. She answered slowly, "No, but you can tell the author knew a lot about the world."

"We also got these books," Cobra added, holding up the books he'd retrieved.

Roselin looked up at them and nodded. She gently took one from Cobra's hand. She looked at the writing on the spine and then flipped through the pages. She spoke casually, "These may be helpful with information about the treasure, but I don't think they'll help in regard to figuring out this map."

"Do you know of anyone who would be able to decipher this thing?"

"Possibly." She stood up from the map and looked at the men. "There is a sailor who comes by often in the evening. I expect him tonight, as a company of boats are coming in from a trade route. It should be a busy night for the restaurant."

"Great!" Marc-Claude announced. "We will enjoy a little food, a little ale, and meet this fellow. It should be grand."

"Good," said Roselin. "Speaking of tonight, I better go and start preparing myself for the high traffic. You men may want to go ahead and secure a table as the place should be filled in an hour."

"We will do that right away." Marc-Claude said. "And by the way, who is this fellow that can help us? What is his name?"

Roselin put her hat back on her head. "I'm not sure what his real name is, but they refer to him as 'Hooks.'"

"Hmm... I wonder why," Marc-Claude said under his breath.

"Just be sure to secure a table," Roselin said as she exited the office.

Chapter 9

"Where did they go?!" Riché shouted out, trying to sound intimidating.

"I don't know where they went. I would gladly tell you if I knew," Governor Pasure spat back harshly. He wasn't having any of this intimidation by this young sailor.

The news of the governor's party ending in disaster traveled quickly, and Riché had gotten word of it. He had a hunch that Marc-Claude was involved. Upon arriving in Bourges, it only took a little bit of investigating to confirm that Marc-Claude was the one who brought the disturbance. Riché had hoped he could talk the governor out of more information and try to find out what they wanted with the governor's mansion, or better yet, if he had any idea what their plans were after leaving Bourges. Unfortunately, the governor was proving himself to be unhelpful to the young explorer.

The two men argued in the courtyard of the governor's mansion. Riché had his crew behind him, while the governor had a number of guards standing at attention for him. Riché was wearing a full formal captain's attire, trying to convince everyone that he was a person of influence and wasn't to be trifled with.

"Listen, you," Riché pointed his index finger toward Pasure. "I work for Von Dechauer. He's not going to be pleased with you if you don't help us find them."

The governor snickered. "What do you think this is, Mendolon? Von Dechauer's not going to send troops this far east, and besides, pirates are stealing from him these days."

Riché clinched his teeth. He was angry and a little out of control. "Fine, is this what you want?" He pulled a sword from his side. "You want to duel? We'll see how tough you are, you fat governor!"

A couple of the soldiers beside the governor pulled their swords and stepped forward. Most would describe the governor as a man of pride, but even he could recognize this situation as a foolish exploit by a young, spoiled sailor. He didn't want to even give him the joy of riling him up. He waved his hand and turned away. He spoke pointedly to his guards. "Say goodbye to the little sailor. Be sure he gets back to his mother for his evening feeding." Some of the guards laughed in return.

Riché stood, frustrated, full of anger. A part of him want to charge toward the governor and slay him right there, but then again, he knew when he and his men were overmatched. He would have to walk away from this one. As the governor's men began walking away, he sheathed his sword. He himself then turned and left the courtyard. The three men behind him followed suit.

As the young sailor walked from the mansion and back toward the town, he yelled out curses and shouts of fury toward the governor. He'd never been so embarrassed in all his life. He thought to himself, *If only he could see what I've done. Or how rich my family is. He wouldn't talk to me like that. One day people are going to fear me.* In the west his name carried weight and respect. Here, people didn't know of his family's business, and he couldn't intimidate them based on that alone.

Riché and his men walked back to their ship. Four of his other men had gone into the town to see if anyone had heard or seen Marc-Claude leave and knew more information. Three stayed on board, and three followed him to the governor's mansion. As of right now, he hoped they were all back at the ship as he was ready to leave this town forever.

As he was walking through town, one of his men called out. "Riché, sir!" He turned to see one of the crewmen who had gone into town. Running up to Riché, he spoke quickly. "We found two individuals with information you need to hear."

Instantly he was intrigued. "Oh, yeah? Who is it?"

"Two young women who attended the party. It's said they were seen with Marc-Claude."

"Did they come with him?"

"Apparently, they met sometime before the party. A few people saw them walk in together."

"Lead me to them."

"Right away." Riché and his crewmen weaved through town, passing people on the busy streets. Even though it was getting close to the evening, the people were still out working heartily.

As Riché walked through the crowd, he pushed people out of the way without regard. "Hey, watch it!" a man responded. Others said similar things as he moved through them. A sense of entitlement filled him. One day he hoped to be famous and recognizable enough where people would move out of the way upon seeing him.

They arrived at an abandoned shop and went in without hesitation. Instantly they saw the two girls, Leah and Rachel, sitting in the middle of the room with crewmembers around them. The girls weren't tied up, and the men didn't have any weapons pulled. But though the atmosphere in the room wasn't volatile, the girls knew they were being held captive. They simply chose to comply as there was no other option.

Riché cleared his throat and stepped toward the girls. "Were you with the pirate Marc-Claude?"

Rachel looked scared, while Leah sat with her arms crossed, looking slightly angry. Leah looked off to the side of the room, refusing to make eye-contact. She spoke with frustration in her voice. "I think you would know the answer to that question by now."

Riché cracked his knuckles in an effort to look intimidating. "You must comply!"

"Or what?"

He pulled a knife. "We could hurt you or her," he said, pointing it at Rachel.

Though Leah had a resolve about her that made her feel like she could withstand anything, she would do whatever it took to protect her younger sister. She knew the quickest way to release would be to just give the men a little information. "I think they were going northeast, not sure where."

"Where did they come from?" Leah didn't respond. She felt as if she was done with answering questions. "Fine," Riché said under his breath. He held out his knife again and walked toward Rachel.

Leah realized this was serious, and she would have to say all she knew immediately. "I believe they had just come from the northeast as well and were going back that direction, but I'm not sure."

"Sir." One of Riché's men pulled him aside.

"What is it?" he said, upset he was interrupted.

"I don't think they know anything else. Earlier they said Marc-Claude met them before the party and gave them a fake name."

"Do they even know for sure he was traveling northeast?"

The crewman shook his head. "Yes, his companion Cobra told some of their plans to the younger sister."

Riché looked over at Rachel and saw her sitting, looking a little scared. A plan formed in his mind. He turned and looked at everyone in the room. "Tie them up. We'll bring them along for leverage."

◈

In the evening Roselin's restaurant was packed. Various men and women of the sea had stopped by for dinner. There were soldiers, pirates, merchants, families with children, and everyone in between. The place was highly esteemed and most loved the place enough to know that it should be respected. Fights would not be tolerated between patrons. This evening was seen as the end of the trade season. The restaurant would be considerably less busy for the next few weeks.

Marc-Claude saw a number of people he knew, some he hadn't seen in many years. He enjoyed himself, walking from table-to-table, giving his greetings, and telling a tale or two. Many people asked about his family and particularly his sister, Clara. Others heard rumors about how he was involved in the Mendolon Chaos. This only led to more stories and laughs. He was thankful for these moments. He couldn't remember the last time he had so much fun.

The atmosphere was gorgeous on a night like this. A gentle breeze flowed through the outdoor eatery as the light of the moon shone above. The stars shone above on this cloudless night. Many of the patrons went out by the sand and had drinks while they looked up at the stars. Others on this evening enjoyed the food, while a few men and women sat together playing music and singing songs from various lands. An onlooker would describe the scene as one of peace and tranquility.

Lin decided to sit off by himself by the shore and do some reflecting. The last dozen years he had spent living the life of a criminal, and many of those months had been spent in prison. He was ready to say goodbye to that old life. Sitting here by the shore felt peaceful, and he felt ready to begin anew. He looked up at the stars and thought deeply about life and the future. He now tried to clear his mind of his past. Slowly he gazed again at the ocean in front of him. At the moment, all he wanted to do was sit and watch the waves roll along the shore.

Cobra was sitting at a table enjoying his fill of the fish. He had always had a hearty appetite. Occasionally, a few people he knew would come and give their greetings, but other than that, he simply kept to himself and enjoyed the evening. It proved to be a great time of rest from yesterday's mission in the governor's mansion. He looked across the room and saw Marc-Claude talking with a couple of sailors. Strangely enough, he could hear him start to sing a few bars of his song from last night. The sailors at the table were laughing as he told the account. Cobra laughed to himself before taking another drink of ale.

It wasn't much longer when Roselin dropped by his table. She spoke urgently. "Our man is here. I want to catch him before he leaves."

"Ok," Cobra said, rising from the table.

The two of them walked over to Marc-Claude. She tapped him on the shoulder and mouthed the words, "He's here."

"Pardon me," Marc-Claude said to those he was speaking with. He left their table and followed where Roselin was leading. He looked toward Cobra, "Do you have the map?"

"It's right here." He opened his coat and showed them the map concealed on the inside of his jacket.

The three of them weaved through the tables on the way to the edge of the eating area. Along the way people called out to Roselin and commented about the food. She smiled and casually said, "thank you," as she passed.

The group came to a table where four men were playing a game of dice. The mood was tense as there was money on the line. It was easy to tell which man was 'Hooks.' He looked to be close to forty with a brown beard with a little bit of grey. He was dressed like a pirate with a large-brimmed hat. What was most noticeable was that in place of his hands were hooks. On one hand he had two that he used to scoop items with such as cups, and on the other, he had one large hook. Upon walking up, Marc-Claude also noticed that the man's right leg was gone under his knee and in its place was a wooden peg leg.

"Hooks, we need to speak with you," Roselin said as they arrived at the table.

"Can't you see I'm busy?"

"This is important," Roselin said firmly.

Everyone at the table stopped and looked toward Roselin. For her to say something was important, the men knew she was serious.

"Alright... give me a minute."

"Fine, we'll meet back behind the kitchen area. I have a table reserved back there." Hooks just nodded in return as he went back to his game.

Roselin, along with Marc-Claude and Cobra, went back to a table behind the kitchen area. It was reserved for employees to eat on their breaks. Currently there was a young cook casually having a drink at the table. Roselin easily dismissed him and took a seat. Cobra spread the map along the table and the three of them looked again at the magnificent piece.

About five minutes later they saw Hooks slowly approach the table. The peg leg slowed his speed. As he approached, Marc-Claude could see he was a very short man. He wondered if the man was even five feet in height. Arriving at the table, he took a seat in one of the chairs. "So, you got something you wanted to show me? ... Whoa, ho, ho... what is that?" he said, immediately noticing the map.

"We got it from a collector," Cobra said.

Hooks looked up at Cobra. "Well, aren't you a tall glass of ale. After we talk here, I got some guys I want you to beat up for me."

"Can we stay focused?" Roselin said.

Marc-Claude spoke up. "We were wondering if you could decipher some of the symbols in the east, mate?"

Hooks glanced down at the symbols. "You men looking for treasure or something?" They said nothing in response. Hooks smiled. "I'll take that as a yes." He took time to look at the map in front of him. Like the others he struggled with what the symbols meant.

After a minute Roselin asked, "Can you figure out what some of these mean?"

"Hmm... not sure. These may be above my knowledge." He then looked straight at Marc-Claude. "Where is the treasure you're looking for anyway?"

Roselin spoke, "We're looking to go to the far east in parts that are viewed as uncharted."

This last statement caught Marc-Claude's attention. "Wait, wait... what do you mean by 'we'?"

"Yes," said Roselin, looking straight at Marc-Claude. "If you are really attempting to do this, then you will need as much help as you can get. I've learned bits of knowledge about these areas. I can be of help to you."

"But what about your restaurant?"

"After tonight, the trade routes slow down dramatically. As of tomorrow, business will practically be dead for two weeks. I was planning on taking some time off anyway, and if necessary, some of my employees can keep things running."

"We'd love to have you," Cobra added.

"Well, if she's in, then I'm definitely joining." Hooks added. "You men are going to need some help navigating these waters in the east, and I'm the best captain around these parts."

"Thank you, mate, but we'll be just fine. Cobra here, and I can handle these parts fine."

"Marc-Claude, you need him," Roselin interjected. "From what I've heard, these waters are not to be trifled with. You need someone with experience."

"That's right. Listen to this lady," Hooks added.

Marc-Claude took a deep breath, knowing they were right. If they were ever going to find this treasure then they would need more help, and besides, having a crew might be of some assistance. "Fine, you guys can come aboard. I'll pay you ten percent of any treasure we find."

"Ha... twenty percent, you cheap pirate."

"I'll up it to twelve, but don't ever call me a pirate again."

"How about fifteen, and I can take us to someone who can definitely read the map."

"That's a deal, mate, fifteen percent."

The terms were set, and they all shook on it. The crew was established. Together they would hunt for the Lost Treasure in the East.

Chapter 10

Another day passed before they left Roselin's island. The men could already tell that the traffic had slowed dramatically from the night before. When the time came, Roselin felt a little worried leaving the restaurant in the charge of her manager, but once she got onto Marc-Claude's boat, she felt instant relief. It had been too long since she was out to sea. She spent most of her time at the front of the boat, feeling the wind in her face and taking in the sounds of the ocean. Her appearance even looked different, more relaxed now that she was on the open sea.

Upon leaving the restaurant, she brought some food for everyone, along with a few spices and an assortment of wine. She was also skilled at fishing and brought some of her personal equipment. Overall, Marc-Claude and Cobra knew that their conditions would be improved now that she was joining the voyage.

Hooks was at the helm of the boat, continuing to get a feel for the vessel as he navigated it through the seas. It was now close to mid-day, and he hadn't left the wheel yet. Being as short as he was, he used a wooden crate to stand on to be able to look over the wheel of the ship. Marc-Claude was a little hesitant to let him have complete control, but in the end, he was relieved to have a break and focus more on analyzing the map and reading the books Cobra had taken.

Earlier that morning, not long after leaving Roselin's, they came to a shallow area of the sea that was plagued by coral reefs and odd rocky formations. Knowing the area well, Hooks was able to make the correct turns to avoid tragedy. Only once did he bump the edge of a rock formation, but thankfully it wasn't a very hard hit. Marc-Claude was immensely grateful they decided to bring him along.

The look on Hooks' face varied between one of pleasure and that of a snarl. He sang songs of islands and treasure chests as he navigated the boat. The others could tell he was enjoying himself. Roselin told the group a little about his past. She knew he had lost one of his limbs in a fight with a bounty hunter, and another was lost to a shark bite. Cobra particularly was interested to hear more of his past when he the chance arose.

As of late, Hooks had been working as a "captain for hire" on these eastern waters. Traveling and picking up jobs wherever he went. He had built a name for himself as a skilled shipman. In the past he had seen much of the world and had many different experiences. Over time he had made his living as a deckhand, a gambler, a full-fledged pirate, and a soldier for his homeland. In addition to his navigating skills, Marc-Claude hoped his life experiences could be a help.

Lin had spent the morning on the deck, practicing his fighting skills with a staff. Even though he was exerting energy, the workout felt relaxing. The past months he had spent too much time destitute and with a bottle. Though his future still seemed like a mystery, just to have his blood flowing and working on this skill brought a sense of purpose. Occasionally, Hooks would yell something about him being too distracting and ruining the view of the peaceful sea. Lin would only smile back and move to a different spot. Nothing would disturb his state of mind.

Currently, Marc-Claude and Cobra were sitting on the left side of their vessel. Marc-Claude was looking over the map thoroughly, while Cobra read from the books. Little by little, they were learning bits of information regarding the treasure. Both felt as if they were unlocking the doors to a mystery that had remained hidden for over a century.

Their plan was to sail for an island realm called Seul. It was one of the last places in the southeast that was charted. Hooks knew of a woman who was skilled in interpreting maps. She was known as the Decipherer. Roselin had also heard rumors of her and knew she was skilled at deciphering symbols and maps. She was a bit of a traveler but usually stayed on the island of Seul. This would be a valuable stop as well since it would give them a chance to gather more information and restock their supplies before heading into the great unknown.

"You getting anywhere with that map?" Cobra asked as he took a break from the book.

"I think so. Look here, mate." Marc-Claude turned the map over and pointed to the artist's name. "Does this look like anything to you?"

Cobra looked again at the name. Once again, he could tell it was trying to spell out a name, but the symbols were so interwoven that it seemed indistinguishable to him. "Hmm... it don't look like nothing to me."

"Yes, but look at this." Marc-Claude ran his finger along certain designs, showing him how the letters were distinguished.

Cobra turned his head to the side, trying to decipher what Marc-Claude was showing him. Suddenly he felt it was almost magical as the letters became clear to him. There was no doubt that he read the word Sophia. His eyes grew wide as he knew he had stumbled upon a great asset.

Marc-Claude chuckled. "I think you see it too."

"Marc... Marc... Marc-Claude!" he smiled back.

He turned the map back over as he continued to talk. "It seemed like ole Dumpas was a collector of things involving treasure hunting."

"Do you think he knew what he had?"

"I don't know, mate," he said with a chuckle, "but it's ours now, and we definitely know what we have. Obviously one of the major clues left behind by Princess Sophia herself."

This new discovery gave the two men even more motivation to keep interpreting the maps and reading the books. They wondered if they were closer than anyone else had ever been to finding this treasure.

Looking back at the map, Marc-Claude pointed to an eastern area on the map. "It looks like the island of Seul is here, so I'm guessing their treasure is by one of these symbols not far north from there."

"Hmm... I think you may be right." Cobra pointed at a different spot on the map. "So, I guess you would say we're right here."

"That's correct. It looks like we're a few days from Seul, but... then again, this map is not to proper scale."

Cobra took a few moments to look over the map. He then looked curiously at a different symbol, close to where they would be traveling tomorrow. "I wonder what that is."

"Not sure," he responded, looking closely at the spot where Cobra was pointing. As best as he could tell, it looked like a cluster of clouds with streaks coming down from the clouds. The interesting thing was that the clouds looked like different colors of blue, green, and white. Even this symbol looked like another beautiful little picture in the midst of this overall masterpiece.

"Oh, well, no bother. You find anything interesting in the books?"

"Yeah, a whole lot. They say that this princess hid a whole lot of gold, but it looks like she also brought with her another treasure."

"What do you mean?"

"The book says this treasure is better than the gold."

Marc-Claude's eyes lit up. "Like diamonds!"

"No, not quite, like there is some type of power with it. Not something that can be touched or handled, but something that can change who we are. I think it's like the other rumors we heard, and I'm thinkin' it's probably true. There's some sort of great prize the princess had. That she wanted to give away freely, but people only wanted her riches. I heard this before, and it makes me think it's better than gold. I think we should pursue this even more that the riches. I mean, do you..."

Marc-Claude chuckled and put his hand on Cobra's shoulders. "You're plagued by disillusion. I hate for you to get your hopes up, mate. If you think some power will change your life and maybe change your appearance, you're mistaken. You're in control of your life. We create our destiny."

"But... but..."

He tried to brush away these ideas. "Listen, mate, I just don't want you to get disappointed. But take heart, this gold will be enough for us. It will be a life-changer. We can buy whatever you want."

"But that's not enough. I want something more."

"Don't be stupid, Cobra! It's treasure! Gold! That's what you want."

Cobra looked out to sea and shook his head. He hated the thought that Marc-Claude might be right. Maybe this journey was going to resort in simply more treasure. That's not what Cobra wanted in life. Sure, the abundance of riches would be a blessing, and would be worth the journey. But he knew there were things in life much more valuable than gold and riches. He was hoping this journey would grant him something more.

Marc-Claude could tell he had disappointed his friend. He took a deep breath and tried to find a way to change the subject. "Well... what else did the books say?"

Feeling frustrated, Cobra decided to share something that would displease Marc-Claude. "There're also some statements of warning with this treasure. You might even say, a few lessons for you."

Marc-Claude rolled his eyes. He knew Cobra was partial to statements like this. "Fine, what did the books say?"

He turned to face his friend. "Both books confirmed that part of this treasure is cursed. That the gold is only an illusion that draws you in and entraps you. It's trying to tempt you and lead you to a place of wickedness."

"Entraps you... ha!" Marc-Claude snickered and waved his hand in a dismissing manner. "Cobra, these are simply rumors, and nothing more. Someone probably shared that to keep people away from it. You know very well that there is an abundance of treasure that Sophia brought to the island. Everything we've read, including those books, say so." He stood to his feet. "Gold! Jewels! Remember, that's what we're after!"

"I know." Cobra looked down at his feet. "There's going to be riches, but..." he paused for a moment. "You know

I just worry about you getting too far ahead of yourself. And especially with this treasure, there might be big dangers."

He laughed out loud. "We'll be fine. What's the worst that could happen?" He began walking away.

Cobra shook his head as he watched his friend walk away. Though he felt disappointed, he hoped there truly was a magical power associated with this treasure. One that could fill his heart's desire. He feared for the dangers as well, but even if there was a little hope of something greater, he would keep pursuing this treasure with his whole heart.

∞

Marc-Claude couldn't sleep. He sat at the front of the boat watching the water move past him as the light of the full moon shone down from on high. It was a peaceful night. Beside Roselin, the others were asleep. Hooks was grabbing a few hours of sleep while Roselin steered the vessel. Marc-Claude had tried to sleep earlier, but his mind was stirred by earlier conversations. Talk of the treasure and riches excited him, and the added discussion of a mystery surrounding it brought a great eagerness to find this prize.

He took a sip from the bottle he was holding. It was a unique drink made from fermented sugarcane, called rum. He had recently discovered it over the last six months, and he was hooked. He only had one more bottle on deck, so he wanted to be sure to savor every drop.

Being up front on the boat appealed to all his senses. The sights of the ocean night were relaxing. The sounds of the water against the boat were soothing. The gentle breeze against his face was refreshing. And the rum was satisfying both his taste and his smell. A passing thought came to mind that he ought to go talk with Roselin and see if he could spark any interest from her with his charm. He quickly thought otherwise as she was focused on the task at hand, and on top of that, he didn't want to disturb this relaxing moment he had for himself. Flirting with Roselin would have to wait for a later time.

On nights like this Marc-Claude's mind often drifted to his family. He was the middle child in a line of five. His parents were well-respected citizens of the Empire before moving to the forest of Saison. He didn't see them much, but he was thankful for the time spent with his mother and father nine months ago. He wondered what they would think if he did find the Lost Treasure of Sophia.

Marc-Claude particularly thought of his younger sister, the one that was just below him in age. She was a lover of the sea, and her heart's desire was to come out with Marc-Claude on his boat. Those were simpler times for Marc-Claude. He thought deeply about some of those memories with his younger sister on his boat. At times he wished he still had that particular boat, but it was long gone. When he thought long enough about it, he was glad he had sold it. That was another time, a past life.

Suddenly, Marc-Claude yawned deeper. He wasn't sure where it came from, but he took it as a sign that it was time to get some sleep. Looking behind him, he saw his hammock gently rocking in the wind. It called to him. He stepped away from the front of the vessel with his bottle of rum in hand. "Good night," he called out to Roselin. She nodded slightly, not taking her eyes off the sea in front of her.

Lifting himself into the hammock, he fell asleep nearly the moment he closed his eyes.

Chapter 11

Marc-Claude was fast asleep in his hammock on the deck when he was awakened suddenly. "Wake up! Wake up, you idiots!" He sat up suddenly to see Lin and Cobra a few feet away, slowing waking up. He looked back to see Hooks shouting and pointing to a boat on their left. "A ship's coming quickly toward us!"

Looking closely, Marc-Claude could see he was right. There was a boat coming toward them from the west at an angle. Seeing another vessel wasn't that concerning, except this boat looked to be a war ship or an explorer's vessel. He quickly got out of the hammock and walked over to Roselin who was inspecting the boat through a monocular. "What do you see?"

She handed the instrument to him. "Look at the side of the boat. Do you recognize the name?"

Marc-Claude inspected the side and saw what she was referring to. On the side he read the words 'Riché the Explorer.' He continued to look at the boat through the lens. There was no doubt that it was coming toward them. "Oh, what luck!" He handed the monocular back to her.

"Do you know this explorer?" she asked.

"I do." He smiled back at her. "And I'm surprised I know someone you don't. This brings me joy."

"Marc-Claude, this is not the time for your pride. Tell me who he is!"

He cleared his throat, and his tone changed to that of lecturing. "He's an explorer based in the Northern Empire. He comes from a family of wealth. He's young, seventeen or eighteen. I've crossed paths with his family's business, but never him personally."

"Eighteen? That's quite a boat for an eighteen-year-old!"

"Oh yes! His family's quite wealthy."

"Any chance he's friendly?"

Marc-Claude shrugged. "Well, I guess if we can't outrun them..."

"Watch out!" Hooks called out.

Roselin and Marc-Claude jumped back as they watched a half-dozen arrows fly through the air toward the boat. Thankfully the arrows landed in the water and not in the boat.

"What are they doing?" Roselin said, surprised by this sudden act of aggression.

"I guess that answers the question about their friendly spirit," Marc-Claude answered.

The boat looked as if it was quickly gaining on them. It would only be a matter of minutes before it was right on them, and Marc-Claude's deck within range of their arrows. Riché stood on his boat passively watching, hoping to intimidate them. A sinister smile formed on his face. This mission seemed too easy. In his mind he was already counting his reward from Von Dechauer.

"Should we fire another round of arrows?" one of the archers asked Riché.

He licked his lips and smiled. "Yes, go ahead. Let's make them surrender."

"Very well." The archer turned to the others. "Archers, fire again at will!" It was only a matter of moments before the arrows again flew through the air toward the boat. Except this time, a few of the arrows reached the boat and stuck into the side.

Back on Marc-Claude's boat, they were getting worried. Hooks shouted down to Marc-Claude. "You got a plan, Captain?"

He looked around briefly before turning to Cobra. "Put up the white flag!"

"We're surrendering?" Cobra said, puzzled. "This doesn't seem very much like you."

"No, but I hope it'll slow them down, or at least stop them from shooting at us. Make them think they've got us."

"I see." Cobra did as he was told and ran the white flag up the mast.

About a half a minute passed before Roselin, while still looking through the monocular, shouted out. "I think it worked! It looks like the archers are no longer in position."

"Good," Marc-Claude said under his breath as he continued to frantically look for a way of escape. Their capture seemed inevitable, but he wasn't ready to give up this easily. "Think, Marc-Claude, think," he said to himself. He paced around the deck as he was starting to grow more nervous. He began moving up the right-side stairwell of the boat toward the helm when he noticed something stuck to the side of the boat. It looked like a large stone, about four feet wide, yet light was reflecting through it and back out again. It was a very curious scene. Interesting enough, he saw another of these odd 'rocks' floating in the water close by before it then got stuck to the side of the vessel. "What is this?" he said quietly. He looked out to the east and saw an ocean full of these things bobbing up and down in the water. Hundreds of them could be seen as far as he gazed. Light was reflecting off them, causing an array of colors and, in consequence, a beautiful scene in the ocean. Suddenly, he realized what they were. It was what he had observed as a symbol the day before on the map.

Quickly he shouted out. "Hooks, turn the ship starboard!"

Hooks looked toward the east. He was taken aback at what he saw. "What! You imbecile! Do you know what those are?"

"Oh yes, mate, but I think we have a better chance with them, then that ship."

Hooks looked back at Riché's ship before looking back east. He knew Marc-Claude was right. "All right, Captain. Let's do this." Quickly he turned the wheel sharply toward the east... right into the path of the colony of large man-eating jellyfish.

This area was known to many who sailed in the east. Some had seen it from a distance, while others knew to not even get that close. The area was called the Poison Sea. Some guessed the area was about two miles in diameter, but many who accidentally ventured into it didn't come out alive. The sheer number of the jellyfish attaching themselves to one's boat was enough to sink a large vessel if one was not careful. And if that wasn't enough, if one were to sting a person, the poison would instantly cramp one's muscle, causing excruciating pain. Originally, Hooks had planned to stay at a comfortable distance from this area, but at first sight of the other vessel, instinctively he began directing the boat more toward the east.

Marc-Claude shouted out. "Everyone look to the sides of the boat! We're going to have a visit from school of jellies." Lin and Cobra instantly came over and looked over the side of the boat and could see a half-dozen had already attached themselves. The blue tentacle of one was creeping its way up the side of the boat. A sharp six-inch stinger on the end of the tentacle was easily visible. On instinct Lin took his staff and fiercely jammed it into the creature's side. The staff punctured the jellyfish's skin, and also knocked the creature back toward the water.

"Take cover!" Roselin shouted as more arrows came flying toward them. Everyone on deck ducked. Hooks had to jump off of his box as an arrow flew his way. Roselin ran up the steps to check on him and make sure all was well. By the time she made it to the wheel, he was already standing back up.

"I'll take the wheel. Help the others with those jellyfish," she pleaded.

Hooks conceded. "Ok, keep us moving with the wind. After that boat stops chasing us, look for a way out."

"I will... help them!"

Marc-Claude and Cobra each grabbed a sword they had on deck. Tentacles were now over the railing as the jellyfish were ascending onto their boat. As fast as he could, Marc-Claude began cutting any tentacles that were over the deck. Cobra went to the left side of the boat as the jellyfish were starting to climb on that side as well. Lin was using his staff to pry the jellyfish off the side of the vessel. Hooks got to work helping them, using his hooks to help Marc-Claude cut through the tentacles.

Riché's boat arrived at the edge of the Poison Sea. A few jellyfish latched onto the side of his boat. Realizing what was occurring, he quickly shouted to the one steering. "Turn us... turn us!" It wasn't long before the vessel started to turn. He then looked toward his archers, "Shoot them!" The archers began aiming high in the sky. He grabbed one by the arm and shouted angrily. "No! Not them! The fish! Shoot the jellyfish!" The archers then leaned over the side of the boat and started implanting arrows into the bodies of the jellyfish. Marc-Claude's boat was no longer their first priority.

Meanwhile, back on Marc-Claude's boat, Cobra was doing all he could to get the jellyfish off his side of the boat. He was frantically moving from tentacle to tentacle, stabbing the jellyfish and cutting their tentacles. He was leaning over the side of the railing, focusing on one particular creature, when he heard a sound like a sponge splashing behind him. He turned to see that one of the creatures had made it onto the deck. "Oh no," he cried out. "I'm gonna need some help here."

"I got this," Hooks yelled out. He ran from behind and jumped on the jellyfish, landing his hooks into its body. The jelly made a strange noise that sounded like a watery screech. He pulled back his arm and landed another swipe into the body of the creature. Cobra saw the tentacles of the creature curl around and reach out for Hooks. Instantly swiping upwards, Cobra cut through one of the tentacles, before grabbing the other with his bare hands and cutting off the end stinger. He pulled back and then ran the jellyfish through as far as he could with the sword. The jelly made a sound like it was dying and Hooks climbed off.

On the other side of the deck, Lin was now standing on the side railing of the boat, rapidly swinging his staff. He was fighting off a half-dozen tentacles that were trying to sting him. Occasionally, when he got a free moment, he would take a hit at the body of one of the creatures that was making its way up the side of the boat.

The tentacles were starting to come faster and more in abundance. Suddenly a larger one wrapped around his waist. He dropped his staff and grabbed onto the railing of the boat. He strained as he held on with all his might. Marc-Claude saw he was in trouble and swung his sword and sliced through the tentacle. The pressure instantly relaxed and Lin was able to pull himself back onto the boat. "Thank you, my friend," he said through heavy breathing. Marc-Claude was barely able to respond before a couple more tentacles came his way. He quickly made short work of them, cutting them off.

Marc-Claude knew they couldn't keep this up. Eventually, the jellyfish would overtake them. They would need a different plan. "Take the sword," he shouted to Lin. He gently tossed it toward Lin, who easily caught it in return. He wasted no time in starting again to battle the creatures.

Running into the cabin, Marc-Claude frantically looked around for anything that could help. He had a few other miscellaneous weapons and some other odd items that could possibly help. He quickly opened a treasure chest and then a few drawers. All along the way, he pushed items aside, trying to think quickly about anything that could be used. After a minute he knew he couldn't take any more time, the others would need his help. He was about to run outside when his eye caught something on the side of the cabin. It was the food, and particularly the spices Roselin had brought with her onboard.

Marc-Claude ran to the table and began looking through the different items, seeing if maybe something would lure the creatures away. It was then that he picked up a large jar of spices that read 'Crushed Grimdolon Peppers.' He knew he had found what he was looking for. Grimdolon peppers were known for their incredible heat. Especially in a crushed form, Marc-Claude imagined they were even more potent. He hoped the peppers may be what was needed to at least cause a distraction. As fast as he could, he ran outside to join his friends.

Cobra and Hooks were still battling three creatures on his left while Lin was continuing to fight frantically on his right. It was also easy to tell by the rocking of the boat that the jellyfish were continuing to latch onto the sides of the ship. Roselin struggled with the wheel as the uneven weight of the creatures rocked the boat off balance. Looking to the north, she spotted the border of this area of jellyfish. As best as she could, she aimed for the clearing.

Marc-Claude ran toward Lin, who was jumping away from incoming tentacles from a couple of jellyfish that were on the deck. He quickly opened the jar of crushed peppers. The smell of the spice was pungent as he poured some into his hand. Almost without thinking, he ran toward the smaller of the jellyfish, dodging a strike from a close tentacle. He got close to what he thought was the eye of the creature and threw the palm of his hand against the slimy texture, rubbing it in as hard as he could. The creature screeched out terribly.

A tentacle from the other creature curved around and struck Marc-Claude in his calf muscle. The pain took his breath away as it felt like his muscle was about to explode. It was so painful he couldn't even scream. He took great care not to drop the jar of spice.

Lin saw what was occurring. With sword in hand, he sliced the tentacle and pulled the stinger out of Marc-Claude's leg. The smaller creature with spice in its eye wasn't fighting at this point. Lin then picked up his fallen staff and jammed it as hard as he could into the jellyfish. Being the smaller of the invertebrates, he found he could lift it. Using all his might and yelling out as he strained, he lifted it over his head and over the ship's rail. The jellyfish slid off the staff, knocking another one off the side of the boat as it fell into the water.

Another creature was starting to climb over the deck. Marc-Claude knew he had to act fast. Before the jelly could see him, he took a handful of spice and sprang toward it. He went right for the eye again and jammed the spice into it. Like the one before, it horribly screeched out in pain. Marc-Claude felt the creature release his grip on the side. He kept pushing forward and the creature slid off back into the water.

Marc-Claude looked over the railing and saw another one coming up the side toward the deck. He took a handful of spice and threw it down in the direction of the creature's eye. Like the others, it screamed out and slid off the side of the boat and into the water. Moving slowly because of the pain in his calf, Marc-Claude then continued this process around the boat.

Hooks was now helping Lin with the other jellyfish on the right side of the deck. This was the biggest of the bunch. Lin was able to keep the tentacles distracted while Hooks went in close, using his hooks to cut into the creature. It was leaving quite a slimy mess on the deck, but nevertheless, their method of attack was slowly working. In a final act of attack, Hooks had climbed on top of the creature and cut into the creature's body. Awkwardly, he fell halfway inside. With his right arm, he stretched out and attacked what he thought was the heart of jellyfish. Almost instantly the creature stopped moving.

Cobra had killed one of the jellyfish on his side and was now battling the last one. He moved closer to the creature, while it backed up. Cobra was about to move in for a final attack with the sword, when Roselin yelled out, "Cobra, on your left!" Over the side of deck, a tentacle reached out from another jellyfish. He stepped to the side and took a swipe, cutting off the stinger. The jellyfish on deck saw his opponent was distracted. It reached out its tentacle and stung him in his bicep. Cobra screamed out in pain as his muscle instantly cramped up like never before. Slowly he grabbed the stinger with his left hand and pulled it out of his arm. In anger, he then ripped the tentacle out of jellyfish entirely. By this time Marc-Claude had made his way toward this side of the deck. Grimacing in pain, he limped around the back of the jellyfish. Quickly he lunged forward and splattered a handful of spice into the eye of the creature. Like the others, this paralyzed it for a moment as the spice burned its eye.

"Ahhh!" Cobra screamed as he held his bicep in pain. It was like nothing he'd ever felt before. His blood was boiling as he looked back at this creature. He wasn't thinking clearly, but he did know he was ready to get rid of this devilish fiend. With his anger fully on display, Cobra walked toward this last living jellyfish on deck. As best as he could, he grabbed the sides of the creature. His hands sunk in about a foot on each side. Now with his adrenaline pumping at full quantity, the pain in his arm started to subside. He picked up the creature and threw him overboard. "Leave! Ya' demon of the sea!" he shouted as the jellyfish knocked off another one of the creatures before splashing into the water. The boat quickly moved past it.

Marc-Claude looked overboard, making sure this side of the boat was clear, and the jellyfish were gone. Even better than that, when he looked over, he saw that their boat was out of the 'Poison Sea' and now into clear waters. He then slumped over and grabbed his calf, trying to massage it to relieve the pain. Cobra did the same with his bicep.

Hooks and Lin walked over to where they were seated. They were both exhausted. Hooks was the first to speak. "I'm thinking I'm gonna need an extra five percent of treasure after that." He raised his arm to show them the jellyfish's slime that was stuck to his body. "I'm going to need a bath too."

Lin looked toward Marc-Claude. "How's your leg?"

"I'm ok, mate. The stinger didn't go in deep." He looked over at Cobra, who was sitting down with his eyes closed and his head resting against the side of the deck. They could all see sweat starting to form on the side of his head. "I think we better get him some help though."

"Yeah, he don't look too good," Hooks added.

"Cobra, you going to be all right?" Marc-Claude asked, concerned.

A few seconds passed before he slowly nodded his head. "I think so." He spoke with fatigue in his voice and with his eyes still closed. "But somethin' don't smell too good. Could you take that away please?"

Marc-Claude and Lin looked toward Hooks. The slime from the fish was still dripping off him. He rolled his eyes before speaking. "Ah, just give me some of that rum you got, and I'll stay at the wheel until we reach Seul." He walked away frustrated, while Marc-Claude laughed.

Marc-Claude spoke again to his close friend, this time with more relief. "Well, mate, looks like we'll have another story to tell."

With what little strength he had, Cobra forced a smile.

Chapter 12

The boat pulled into the island of Seul. The island was close to twenty-five miles in width and between fifteen and twenty miles north to south. Its population was around three thousand. Most of its wealth came from corn and honey. Occasionally ships would pass from the north and stop there for food and supplies, but being in the far east, few came by on purpose. Mostly the island merchants needed to ship their resources to other nations and bring back other supplies which would be sold to the islanders. This was the only way to get the necessary resources the citizens needed.

A full day had passed since their encounter with the jellyfish. Cobra had slept very restlessly through the night, breaking out in sweats and occasional screams. Roselin had brought along a few medicines and oils that helped to soothe his pain, but she wondered if he had some type of allergic reaction to the medicine. Marc-Claude on the other hand was doing well with his sting. His calf was still swollen, but the pain had subsided. The main concern on his mind now was helping his dear friend.

Marc-Claude had Hooks dock the boat at the most inconspicuous place he could find. He knew that if this 'Riché the Explorer' was truly after them, then there wouldn't be a way for them to completely hide, but he wanted to be sure the boat wasn't noticed right away either.

The mystery of Riché still befuddled them. Marc-Claude wondered if this young explorer was also looking for the treasure and heard rumors that others were after it as well. Or maybe somehow Governor Pasure was able to quickly hire him to hunt them down. Neither option seemed plausible, but Marc-Claude didn't care; he just knew that they needed to stay away from him.

The crew disembarked the boat onto the quiet island. The first thing the four men did was take off their boots and hats and immerse themselves into the water. The stench from the jellyfish slime could still be smelled, especially on Hooks. Previously the men had washed as much as possible after the attack by the jellyfish, but really what they needed was a full-fledged bath. Thankfully, when they fully submerged in the ocean, the slime cleaned off easily. The men then took an extra half an hour to enjoy the cool ocean water. Roselin, on the other hand, took some time to get a few minutes extra sleep. She had taken a long shift to steer the boat through the night and figured even a little nap would benefit her.

As the men finished up, they went back onboard and changed their clothes before disembarking again with Roselin. A few people passed by their boat. They stopped to take notice of this group of newcomers. With his hook, Hooks passed a casual wave to one man, but other than that, no one said anything. The islanders too were content to go about their business.

The crew walked along a dirt road that led to a town about two hundred yards to the northeast. "This way," Hooks said, heading in the direction of the small town. As they walked toward the buildings it was easy to notice that corn was growing everywhere, right up to the edge of this dirt road and then to the shore. Sometimes they passed a small patch of grass where only two or three stalks were planted, but other than that, it looked as if every part of land was used for farming. The corn was green and full, and the cobs were ready to be picked. It gave the land a very quiet and peaceful feel, a great contrast to what they experienced at the Borghese port.

The group arrived at the small village. There were probably only ten structures total. A few dozen people were walking the streets, but no one seemed to be in a hurry. Marc-Claude noticed a slightly larger port closer to this small village. Marc-Claude was thankful they hadn't docked there because this would definitely be the first place Riché would look for his boat.

"Are you sure this 'Decipherer' will be here, mate?" Marc-Claude asked Hooks.

"Yeah, yeah, we'll find her, just be patient." Hooks said this with a little anger in his voice. As a whole, the others were starting to get used to Hooks and the way he talked. It seemed that his usual demeanor was one of disagreement. Over the last day, they had learned not to be upset by him. He continued, "You idiots stay here, while I see if anyone knows where she is."

The four others stayed on the road, while Hooks went inside one of the buildings. It was less than two minutes before he came back out. "She's close!" he said victoriously. "Right this way." He reached out his hook, showing the way. The group walked across the street to another building. It looked to be some sort of tavern. The crew went inside and saw a small group of sailors casually drinking. Most stopped their conversations to glance over at the group that had just arrived. They were used to seeing occasional travelers, but Cobra's size often made folks stop to stare.

A few men shouted out casually. "Welcome, Hooks!" He saluted back.

Roselin knew a few of the patrons. She walked over to make conversation. One man said loudly, "So, they finally got you out of your restaurant!" Some started laughing at this comment. Roselin smiled to herself, rolling her eyes.

"Lin!" someone else shouted out to their left. He turned to see an old friend.

"What are you doing here?" Lin asked him. The two men embraced. It had been years since Lin had seen this close friend.

"This is where I've been stationed the last year."

His name was Tai, and he had been a good friend of Lin through many ups and downs of life. Their lives had taken different routes—Lin had pursued a life of crime, while Tai had gone the route of a marine officer, helping to protect the seas from the influx of pirates and thieves. In the past Tai had encouraged Lin to leave his life of delinquency, but it was always to no avail. Eventually Lin would make his way toward Mendolon, where he would be captured by the Knights.

"Come, I'll buy you a drink. This place has the best ale." Tai said, pulling his friend toward a counter.

Marc-Claude and Cobra were now standing awkwardly by themselves. Marc-Claude sighed and took a deep breath. He looked over at Cobra, who was rubbing his bicep. "You going to be all right?"

"Yeah, we just got to find some new medicine before we leave."

"I understand." He then looked over at the bar. "Why don't we first have a drink?" he said with a smile. Cobra didn't reply but simply followed Marc-Claude to the counter. Drinks were ordered and the barkeeper quickly brought out two mugs. As a habit the two men hit their mugs together and began drinking the ale. It tasted great and was refreshing, and for a brief moment, the two sat and simply drank as friends.

Moments like this had been scarce for them lately. Before this treasure hunt and particularly before Marc-Claude's newfound fame, the two men were more casual in their pursuits. Usually they simply followed Marc-Claude's whims as to where he'd like to explore and where he'd like to steal. For this moment there was nothing they could do but simply sit and wait on the others. It was nice to have a drink merely as two friends.

It wasn't long before Roselin came over holding a bowl and a strange looking flower. "Cobra, here, put this on your arm." She laid the bowl on the counter. Marc-Claude looked down and saw that it was full of a reddish honey. Roselin then squeezed the flower and a thin liquid substance ran off her hand into the bowl. She then took a spoon and thoroughly mixed the two together.

"What is this?" Cobra asked.

"It's some of their locally harvested honey. This kind specifically is known for its high acidity. A few travelers have given me some over the years. It's good, but potent." She then pulled out the spoon and spread the substance onto his arm. Cobra winced a little. He could feel a burning sensation on the skin as the concoction began to neutralize the poison of the sting.

"What was the flower you added?" Marc-Claude asked.

"It's called a Salehta. It grows wild on this island." She stayed focused as she continued to work on Cobra's arm. "Supposedly it helps to soothe the skin from a sting. It might be an island folktale, but the locals say to mix it into the honey for jellyfish stings."

Cobra's eyes were squeezed tightly as the honey and flower juice continued to work. He then took a drink of the ale to help distract his mind. He didn't mind the pain since he could tell it was working. There was a fear that if the poison was allowed to sit for too long that it might cause long-term damage to his arm.

Roselin then turned to Marc-Claude. "Your turn."

Marc-Claude smiled nervously. "You sure? I didn't get stung nearly as bad as Cobra. I don't think it's a problem."

"Oh, no, it's probably for the better," Roselin said. "We don't want any chance of you having an infection."

Marc-Claude looked over at Cobra to see what he would say. His friend nodded his head. "You ought to let her do it. We don't want you hurt later."

Looking at others in the tavern, he could see a few other patrons looking at him, seeing what he would do. He swallowed hard before reaching down and pulling up his pant leg. Roselin then took a generous portion of the mixture and rubbed it on his leg. Instantly the fiery sting of the honey shot through the nerves in his leg. He covered his mouth with his fist to keep him from screaming. Sweat drops started to form on the outside of his forehead. A few of those looking on began to snicker, seeing him struggle in this manner.

On instinct Marc-Claude began to sing to distract himself. "A sailor's night is my delight. Watch the waves and try to be brave. Yo, ho, ho, to-dal-dee. Close my eyes and..."

he trailed off, grimacing in pain. The sting of the medicine became too much.

Hooks walked over to join the group. "Hey, good news. The Decipherer is in the back. She…" he paused as he caught sight of Marc-Claude. "What's with him?"

Cobra looked back over at Marc-Claude before speaking up again. "Roselin's making him feel better."

Hooks laughed before continuing. "All right, as soon as you're ready, she'll see us in the back."

Marc-Claude just needed another minute or two before the pain started to subside. He was still limping a little, but overall, he thought he'd be fine. The three of them then followed Hooks toward a back room where the Decipherer would be waiting. Lin, on the other hand, stayed with his friend Tai.

The group walked down a short hallway in the tavern. The area was dark and gave them an eerie feeling as the group of four approached the door. All seemed quiet except for the knocking of Hooks' wooden leg against the wood floor. Marc-Claude and Cobra felt a mixture of curiosity and anxiety as they moved closer.

Reaching the door, the others could see it was slightly open. Hooks gave a couple of taps with his hook. "Hello!" There was no reply. He tapped again and pressed his ear on the door.

Eventually he heard a faint call, "Come in."

"Let's go," he said confidently. He pushed open the door and they all walked in together.

This room was dark with a handful of candles glowing at the far end of the room on a table. Sitting by the table was a woman. She was seated at such an angle that her face couldn't be seen. Her grey hair flowed down her back, just about reaching her waist. She didn't look up as the others approached her. In front of her on the table was a plate with food. Meticulously she was cutting into a piece of meat.

Hooks stopped the group a few feet away. The others stood behind him, wondering what to do next. Hooks cleared his throat loudly before speaking up calmly, "Hello there."

Slowly the individual put down her knife and fork and turned to face them. Right away she saw Hooks. "Well, well, well," she said joyfully. "If it isn't my old friend, Sir Hooks, how are you doing, my friend?"

"Oh, just fine, Maud, just fine." He tipped the front of his hat in effort to greet her.

Marc-Claude's eyes grew wide as the Decipherer then looked at him. An even bigger smile formed on her face. "Marc-Claude, is that really you?" she said, standing up from her seat.

He was paralyzed with silence and didn't know how to respond. "Y... yeah," he said hesitantly.

"Well, you don't say! I haven't seen you for years." The woman, who looked to be in her mid-sixties, went forward and embraced Marc-Claude.

"Hello, Maud," he responded somewhat hesitantly.

"Sounds like you two know each other," Roselin added.

"Oh, absolutely!" Maud responded, walking toward a window. She pulled back the curtains, letting much light into the room. She sat down and explained everything. "Marc-Claude, here, is my oldest sister's grandson. I used to help take care of him for his parents. He was a spirited little boy. Played hard, cried often, and needed lots of help. I think he probably wet the bed till he was eleven years old, and you ought to have heard him cry that time he lost his dolly. You wouldn't believe the size of those tears, and then there was that time…"

"Thank you, Maud," Marc-Claude said, trying to get ahold of the situation. "It's great to see you, but there seems to be a mistake. We were looking for someone known as the Decipherer."

Hooks laughed. "Aren't you the observant one. Maud is the Decipherer."

She slapped her knee. "Yep, that's right! You know I travel the world. I've seen maps and messages upon messages in different languages. You ought to see the way people write these days. And the maps! Oh, my ocean breeze!" Maud moved her hands in the air in excitement as she spoke. "The maps people are making these days with the detail and the colors. Truly extravagant! Sometimes they're of different colors, sometimes they're of the same colors, yet different hues, truly wonderful. You wouldn't believe it. One time there was this…"

"Yes, maps are… uh… good!" Marc-Claude said, interrupting her. She would have gone on much longer if he hadn't stopped her. Even though he hadn't seen her since his teenage years, he remembered Maud's tendency to tell random stories at length without stopping. It was as if she had a wealth of information in her mind but didn't know how to organize it or when it was appropriate to share it. This was helpful in deciphering maps but made it difficult to carry on a conversation with her.

Hooks stepped forward. "We have a map we think you should see."

Before Maud could say anything, Cobra pulled out the map and placed it on the table in front of her. Her eyes grew wide as she saw the beautiful depictions in front of her. "Wow! Incredible! Where did you find this? Look at the detail in these different depictions. The map is clearly about a hundred and fifty years old. Look at how it shows the Northern Empire, Mendolon, Grimdolon, along with the kingdoms in the south. Such detail! Where did you get this? Oh, no bother! Hey look, there is a place where the Poison Sea is depicted. Though it's not that big. Did you know there was an area to the southwest of here where a colony of large man-eating jellyfish gather? One time someone caught one and brought it into the tavern. They cooked it just for fun. It was awful, but that's ok. It was still fun to eat."

As she continued to talk, Marc-Claude was a little surprised by how much she had deciphered so soon. He thought he would let her keep going with her initial observations before he chimed in and directed her attention to the territory east of here. There was no telling how she would respond to the idea that they were looking for the Lost Treasure of Sophia.

Maud continued on for a full five minutes before Roselin leaned over and whispered to Marc-Claude, "Don't you think you should stop her?"

Marc-Claude cleared his throat and spoke up. "Well, Maud! I want to tell you something. We are looking for treasure in the east and wanted to see if you could see anything on this map that might indicate where this treasure might be."

Maud grabbed Marc-Claude's elbow and shook it back and forth as she laughed. "Oh, I knew from the time you were a little boy that you wanted to explore the seas looking for treasure. I remember that one time you, when you were five, you made that sword out of sticks. You told me you were going on a sea voyage. I couldn't understand you well because you were sucking your thumb." She turned to the others. "I think he sucked his thumb till he was nine."

"I did not!" Marc-Claude objected.

Roselin stepped forward, trying to keep the situation on track. She addressed Maud. "Please, we're not looking for a simple treasure chest, but rather we're looking for the famous Lost Treasure of Sophia. We wanted to see if there was anything on this map that would indicate where it would be."

"That's amazing!" She grabbed her glasses and put them on. "That treasure has never been found. Some people don't even believe in it anymore."

"Yes, we know." Marc-Claude said. "We think it should be somewhere over here." He pointed to a place northeast of Seul. "But the symbols don't seem to be signifying anything that looks like treasure."

"Hmm..." The Decipherer went silent as she carefully looked at the map. She studied the symbols carefully. She smoothed out the map with her hands as she continued to look at it up and down. A full minute passed before Maud spoke up again. "Ok, listen here, you scoundrels," she paused to laugh at her use of the word scoundrels. The others were not amused. "I think you may be looking at the wrong spot. The treasure would be here in this group of islands to the southeast of here."

The others looked at the map and saw a golden symbol with different disjointed symbols along the outer rim. They thought it resembled some type of compass. "That doesn't look like islands," Marc-Claude said.

"Oh, it is. Look at how the artist depicts islands in other parts of the map. You can see these symbols in this golden circle. He's trying to cleverly disguise them in the midst of the map, while also showing there's something majestic about this area. It's very clever, but he can't hide anything on me. Haha... I remember there was a man who brought me a scroll full of riddles. He didn't think I could figure out any of them, but old Maud was able to get them all. Then there was another time..."

"I've heard rumors of these islands," Roselin interrupted. "But I've heard they're mostly desolate. They're pure rock, or worse yet, desert. And that's if they're even out there in the first place."

"Oh, they're out there. Between the rough waters from here to there, the jellyfish to the west of them, and then talk of sea serpents south of them, people aren't very excited to see a group of islands that are boring."

Cobra spoke up. "Then how are you sure the treasure is there?"

Maud smiled. "I just love you people. The artist is obviously trying to show that there's something more to these islands than just sand and rock. Look at some of the other islands on this map, they aren't painted with golden designs like this. The author is disguising this, by making it look like some type of compass."

"So, Maud," said Hooks. "Would you have any idea where in the midst of these islands the treasure would be?"

"To be honest, there are a lot of smaller symbols in this area of the map, but once I see it in person, then I can do a little bit better at telling you where everything is."

The room went silent for a few moments as this last statement hung in the air. No one had even entertained the idea of Maud coming along on this trip. Eventually, it was Marc-Claude who spoke up. "Well, Aunt Maud, I hope you get to see it someday, but we must be on our way. Great to see you. Please give my regards to the family when you see them."

"Would you come with us?" Hooks asked.

"Yes, I think we will need your help," Roselin added.

Marc-Claude thought about objecting, but then again, he knew that they were right. She would be a big help as they got closer. In that moment, he just didn't like the thought of traveling for days on a boat with his great aunt. His heart sank.

    Maud stood up in excitement. "Oh yes! I'd be delighted. Thank you so much. This is going to be great. How fabulous! I can tell you more stories about my nephew as we travel."

    "I think I need to sit down," Marc-Claude whispered as he felt light-headed.

Chapter 13

The group talked for a few more hours before Roselin decided they all needed a break. They had been making plans for what their upcoming voyage would look like. It would take between thirty and forty hours out to sea before they could potentially arrive at the cluster of islands. Roselin said she once heard a sailor refer to them as the Islands of Rocheux. They would need to be sure they had enough supplies for going there and back again as the area would be fairly desolate. Sailing routes, food supplies, and the potential distribution of treasure were all talked about. And though it was difficult to keep Maud focused at times, a lot of the particulars were decided upon.

Marc-Claude was now back in the main area of the tavern. He felt as if he needed a drink. He went to the counter and ordered a pint of ale. It had a slight honey taste to it, which made it unique. He had already decided that he would have another, once this one was finished.

He was a little unhappy about the terms that they had finalized concerning the dividing of the treasure. Even though his share would still be fifty percent, he'd been searching for this treasure for a long time. In the past he'd been dreaming of taking it all for himself and Cobra, but now he had to divide it among his crew. Mixed emotions filled him. He was grateful for their help and knew he couldn't complete this journey without them, yet it still felt painful to give away half the treasure to the others.

Cobra came up and sat beside him without saying a word. He had been the most interested in the discussions. For his portion of the treasure, he requested anything that would be considered magical or enchanting, as opposed to anything that had intrinsic value. During the discussions Marc-Claude had interrupted Cobra and demanded that he take at least a portion of the gold that they find. He resisted, but eventually Cobra relented and agreed to take five percent. Marc-Claude was a little upset with him for not fighting for a bigger portion.

Both men said nothing as they sat and drank casually for a few minutes. Eventually Roselin, Hooks, and Maud came out of the backroom and sat at a table. It looked as if they were going to order a little food, as opposed to just having drinks. Seeing that Marc-Claude wasn't talking, Cobra decided to join them. "I think I'll get something to eat." He stood up and walked away.

"Let me know how the food is," Marc-Claude said. He looked back down at his drink and seemingly got lost in it. Maybe all he needed was a few minutes to clear his mind and gain his bearings. Thinking of how close he was to this treasure would definitely bring some encouragement once his mind was clear.

Lin casually walked up. "Marc-Claude, was the Decipherer much help?"

"She was. She's actually going to be joining us," he said, sounding deflated.

"Very interesting." Lin said, rubbing his chin.

"Where's your friend?"

"He just left." Lin then sat down quickly beside Marc-Claude, looking as if he had something important to share. "He helps patrol the seas, and he had to get back to work as his fleet had captured a most interesting prisoner off the coast of this island."

Marc-Claude was suddenly intrigued. "Oh, yeah, who's that?"

"It was a man that I learned about while in the Mendolon prison. He goes by the title 'the Court Jester.'"

"Whoa, mate," he said, shocked to hear this villain was captured here. He'd never spoken with him face-to-face. While the Jester was imprisoned in Saison, his sister hadn't allowed Marc-Claude to speak to him. But he was thankful to have a new opportunity. He couldn't hold back his curiosity. "Do you think your friend could bring me in to see him? I might be able to draw some information out of him."

Lin paused for a moment, thinking about Marc-Claude's suggestion. "Hmm... let me go ask. I might be able to catch him before he leaves." He quickly turned and ran toward the door.

Marc-Claude turned and shouted toward Cobra. "Cobra! Stay here, I'll be back in an hour or two!"

Cobra shrugged. At this point he was used to Marc-Claude running off on his own.

※

Roselin and Cobra sat together and ate a large meal of fish, vegetables, potatoes, bread, and desserts. The food at the tavern was less than desirable, so they had decided to go to a more expensive eatery attached to an inn. An hour had passed since Marc-Claude and Lin had left. Hooks had stayed behind talking with a few old friends, while Maud finished up with a few clients. Roselin wanted to try this restaurant as she had heard passing comments from different sailors about its exquisite preparation of vegetables and potatoes. As a cook herself, she wanted to see if there was anything she could learn from this place. Cobra, on the other hand, was simply hungry and decided to join her in this exploration of food.

This restaurant was busy with different dignitaries and socialites from the small island. All were dressed prestigiously with some in attendance in uniform. Roselin, and particularly Cobra, stood out in this crowd. Everything about the atmosphere communicated that this was a place of luxury. There were silk tablecloths, a lute playing in the background, unblemished wooden walls, and a few extravagant paintings, all of the finest quality. It was as if the designers wanted the décor to look like that of a castle. Thankfully, Roselin had enough money with her to cover the cost.

Cobra tried a little bit of everything. He hadn't eaten much the day before and it showed. The cooks stayed busy filling their orders. When they were brought another dish, Roselin would take it upon herself to order something new. This, combined with Cobra constantly needing his drink refilled, made the servers and cooks a little more strained than usual.

"What's your favorite so far?" Roselin asked as she nibbled on the edge of a piece of bread.

He set down the cup he was drinking from and wiped his mouth and thought for a moment. "Maybe the potatoes, but everything's good."

"Even the fish?"

Cobra smiled. He knew what she was getting at. "I like this fish, but yours is better."

She sat back in her chair, feeling a sense of relief. "I think so too."

A few more minutes passed before the owner of the eatery came by to check on them. He looked closely at Roselin. "Are you and your friend in need of more substance?"

"I think we're coming to an end. Maybe one more serving of your potatoes."

"Very well," he said properly. "I do hope you have the means to pay for all this."

She chuckled. "Trust me. We'll be fine."

"I could use some more wine!" Cobra interjected.

The owner rolled his eyes and snatched the cup. Cobra was taken aback at this display of rudeness. He looked inquisitively at Roselin, as if to say, 'what was that all about?'

"Don't mind him," she said under her breath.

Cobra nodded, trying to shrug it off, but the thought stuck with him. It was then that he began to notice others were staring at him. He could see a few people turn away when one made eye contact. Another man, who was staring at him, shook his head in disgust. Cobra looked away, feeling embarrassed. Maybe it was his clothing, or maybe his size, but one thing was clear, he wasn't welcome here.

Suddenly, many of the trials from his youth came back to haunt him. The teasing and the scorn played inside his mind. He'd heard it his whole life. Here in this place, scanning the faces of those around him, it was all too much. He felt as if he was ready to break something, or better yet show his might. They would all be sorry. He would show them that what he lacked in intelligence and appearance, he made up for in strength.

Cobra was about to stand up and execute his plan, when suddenly from inside of him came words of restraint, flying in like an arrow. The simple adage, "Be slow to speak, slow to become angry," repeated in his mind. He put his hands on the table and breathed slowly, trying to clear his mind.

Seeing his disgruntled face, Roselin could tell there was a battle going on in his mind. "Cobra, are you well?"

He shook his head. "I'm sorry... I have to go," he said, standing up abruptly and walking out.

"Good riddance to the ogre," he heard someone say as he left. Others laughed.

Leaving was the best course of action for him. Cobra didn't want his anger to get the best of him and then for bad things to happen. In his younger years he would usually act out on his anger and start a fight. Most of the time he regretted it and cried about it later. Ironically, Marc-Claude had helped him brush off the insults of others and suppress his anger. Along with that, knowing that Marc-Claude was his friend, no matter what occurred, helped to ease his mind and bring relief. He had come a long way in calming his mind. Yet, through all of this, from time to time, his anger would still present itself again. It was a battle he was always aware of and looking to conquer.

Cobra walked toward the side of the building. It was now evening, and the darkness helped conceal him. He leaned against a wall and closed his eyes. It wasn't too much longer before Roselin came running up. "Hey, is everything all right?" He took a deep breath as he squeezed his eyes tight, still trying to suppress the thoughts of anger. She kept on, "Listen, I wouldn't pay any attention to those people in there. They don't know you. They don't know who you are."

He cleared his throat and spoke quietly. "But would it even make a difference? They'd just see that I'm not smart and nothing more." He paused for a second and clinched his fist. He spoke with more resolve. "But everything will be ok.

Once we get that treasure, then things will change. Nothing will be the same."

A sad expression formed on her face. She took off her hat, trying to show a display of sincerity. She paused a moment and chose her words carefully, greatly hoping they would help her new friend. "Listen Cobra, I don't know what we'll find with that treasure, or what kind of magic there is associated with it, but I don't think it will be the change you're looking for."

His interest was piqued. "So, you think there's magic with it too?"

She took a deep breath, before speaking hesitantly. "Yes, I've heard the rumors. I know more than I've let on."

He took a step toward her. "Then you KNOW there's magic with it."

"Please, hear me." She put her hand on his arm. "Even if this magic is able to change you, then it won't be authentic, or even real. Magic always shows itself to be insincere. Though it might be powerful, I don't think it will give you what you're looking for."

He pulled his arm away. "But the books say it will give me the knowledge I seek."

Roselin shook her head again. She could tell Cobra was at the point where he wasn't listening to her anymore. An obsession was growing within him. A quest for knowledge and intelligence, which wasn't bad in and of itself, but she worried about his purpose behind acquiring this new intellect. She worried if this would bring out the worst in him, instead of the good. She would hate to see this gentle giant turned into a monster.

"Well, I think we better head back to the tavern. Marc-Claude might be back soon, and we'd hate for Hooks to get into any trouble while we're gone."

Cobra snickered slightly as he slowly turned back toward the tavern. Roselin followed beside him, hoping his mind had at least been redirected.

∽∾

Marc-Claude walked down a hallway past a few prison cells. He was on the way to see the man called the Court Jester. Lin's friend, Tai, was able to get him into the prison. It wasn't an easy task as Tai had to convince his overseer that Marc-Claude's family had interacted with him in the past. So far, the Jester wasn't talking much, so the officials were hoping that Marc-Claude could change this.

As he got closer, Marc-Claude reminded himself to stay calm. The Jester was indirectly responsible for the death of his brother-in-law, and for that he felt entitled to a sense of revenge. He loved his sister and wouldn't hesitate to right any wrong that had been done to her. Any action of revenge or justice would have to be passed off to others. For now, he just wanted to meet this man and deliver to him an insult if possible.

The cell was just about in view. He stopped for moment to readjust his collar and to tie his bandana tighter. Taking a deep breath, he then stepped forward in front of the cell of this enemy.

Marc-Claude saw a figure sitting with his back against the side of the cell. He didn't move when Marc-Claude stepped in front. His clothing was that of a commodore, but he had well-applied face paint with diamonds on his eyes and a two-tasseled hat on the top of his head. Marc-Claude stood in front of the cell for a full minute and neither man said a thing. Eventually, Marc-Claude cleared his throat loudly.

"What do you want?" the prisoner said without moving.

"My name is Marc-Claude. You may have heard of me."

"I don't care who you are, leave me."

"Sorry, but I wasn't able to speak with you in Saison, so I came now." He paused and stepped closer to the bars. "What were you doing this far away from Mendolon?"

"Sight-seeing," he said condescendingly.

"Well, please don't touch anything along the way. Your mere presence seems like it ruins everything it comes in contact with."

The Jester didn't respond. Marc-Claude looked closer at him and thought he looked destitute. He shook his head as he figured the Jester wasn't saying anything else. "Very well, mate, I'll leave you to continue playing with your little face paint. Enjoy your cell."

As he began to walk away the Jester spoke out. "You're a fool."

"I'm a fool?" Marc-Claude stopped in his tracks. "Bad choice of words, mate. Lest I remind you that being a fool was your job. Ha! Maybe I am in some regards, but you chose to be one."

"Don't be naïve." He turned toward Mar-Claude. "I know what you seek. I've heard the rumors of it. And let me tell you, your weak mind won't be able to tame it. The desires within will destroy you. You will die by the power of what you seek."

"What are you talking about?"

He turned his head and leaned it against the back of the wall. There was a hint of jest in his voice. "You'll see. I might be wearing the face paint, but you'll see that your worthless life is weak, and in essence your pursuits are foolish in the end."

Marc-Claude was slightly intrigued. He stepped closer to the cell. "You have quite an imagination, and I'm always interested in being entertained. What is this irrational fantasy that is brewing in your mind? I imagine it would be interesting… in a peculiar scientific type of way."

The Jester now said nothing in response, but simply closed his eyes as he leaned against the cell. Marc-Claude took a deep breath. He figured he had spent too much time already on this little escapade. Without saying another word, he simply walked down the hall and out of sight of the cell. In that moment Marc-Claude suddenly didn't seem to care anymore. This enemy was in prison. Justice would be served. Maybe he could somehow check in and hear what the final verdict was, but, for now, all was settled. This seemed to suppress any thoughts he had for trying to harm or seek revenge on this villain. And besides that, there was nothing else he could do at that time, especially if the Jester wasn't talking. The Jester would be dealt with by others, but that wasn't part of his story. His mind was back on the mission, and the Treasure in the East was his complete focus.

Marc-Claude left the prison without much fuss. He barely even spoke to the guards. The night air felt cool and crisp as he stepped into it. He breathed in deeply as the prison air had been a little stale. Briskly, he began walking back toward the tavern. The crew would leave early the next day. He was ready for the journey as he felt he had all they needed from this island, and there was no reason to delay. The treasure called to him; they needed to leave.

To his left he saw an elderly man pulling a cart, looking as if he was selling a commodity. Marc-Claude was curious. He approached the man. "Good evening, mate."

"Hello," the man said, extending the o-sound.

"Just wondering what you're trying to sell at this time of night."

"Oh, ho, ho!" the man said with excitement. "Well, I've got something for you." He reached back into his cart, and fished around for a second, before pulling out what looked like a piece of fruit. He held it up proudly. "Figs! As many as you want. They don't grow here. Brought by a fine sea traveler."

Instantly Marc-Claude felt sorry for asking. "Oh... let me guess, a man named Corleone and his wife, Gabriella."

"Oh yes! Yes! They dropped some off from a kingdom in the south. They have a later harvest. It's wonderful. They come by often whenever they're in the area. Extremely generous. You should meet them sometime. You know, what I think…"

"Please, just…" Marc-Claude began to walk away abruptly. "Just give them my regards."

"Why don't you stay and greet them yourself."

"Sorry, mate, traveling east," he said, trying to get away as quickly as possible. The legendary treasure in the east needed his attention. He couldn't keep being distracted like this.

The man called out again. "But wait! You forgot your figs."

Marc-Claude slapped his forehead and began walking away even faster.

Chapter 14

The crew left Seul in the early morning. A strong wind was pushing them east. Some of them felt a little apprehensive as this area was seen as dangerous and uncharted. Hooks was at the helm expertly moving the wheel as there were a few boulders and reefs along these waters. Lin was helping him navigate and making him aware of different deterrents that were coming their way. Occasionally, Lin would miss one, and Hooks would yell a slew of insults. Thankfully, Lin had grown much more patient during his time in prison.

Marc-Claude tried to get Maud to look at the map again and decipher more of the various places depicted on it. Unfortunately, Maud was too distracted and kept talking about various family members that he had never met. At one point she told a lengthy story about a second-cousin, once removed, who once had the world's largest collection of animal bones. Marc-Claude didn't ask questions—he didn't want to know anything more about this situation. He simply felt embarrassed by his family lineage.

Cobra tried to read more in the books but found it difficult. The rocking of the boat from the sudden turns in navigation made it hard to focus. As best as he could, he persevered in his reading. He wanted to make sure there was no error in finding the treasure. The incident at the eatery on Seul was a reminder that he needed to find this life-changing treasure. Situations like that would never happen again after it was found. He would command the respect of others.

For a few hours they traveled, trying to keep the same course southeast as best as they could toward the islands of Rocheux. Roselin had brought out some food for them in the mid-morning, but very little was eaten as the boat's rocking brought on a slight bit of sea sickness. Through it all, it was easy to see why this area was basically uninhabited.

Roselin had the passing thought that maybe this territory was protected on purpose. Possibly this hindrance was purposeful. She offered this idea to the others, but it was dismissed by Marc-Claude. Even if there was something purposeful trying to prevent them from reaching the treasure, it wouldn't stop him. He would do whatever it took. Eventually when the waters got too rough, Roselin suggested they put it up for a vote whether they should continue on or retreat. Marc-Claude, Cobra, and Hooks voted to go forward, while Lin and Roselin suggested they turn away. And Maud they couldn't get focused enough to vote, but nevertheless it somewhat sounded like she wanted to press on. So, they continued.

After a few hours they came out of the rough waters. They all took a moment to breathe a sigh of relief. "See, nothing to worry about," Marc-Claude said, somewhat sarcastically.

"Don't get relaxed yet," Roselin said. She pointed forward motioning to a dense fog coming into view.

"Oh, uh... probably just a cloud on the water. Nothing to worry about." Marc-Claude said, not sounding convincing at all. No one said anything in response to seeing the fog. Some of Roselin's earlier warnings came to mind. They all worried if this was something mystical trying to prevent them from reaching their destination. Even Hooks seemed a little apprehensive at the thought of entering it, but either way there was no way around it. They would be going through this fog.

Slowly the boat went forward, entering the cloud on the water. Moment by moment their vision was clouded, and they felt a heaviness around them. Marc-Claude walked to the edge of the ship and looked around. He told himself there was nothing to be afraid of, but he questioned why he felt fearful. He wondered if he'd worked himself into this state of panic. Either way, he couldn't answer that at the moment. "Keep moving forward!" he shouted.

He looked back at the others and found them looking anxious, similarly to how he felt. Roselin stepped closer to him and spoke with reluctance in her voice. "I don't know what this is, but maybe it's just the fear of the unseen. We don't know what's on the other side."

"Yeah, I think you're right." Marc-Claude said. He then ran up the steps toward the helm toward Lin and Hooks.

"Hooks, what's this water like?"

"Smooth. Good thing we're out of those rocks."

The boat continued through the cloud for a few more minutes before the outside light could be seen. Instantly the whole crew felt relief. Again, they breathed a sigh of relief, thankful there was nothing to worry about in the fog.

Peace began sweeping over all of them. Cobra particularly felt reassured. He sat down on the steps and wiped his forehead. He laughed slightly, realizing his fears were unfounded. Seeing Cobra's response, a couple of the others chuckled as well.

Their feeling of peace was short-lived as Maud suddenly cried out, "Another boat!"

They looked toward her, but it was too late. A ship was crashing into them. Unable to brace themselves, they fell to the deck from the sudden impact. In a matter of moments men from the other vessel began jumping onto their boat. They were armed with swords. It was obvious that this boat was waiting for them to exit the cloud before they attacked. It had provided a near-perfect shield for them.

Everything happened so fast, they weren't able to react. Marc-Claude, Lin, Roselin were instantly surrounded and knew there was nothing they could do. Cobra began fighting one of the men. He knocked him down and kicked him in the side. Another man approached him, and the result was the same. Cobra easily fought with him and knocked him off his feet. He was about to fight another, when a voice shouted out. "Surrender now, or these three die!"

Cobra turned to see a younger man dressed like a captain. Half a dozen of his men had drawn swords around the others. Cobra knew he would have to surrender. He got down on his knees and put his hands in the air. A couple of men came forward and tied his hands behind his back. They then threw him down on his stomach and put a sword to his neck.

Two men held Hooks' arms in the air, while another held tightly onto his waist. All the while he was struggling to break free, yelling insults to the men carrying him. His legs were tied together around the thighs. A wooden board was brought off of their ship and his arms tied against it, thus immobilizing them. Even while being completely helpless, he still rocked from side to side, yelling out and trying his best to break free.

Marc-Claude cleared his throat and spoke out loudly among the chaos. "I presume you are Riché the Explorer."

The young man smiled. "Yes, and it will be a name you'll never forget."

Instantly, Marc-Claude disliked him. He could tell by his clothing and his mannerisms that he was trying hard to put out a façade that he was a well-seasoned explorer. Though he figured this young man was well trained, he knew any success or prestige this young man had was bought and paid for by his rich family. He spoke unafraid to his captor. "If you've come looking for the treasure, then you're fooling yourself. We have not acquired anything, nor will we share any secrets with you."

He laughed. "Oh no, my treasure is not from a map or a chest. I work for the one and only Von Dechauer. He will reward me bountifully once I bring you back to him."

Instantly Marc-Claude was lost in a daydream. "Oh yes! My old friend, Von Dechauer. Be sure to tell him thank you for helping to make me famous."

"You can tell him yourself."

Marc-Claude looked around and tried to think as best as he could for a way to talk himself out of this one. More than anything he knew he didn't want to face Von Dechauer. He had heard the horror stories of what he did to prisoners. That was not a fate he wanted to endure. He thought he'd press his luck. "Too bad he's just using a rich kid's resources to get the treasure for himself."

This upset Riché a little. He took a step closer to Marc-Claude. An angry look formed on his face. "No, he doesn't want the treasure. He thinks it's a fool's errand. This is simply a manhunt."

Marc-Claude laughed insultingly before speaking. "Kid, it seems like you're a good captain, but you've got a lot to learn. He's using you for his purposes."

"No... no! He wants you. His payment and the reputation I gain will be enough."

Marc-Claude laughed even harder. Roselin and Lin were doing their best to stay level headed, wondering where he was going with all of this. He stopped laughing and looked right at Riché. "You know what, mate…" He paused for a moment staring intently at his captor. He smiled. "Oh, never mind."

"What? ... what!" Riché said, getting upset.

Marc-Claude simply shook his head and looked off to the side. "Nothing. Just please tie us up."

"No, don't tie them up." Riché pulled his sword. He stood there in front of Marc-Claude, waiting for him to say more. Marc-Claude just stayed on his knees, trying to look as relaxed as he possibly could.

Riché couldn't stand it. He felt insulted by the silence. Stepping even closer, he brought back his hand and struck Marc-Claude in the cheek with the back of his hand. "Uh," he groaned as he fell on his side. It took a moment for him to clear his mind. "Why couldn't you just tie me up?" he said with exhaustion in his voice.

"Tell me what you know!" Riché shouted.

Marc-Claude took his time sitting back up. He brushed himself off and took a deep breath. He could tell his plan was working. If only he could keep Riché from completely losing his temper. "Listen, kid, Von Dechauer is thinking a step ahead of you. He's outsmarting you. I know you can't see it, but I already can. He's taking complete advantage of you and your resources." Marc-Claude knew none of this was true. Von Dechauer was known as a ruthless businessman, but he was also regarded as fairly true to his word. Marc-Claude could only hope that he sounded believable. He continued. "He's probably not even paying you that much."

"He promised me a year's worth of gold!" Riché said, trying to stay dignified.

Marc-Claude swallowed hard in an attempt not to sound shocked at the large amount. He kept playing it cool. "Is that all? Most who work for Von Dechauer are promised at least twice that."

Riché stuck his sword in the deck before shouting. "Then last year, why didn't you complete the mission for him?"

He chuckled again. "You've got a lot to learn about the world, kid. The fame I got from foiling his plan is worth more than anything he could offer."

"But that's why he wants you! And once I bring you back to him, I will be known as the one who tracked down the prestigious Marc-Claude."

"Are you really that stupid?"

"Shut up!" Riché smacked him again. Marc-Claude fell to his side once more, realizing that last statement went a little too far.

Marc-Claude sat back up. He moved his jaw around, trying to relax it before speaking. "Listen, mate, he wants this legendary treasure. We're so close to finding it. Do you think he's simply going to let that vanish?"

"But he said he didn't want to bother with it."

"He's fooling you." Marc-Claude, feeling braver now, stood to his feet. "Here's what I suggest. I'll help you find the treasure if you let everyone go, except Maud. We'll need her help."

"She's over here, captain!" one of the crewmen shouted out. They all turned to see Maud squatting down between two barrels, being perfectly still. Even when it was clear that she had been spotted, she still didn't move.

"They can see you, Maud. You can come out!" Marc-Claude called loudly.

A few seconds later Maud shouted back angrily. "Thanks a lot, Marc-Claude! They would have never seen me."

Marc-Claude rolled his eyes before looking back at Riché. "She will have to come in order to interpret the map. Does it sound like a deal?"

Riché grabbed his sword and sheathed it. He seemingly looked more comfortable all of a sudden. It was obvious to all that something was on his mind. "No, here's what I propose. I will bring you to Von Dechauer after you and your interpreter take me to the treasure." He paused as a diabolical look formed on his face. "In exchange for this, I will let the girls live."

"What girls?"

"Bring them out!" Riché shouted.

They all watched as two of Riché's men brought out two women in their twenties who were dressed elegantly. Marc-Claude and Cobra instantly recognized them from the governor's party. It was Leah and Rachel. They looked frightened. Immediately, Marc-Claude felt bad that they had to be dragged into this ordeal. Worse yet, he knew that he had lost all of the power in his negotiating. For a moment he felt helpless. "What of the others?" he said quietly.

"I'll let them live."

Marc-Claude spoke much more quietly, and with a tone of resolution. "Fine, take Maud and me with you. We'll do our best to find the treasure. But you must promise that you won't harm anyone."

"Very well," Riché said, now visibly excited. "Bring whatever you need on board, along with the interpreter. Tie up the others."

"But you said you wouldn't harm them!"

"I won't, but I don't want them chasing after us either." Victory was in his voice.

The plans were then put in place. Cobra, Lin, and Roselin were tied around the ships mast, while Hooks was left tied to the board. Cobra felt deflated. They had come all this way, and he had been searching for so long. He had greatly desired this treasure, but now, it appeared to be all over so quickly. Survival was now on the forefront of his mind, and the only thing he could hope for.

Marc-Claude and Maud willingly submitted themselves to their captors. Their hands were tied, and they were led away. Maud had handed over the map to Riché's men. As Marc-Claude embarked onto Riché's ship, he turned and looked back one last time at his friends. He was trying to think of something he could suddenly do for them, but at the moment he figured that trusting Riché to keep his word was the only course of action. Marc-Claude said nothing, but simply walked onto Riché's boat, feeling as if he'd let down his friends.

After Marc-Claude and Maud were taken care of, Riché turned to some of his crew and spoke quietly. "Sink their ship."

Some of the crew were shocked by these words. "But... but that will kill those on board."

"I don't care. You men, each take an axe and go below deck. Chop holes in the sides. Let the water in." The men said nothing in reply, but looked at one another, wondering what the other would say. Riché was growing impatient. "You got a problem with that?"

"No, sir," One replied quietly.

"Good, make it quick." Most of these men were sailors or rough mariners hired by Riché's father. Though they weren't the most trustworthy group, they didn't like the idea of killing anyone. This was not what they had signed up for. Nevertheless, three of the men on the crew went below the deck with axes in hand. They took their time chopping holes below deck. The water began rushing in. None of the men said anything during the process, feeling ashamed for what they had done. They went back up onto the deck and purposefully didn't make eye contact with those that were restrained.

"Is the job done?" Riché asked as the men now came on board his ship.

"Yes," one man responded solemnly.

Marc-Claude had noticed the axes in their hands and knew there was a problem. As their ship sailed away, he stood at the side railing of the deck, watching space grow between the two vessels. He knew that Riché hadn't just left them tied up. The boat was sinking, and his friends would be stranded. Not even pretending like there was no pretense, he turned to Riché and spoke matter-of-factly, "I thought you said you wouldn't hurt them."

Riché slapped him on the back. "Oh, maybe it's you, Marc-Claude, that needs to learn a thing or two. I said I wouldn't hurt them, and so far, they're still not hurt."

"God, help them," Marc-Claude mumbled under his breath.

∽♡∾

Cobra, Roselin, and Lin were sitting against the mast, all with their arms tied to it. They had all heard Riché's commands earlier and knew that the boat was sinking. Lin was straining, trying to pull free from the ropes. Cobra was rocking back and forth, seeing if there was leeway in the stability of the mast. Roselin, on the other hand, was stretching out her foot as far as she could, trying to reach the board where Hooks was lying. The hope was that his hooks could somehow be used to cut them free. Unfortunately for both Roselin and Lin, their plans seemed hopeless as Hooks was out of reach and the ropes were tied so tight that there was no give at all.

"Hooks, is there any way you can slide over here closer?" Roselin asked.

"No, I can't... but I'll tell you something. When I get my hands on that young spoiled, rotten, phony, weak, little teenager, who is full of himself and thinks..." The others paid him no mind to him as he continued with the insults about Riché.

Cobra was having some success pushing against the mast. The boards around it were creaking ever so slightly. It wasn't much, but it gave them a little hope. He kept on rocking with all his might, trying to push and pull it out of the deck. After five minutes of pushing and pulling with his body, he had made progress of a few inches.

Suddenly Roselin called out, putting their two plans together. "Cobra, Lin, try with all your strength to pivot the mast toward my side. It might be all I need to reach Hooks."

Cobra and Lin established their footing and strained with all their might. They probably gave Roselin about six extra inches, but it was just enough for her foot to interlock with Hooks. She pulled her foot time and time again, very slowly making progress and pulling him closer to her. "Come on, you can do better!" Hooks shouted.

"Quiet!" Roselin shouted back, trying to stay focused. Eventually she pulled Hooks' board to a spot where Lin could help position it to an advantageous spot. Using his feet, Lin moved the board into position where one of his hooks could slowly start to cut part of the rope close to Cobra.

"Now, cut the ropes!"

Instantly, Hooks got to work. Strand by strand, they could see he was quickly making process. The holes Riché's men had made below deck weren't very large and made for a slowly sinking boat, but even still, time was of the essence. The three of them didn't want to be tied to this mast when the boat went underwater.

"Ok, I'm goin' to give it a try," Cobra announced when he saw the ropes were adequately weakened. With all his strength, he pushed against the ropes, yelling out as he tried to break the ropes. Lin and Roselin tried to help, but they could tell, they weren't much good.

"It's working!" Hooks yelled out. Cobra stopped. Hooks went back at it with his hook, cutting the rope. "Try it again, you big buffoon!"

Cobra ignored the insult and pushed his arms out. This time there was success. The ropes loosed enough for Lin to slide out. The other two could then slide out easily as there was now more than enough slack. Without thinking, they then quickly untied Hooks and put him to his feet. "I knew you could do it," he said, bumping Cobra with his forearm. "Love you, man!"

The others looked around and now had to face their other problem. The boat would soon be sunk with no land in sight. "Grab what you need!" Roselin shouted out. "See if we can find anything that will float. It won't be long till we're under." The four of them got to work quickly looking for any necessities, or anything that would help in their survival. Cobra immediately grabbed some of his favorite books, including the ones taken from Governor Pasure's mansion. He wrapped some of his clothes around them and as best as he could secured them in a cloth bag. Roselin grabbed a few items from the food she'd brought along, mostly bread and fruit. She knew this wouldn't last very long, but her hope was that it would buy them a little time. It seemed like the only thing she could wish for at this point.

Their fate had changed so quickly. It wasn't long ago that they were thinking about finding a majestic, mysterious treasure, but now their minds were occupied simply with staying alive. As the boat went under, they simply prayed and hoped.

Chapter 15

Cobra, Roselin, Lin, and Hooks floated in the water, clinging onto a few boards. A few of their miscellaneous items were sitting atop of the boards. No one said anything as they felt discouraged by their present state. It had taken a little longer than expected for their boat to sink. This seemed to only add to their despair as it built the anticipation for their stranded situation of floating along in the water without hope.

Their situation at the moment was slightly stable. The sun was shining, and the temperature was pleasant. Also, the water seemed mild as well. They didn't fear freezing or any type of problem related to their body temperature. Between the slightly warm weather, and mildly cool water, it formed a near perfect swimming condition for the group. The biggest threat they figured was a shark or a random jellyfish from the Poison Sea.

No plans were on their mind. Before the ship had gone down, they all had looked as far as they could for an island. Each took a turn with the monocular and searched in all directions. Eventually they discovered that it was pointless, no land was in sight. Swimming would be out of the question.

More time passed before Hooks spoke out angrily. "You know what, this is all your fault!" He looked toward Roselin.

"My fault?" Roselin said, clinching to a board with both hands.

"Yes, your fault. If you had never brought me into this situation, I would have never met these guys, and I'd be on some beach somewhere enjoying some high-quality ale."

"I didn't force you to do anything. You agreed to this on your own."

Hooks pushed his arm through the water, moving closer to Roselin. Being a small individual, half of his body was atop of the board. "I only agreed to it because I could see these scums didn't know what they were doing. I thought it might be a bad idea, but then I thought, 'Surely, Roselin isn't an idiot. She would know when a job is a failure or a good idea.' But no, even the enlightened Roselin is apparently lacking in intelligence as well. Intelligence must be in shorter supply than even gold or treasure."

Cobra tried to ignore them as they continued to argue. His large hat rested on top of his head. He pulled it down further, trying to drown out the sight of the two of them fighting. This argument wasn't going to help the situation, and it only further sent him into despair. Of the four, he was the most discouraged. Not only had he lost his purpose from the last year, but he had lost a friend as well. He feared that even if they somehow got out of this situation, it would be too late. He would probably never see Marc-Claude again.

"I don't think you'd ever find this treasure anyway." Hooks continued to yell at Roselin. "All we have to go on is bunch of loose bits of information that these pirates threw together. Foolish trust like this makes me see why your restaurant is run so poorly."

Roselin's eyes grew wide. Now it was personal. It took her a minute to recover from what she'd just heard. "How... dare... you!"

For a very brief moment Hooks thought about apologizing, but that moment passed quickly. "Yeah, it's true," he said quickly, knowing he'd gone too far, but he felt like he couldn't take it back either.

Roselin pointed right at him. "Well, let me tell you. You are nothing but an idle scoundrel. You never even pay fully, you freeloader. Your rude attitude keeps customers away. You're loud, take too much time to eat when we're busy, and if we're talking about intelligence..." She stopped suddenly when she noticed Lin. His eyes were closed, and his hand was on the top of water as if he was trying to feel the current of the water.

"Come on, just give it to me!" Hooks said, looking for the rest of the insult. "Don't hold back now."

"Shh... quiet," Lin said.

Half a minute passed before Roselin spoke up. "What is it, Lin?"

"I think something's coming," he said stoically.

"Are you sure?" she asked.

"Yes. I feel it on the water, and you can hear it if you listen closely."

All the arguments ceased as they listened carefully to the world around them. Being this far east, in basically uncharted waters, had erased a thought of rescue. There was a sense of wonder as to what this could be. They all knew if they could hear or feel anything it meant something was fairly close.

Hooks spoke out among the silence. "I'm thinking you're crazy. There's nothing around here."

Lin then opened his eyes and looked toward the others. "It's coming from the fog."

They all turned and looked, and there they could see emerging from the fog a large merchant ship coming close to them. A white sail was helping to move the ship toward their position. They could see a few people peeking overboard. Some of them began pointing at the stranded individuals bobbing in the water from the waves of the boat. Lin wondered if these individuals would be friendly or if he and his friends would be taken captive. On the other hand, Roselin, Hooks, and especially Cobra, had no fear. For they knew that this boat belonged to a friendly merchant named Corleone and his wife, Gabriella.

"Hello, there!" a voice yelled off the side of the boat. They all looked up and could see a man with large golden curls smiling as he waved. A beautiful woman dressed royally was by his side. She was waving as well.

"Hey! Can you get us out of this water?" Hooks yelled out.

"No worries, my friend." Corleone responded joyfully. "We'll have you up soon."

The next few minutes went by quickly. Instantly a half dozen crewman got to work preparing for their arrival. A couple of men on board even dove into the water to assist the stranded individuals. Ropes were let down and no energy was spared with helping them onto the ship. Warm blankets were wrapped around them, while Corleone's men retrieved all their items that were floating on various boards. Ironically even the boards they were floating on were retrieved. Roselin tried to tell them this wasn't necessary, but they wouldn't listen. Everyone displayed hospitality to a fault.

"Please, bring out our best rations." Gabriella commanded with elegance.

"Right away," a crewman responded.

"Ahh, Cobra, my friend, great to see you." Corleone said with a big smile.

Cobra chuckled. "But it's truly great to see you even more." The two men then embraced like old friends. This would have been odd with any other individual, but after knowing Corleone for only day, one felt like they'd been friends for a long time.

"How'd you find us?" Roselin asked. "Or rather, why are you out here?"

"Oh, yes," Corleone said, laughing. "We stopped at Seul to drop off a supply of soybeans. It was then that I stopped to see a man I often give figs to when we have a surplus. Well, he mentioned that a man told him to give us his regards. Do you know it? I asked him what who it was, and he described Marc-Claude."

"But then how did you find us?" Cobra asked, still confused.

He slapped Cobra on the back. "Oh, it was very simple. He said you were traveling east, and the only thing out that way is the Islands of Rocheux, and I've always wanted to see them. It's our slow season, and I wondered if we could catch up with you. So, I then asked the crew, and they all agreed we should try. Especially with the dangers of this area, they thought you might need help."

Food was brought out to the four individuals in generous portions. As it was being served, Gabriella spoke up. "By the way, where is Marc-Claude?"

"Well, that's quite a story," Cobra said. While the others ate, he began a long account of their travels since they last saw them. Corleone and Gabriella's kids joined them and were listening intently to this story. At times the others would add in helpful details or remind Cobra of a major point he'd left out. Nothing was hidden, and Cobra disclosed everything he knew about the Treasure in the East. These people had saved their lives. He felt they were entitled to know the reason why they were in this state, and what had led them here. By the end of the account the whole crew was around them hearing of the adventure.

As Cobra wrapped up his account, the crew started mumbling amongst themselves. "Interesting," Corleone said. Slowly, his wife reached over and grabbed his hand. They then locked eyes, seemingly knowing what each other was thinking. It wasn't long before Corleone cleared his throat. The crew went silent as he began to speak. "Very well, there's only one solution for us. We will travel east and rescue Marc-Claude."

"Hooray!" the crew shouted out in celebration. Cobra, Roselin, Hooks, and Lin all looked at each other, surprised at how, once again, their fate had changed so quickly.

∾

Marc-Claude leaned against the railing on the side of the boat. He wasn't tied up anymore as he was watched closely by some of Riché's men. Maud, on the other hand, was taken below deck where she was made to further interpret the map. A few hours had passed since they were taken captive, and it was the early evening. The atmosphere became more and more hazy as they traveled east. Marc-Claude saw many random rock formations coming out of the water. These were an obvious indication they were getting closer to their destination. The boat made several dramatic turns, missing the upcoming rocks.

His mind was on his friends he'd left on the other ship. He feared for them as he could think of no way in which they could survive more than a few days. He wondered if there was any way, in which he could escape and possibly make his way back to them. At this rate it would be a couple of days before he would be able to make it back. Hopefully they would somehow find a way to hold on and survive.

Marc-Claude could see Leah and Rachel on the other side of the deck. They huddled together, and thankfully they looked unharmed. He felt sorry for bringing them into this mess.

After a few more hours passed, a crewman came along and ordered him to lay down on the deck. Marc-Claude thought this was odd, but then he was told that they were still a few hours away. They would sail through the night and arrive sometime in the middle of the day. A parcel of food was brought to him, and then as best as he could, he tried to sleep. This proved futile as the ship was constantly bumping rock formations. On top of this, Riché was yelling out commands and insults upon each striking. Halfway through the night Marc-Claude gave up and simply sat upright as they made their way through the rough waters.

As dawn approached Marc-Claude found himself dozing off. The light of the new day brought somewhat smoother sailing. He dreamed of terrible things about his friends. Even in sleep he couldn't stop worrying about them.

He awoke after a few hours. The crew was moving about speaking urgently. Quickly he rubbed his eyes and stumbled to his feet. He looked around and could see the haze was even stronger, but yet through it all, he saw larger rock formations all around the boat. Some of these formations were large enough for vegetation to grow on them. Possibly these were the result of some type of volcanic rock. Overall, he couldn't tell for sure of this area's origin, but one thing he was sure of was that this area had an ancient feel to it. There was probably history here that had been lost for centuries.

Marc-Claude looked to the side. A few feet away he could see Riché holding out the map and Maud pointing to various places on it. She looked like she had gained a point of reference regarding this area and could possibly see where the treasure might be located. Marc-Claude quickly became curious and walked in their direction. A few guards instantly took notice. They pulled their swords and commanded him back to where he had been standing.

They kept sailing through the various islands until they came to another dense fog. Many of the men went silent as they worried about what was ahead of them. Riché could see the fear on their faces and shouted out, "Do not stop! We move forward!" The boat moved into the fog. Many held their breath entering it. Marc-Claude closed his eyes. He could hear Maud say something, but it was unclear.

The fog didn't last long before they emerged on the other side. There Marc-Claude saw an island that looked to be about two miles long. There were two large hills. A smaller one was on the front side closer to them, along with a larger one on the opposite side to where they were steering. A small waterfall could be seen to the right side. Mostly around the island was a rocky coast, cautioning any who would think of coming close. There was one section that looked somewhat clear. The captain headed straight for that section.

Something they all noticed right away was the depressing vegetation. There was lots of greenery, but most looked either waterlogged or dying, which was an odd combination. Though the plant life was abundant, it looked like it struggled to grow and was weary of life. This gave many of those on board a feeling of uneasiness.

A strange species of birds flew overhead. They looked like a mixture between crows and vultures. A dozen of them were circling above, and a handful of others could be seen around the island eating from trees and various other parts of the dilapidated greenery. One of the crewmen with a bow pointed an arrow overhead, just in case a bird got the notion to swoop upon them. But after a minute or two passed, it was clear the creatures weren't looking to harm them.

Maud was then thrown down onto the deck close to where Marc-Claude was standing. He quickly helped her up onto her feet. "Are you all right?"

"Yeah, I guess they didn't need me anymore, so they just threw me aside." She took a moment to brush herself off. "I didn't want to lead them here, but they said they were going to hurt you, Marc-Claude. And I just couldn't let them do that. Being my sister's grandson, there ain't nothing I wouldn't do to save you. We're family, and our family bonds are strong."

Marc-Claude smiled a tired smile. "Thanks, Aunt Maud." In this moment, he found himself appreciating her. Though she had driven him crazy in the days before, hearing her mention his grandmother and their family bonds brought a sense of love. Amidst their dire situation, having someone close who loved him gave him an immense sense of comfort.

Riché shouted out, interrupting the moment. "Listen up! We'll get as close as we can to the island. I'll go ashore along with these two prisoners. I want two of you men to come along with us. The others can stay on board. This will hopefully be a short exploration. We'll quickly find any treasure there may be and then we'll depart." No one responded at first, but soon afterwards, a few of the men started arguing about who was to go onshore. Riché saw what was transpiring and put it to a stop immediately. He then simply picked two men out of the group, leaving eight behind.

The boat stopped about twenty feet from the shore. This was as close as they wanted to get to the rocky coast. "Let's get moving!" Riché commanded.

Marc-Claude took a deep breath. Three men walked over and grabbed him and Maud. They quickly tied Marc-Claude's hands behind his back. Being an older woman, they allowed Maud's hands to be free. The crewmen then pulled the two of them to the edge of the boat... toward the island.

Chapter 16

Marc-Claude stepped onto the edge of the island. His boots and part of his pants were wet as they had walked through shallow water to get to the land. Maud was completely wet because she had fallen in. The crewmen were leading them along, while Riché held the map in front. At first glance, it didn't seem like the map would help them at this point, but nevertheless it had proved itself profitable thus far, so Riché was sure to bring it along.

A soggy, grassy area greeted them as they stepped onto the shore. The crewman quickly pulled the prisoners forward. An unnerving feeling crept over Marc-Claude the more he stepped onto the island. The depressed plant life, the birds circling overhead, and a slight fog made it seem like a warning to those who moved on the land. Especially with his mind still on Cobra and the others, he wanted no part of these dangers. He walked along lazily.

Almost as if on cue, a bit of thunder echoed out in the distance. Dark clouds moved in quickly. One of Riché's men stopped in fear. "Keep moving!" Riché commanded.

The group kept walking. The elevation was rising quickly as they moved up the first hill. There were no paths, but they simply trekked through tall grass. A light rain started to fall upon them. They could see halfway up the hill, where there were two dead trees separated by about six feet. Their trunks looked white, and their branches were spread out like fingers in all sorts of directions, interlocking at the top. Between the trees was a metal gate that was falling off its hinges. Riché led them to it.

As they arrived, Riché took a moment to examine this metal gate. It was only four feet in height and covered in rust. The metal bars of it were spiraled and by the look of the hinges, it looked as if they were replaced at one point. Riché looked back at Maud. "Can you decipher any of the patterns here? Can you tell exactly how old this is?"

"No, but I can tell you something for sure. This is really old, like ancient."

Riché simply nodded, "Fine, let's keep moving."

Without hesitation, the group moved through the gate and further up the hill toward the peak. The humidity was strong and the air felt thick. Marc-Claude pulled a little at his ropes. He wondered if the sweat from his arms could somehow loosen the ropes, and he could pull free. Whenever he thought the crewmen weren't watching closely, he would take another tug at his ropes.

The group made it to the precipice of the hill. They paused as they could see more of the island. Another larger peak sat in front of them. Between them was close to two hundred yards of forest and vegetation. Some of the trees looked like they were flourishing, while others were dead. The five of them looked closely at the wooded area and tried to see if there was anything that could give them a clue as to where the treasure might be. It didn't take long for them to realize that this was pointless. Nothing substantial could be seen from this viewpoint.

Riché stuck the map in front of Maud and spoke forcibly. "Now tell me if you see anything."

Maud took the map. She looked closely again, studying some of the symbols around the compass. Being on the island gave her a better indication as to what some of the symbols represented. After a minute passed, she looked up at Riché again, but said nothing. She was debating internally with herself what she should do.

He was frustrated with the silence. "Tell me what you see, or I'll kill those girls."

"Calm down, please. I'll tell you. Don't hurt anybody." She quickly pointed out toward the other hill. "I think it's somewhere around that other mountain. Maybe at its base. Maybe midway up. I don't know. This map ain't known for its exactness."

Riché clinched his teeth. "If you're lying to me, old woman, I'm going to make it so miserable for you. Now, just get us to the treasure, so we can leave."

Maud looked away, afraid of his temper. Marc-Claude felt so angry. No one ought to speak to her in this way, particularly someone as young as Riché. Even though Maud was a little crazy at times, she was family. He would have easily fought for her had the chance availed itself. "Leave her alone!" he called out. Reacting swiftly, Riché smacked Marc-Claude with the back of his hand. He fell off his feet, groaning as he hit the ground.

"I'm tired of this. Let's move down the hill quickly and get through that forest."

∽৩৩∾

"I see a ship!" Corleone called out as they moved through the islands of Rocheaux. "Adjust our route toward the east." Others on board looked on, trying to see the ship he spotted. Corleone handed his monocular to the others around him, and they could see what he had spotted. He continued, "Brace yourselves, a small clash might ensue as we get closer."

Corleone was poised in all his instructions, never seemingly rattled or flustered by the circumstances around them. The others respected Corleone and Gabriella and were comfortable with following their lead. This was not just because they had rescued them, but because the two of them displayed superior leadership qualities, while also showing concern for those around them. Cobra thought they reminded him of his friend, Belle of Mendolon.

The crew pulled their swords, while Cobra, Lin, and Roselin were handed weapons. Roselin particularly wasn't a trained fighter in any sort of fashion, but nevertheless, she hoped she could at least pose a threatening presence toward Riché's crew. They all liked their odds in the course of a skirmish, especially now that the element of surprise would be in their favor.

As they got closer it was obvious that they were spotted. "Their crew is getting into position," Gabriella called out, now the one looking through the monocular.

Corleone's boat continued moving at a brisk pace. It became apparent that they weren't slowing down as they approached the other boat. "Brace yourselves!" Corleone called out.

Their boat rammed into the side of the other ship. They first ducked as a few arrows flew their way. The next few moments were chaotic. They jumped on board the other ship and immediately entered into a clash with Riché's crew. Instantly, it became apparent that Corleone and those on his ship would overwhelm the eight men Riché had left behind. Corleone had eight in his crew, plus with Cobra, Lin, and Hooks actively fighting, it was obvious that one side had the advantage.

After only a few swipes of their swords, Riché's crewmen decided to retreat toward the captain's quarters. The man Lin was fighting was only able to get one step away before he was swept off his feet by Lin's staff. His chin hit the deck and he was stunned. Lin put his foot in his enemy's back, neutralizing him as a potential threat.

Cobra's man also tried to run away, but Cobra grabbed him by the collar and threw him to the deck. He dropped his sword in the process. Cobra picked him up and slammed him back down on the deck. He then picked him up and held him high over his head. Cobra then walked toward the edge of the ship and was about to throw him over, when Roselin grabbed his arm. He stopped suddenly.

"The water is shallow, and there are rocks," she said. "He might die, if you toss him overboard."

Cobra instantly softened. He knew that anger was fueling him in this present attack. He wanted revenge for them sinking their ship and kidnapping Marc-Claude, but he realized he was out of control. He lowered the frightened man back to the deck. One of Corleone's men came up to him with a sword, making sure he was no longer a threat. Cobra calmed himself. He felt ashamed for letting his anger gain control of him like this.

"Let's finish them off," Hooks called out, anxious to take advantage of the situation. There were only six of Riché's men left.

Lin, holding firmly to his staff, led the way. The others gathered in behind him. Slowly he opened the door to the cabin. The others backed out of the way as they wondered if arrows would be greeting them. After a moment they realized that arrows were not coming.

Feeling anxious, Hooks peeked in the side of the doorway and saw the men shaking. He smiled to himself as he looked toward Cobra and Lin. "Let's go in. These guys are dupes."

The three of them entered, looking as fierce as they possibly could. Corleone's crew was behind them. Lin twirled his staff into a better fighting position. "I would advise that you men surrender before anyone else gets hurt."

Riché's men backed up further before looking at one another, trying to see what their fellow sailor would do. It wasn't much longer before the man situated in the middle threw down his sword. The others followed suit and gave themselves up.

"Oh, come on. Be men!" Hooks yelled out, clearly disappointed no fight would ensue.

Cobra quickly looked toward the crew. "Please tie them up. We got to get on that island and find our friends."

"We understand. We'll take care of them. You go ashore."

"Thank you." That was all Cobra needed to hear. He turned to leave the cabin. Roselin, Lin, and Hooks came with him.

As Cobra was leaving, Rachel came running up toward him. "Cobra!" He turned and the two of them embraced.

"Are you okay?" he said, pulling away from her.

"I'm fine, but they took Marc-Claude and his aunt on the island."

"I've heard. I'm going after them."

She nodded as she went silent. The two looked into each other's eyes. Half a minute passed before she spoke again. "Please, be careful." There was great concern in her voice, but nevertheless she knew nothing was going to stop him from continuing onto the island. He threw caution to the wind as he jumped over the railing.

Landing in the water, he took a moment to gaze on the ominous view of the island in front of him. Knowing there may be dangers ahead, he suppressed any fear in his mind and ran forward. "Cobra, wait for us!" Roselin called as she, Hooks, and Lin followed behind.

∽∘∾

Riché, Marc-Claude, Maud, and two of the crewmen walked through the decrepit forest. Some of the trees looked healthy while others were dead. Marc-Claude took in his surroundings. He couldn't figure out a pattern as to why some of them were dead. It seemed odd and uneven. Other bushes and vegetation looked tired or water-logged as if they'd given up on life in this forbidden island.

They journeyed forward, dodging fallen trees and cutting through plant life when needed. Occasionally Marc-Claude would slip and fall as his hands were tied, and he wasn't able to steady himself along the way. This would lead to a verbal assault from Riché. He had hoped this would be a short excursion. The more they walked, the more frustrated he became.

After walking for twenty minutes, one of Riché's men called out. "Sir! Look at this."

Everyone stopped immediately to see that the crewman had crouched down and was looking at something. Riché came close, and the crewman pulled something out of the ground. He held it up and passed it to Riché. It was easy to see it was a gold coin. Riché snatched it from him and held it in his palm. There was much wear on its sides, but there was no denying what it was. His eyes lit up. "We're close. Look all around, see if there's any more."

They all looked to their sides, trying to see if there was any more treasure within sight. Even Marc-Claude and Maud glanced around them, curious to see if they were indeed close to the treasure. The crewmen walked a few steps in different directions, looking to see if there was anything in the tall grass surrounding them.

Riché grew more anxious, now knowing that they were close. "Do you see anything?"

"No, nothing more."

"Fine, let's press on."

The five of them moved through the wooded area. The light rain continued, and more thunder could be heard in the distance. They moved even slower now that there was a possibility that gold could be found. Marc-Claude particularly slowed his pace, hoping to give himself more time and therefore more of a possibility of an escape. The difficult thing would be that Maud would have to be freed as well. This created an even deeper conundrum.

As the group kept moving, more coins were found, and even a couple of small jewels. With each find Riché grew more obsessed with finding more and more gold. This slowed their pace even further as he didn't want to go more than a few feet before searching the area for treasure. Fortunately, their searches were turning up more and more fruitful. One of Riché's crewmen was now carrying a satchel full of gold coins.

As they got closer to the base of the other mountain, they saw a stone structure in front of them. "What is this?" Riché said under his breath. His pace quickened a little as they got closer. At about twenty feet away, they could see that it was a stone archway, approximately twelve feet in height. The group stepped over fallen limbs and cut through hanging vines as they got closer.

Arriving at the structure, Maud stepped forward to read the writing on the sides. It was weathered and every third word was incomprehensible. Riché didn't hinder her as he could tell she was trying to decipher the meaning behind this structure. They all waited patiently.

Marc-Claude looked up and down the structure, seeing if he could discover anything of significance. Across the top he could see a few pictures that seemed to depict a battle. There were symbols and weapons of war, along with descriptions of soldiers. "Did a battle occur here?" he asked. This caught everyone off-guard as Marc-Claude hadn't spoken in a long time. Riché thought about reprimanding him, but he was curious as well.

"No, I don't think so," Maud responded. "It looks like this writing is depicting history." She paused a moment and squinted her eyes. "Difficult to tell, but maybe this place was significant to the war. Like maybe it was the base for the enemy, or wait..." She then kept reading closely. The other four stood silently, eagerly waiting for what she would say. The expression on her face grew confused.

After a minute Riché couldn't bear it any longer. "Tell us what you know, you old hag. Don't hold back!"

She didn't take her eyes off the writing. She spoke quietly, "Most of this writing is a warning."

"A warning for what?"

"Not sure, but it's telling us to get off this island." No one said anything in response to this. The fear of the unknown began to encompass them.

"Sir!" one of the crewmen called out. He was standing a few feet away from the others, looking around the right side of the archway through the trees.

"What is it?"

"Something else is up ahead, through the archway."

The others looked through the archway and could see what he was talking about. There was some type of statue about thirty yards away. "Let's go," Riché commanded.

The group proceeded through the archway and close to the statue. The ground was much clearer on the other side of the archway and made for an easy progression forward. There were a few vines growing over the structure. It was seven feet in height and appeared to be depicting a cloaked man. Numerous cracks were weaving through the body, and a large chunk of the left shoulder had fallen aside. Its arms were crossed, making an "x" with its forearms. Its head was looking at a downward angle. Crouching a little to look upward at the face, Riché could see that the artist didn't take the time to carve a face on the structure.

Maud spotted some sort of stone plaque a few feet away. Curious for more information, she walked over to it. Out of everything she'd seen so far, this plaque looked the most out of place. The gate, the archway, and the statue looked ancient, whereas this plaque looked less than two hundred years old. It was covered in greenery and other undergrowth.

The others saw she was trying to decipher this plaque and joined her. One of the crewmen brushed aside the leaves and plant life that were around it. There were very few words written on this one. The language was an older dialect of a modern tongue, not too difficult to understand. Even Marc-Claude was almost able to interpret it.

"What does it say?" Riché asked.

"Whoa, this is not a good thing."

"Just tell me!" he shouted.

Maud spoke with concern. "This one is another warning; except this time, it is warning us about the roots of evil taking ahold of our lives."

Riché shook his head. He paced a little as he scratched the back of his neck, wondering what he should do.

Marc-Claude looked back at the inscription. He recognized a few words and could tell that what Maud had read was true. He whispered under his breath, "Where are we?"

Chapter 17

Cobra, Lin, Hooks, and Roselin ran along the beach on the north side of the island. The others followed Cobra as he was running at a full sprint. "Slow down!" Hooks yelled as he wasn't nearly as fast as the others. Thankfully the rain had stopped at this point. Moving past the smaller hill, the group turned into the interior of the island. Cobra didn't have a specific plan, but rather he was motivated by a desire to save his friend. He would run through any forest and face any enemy if it meant rescuing Marc-Claude.

His pace naturally slowed as he now had to trek through taller grass. He was about twenty feet from the edge of the beach when Roselin called out to him. "Cobra!"

"What?" he said, without stopping.

"I think it's best if we stay on the beach and move toward the mountain. We can move faster there than in this tall grass."

Cobra now paused. He wasn't sure what the best strategy was, but he figured Roselin was probably right. Maybe they could move up the mountain and get a better view of the land below. But also, he figured Riché may be moving through the wooded areas since they didn't initially see them on the beaches of the island. He felt paralyzed by indecision.

Roselin continued, "Unless you see something here, I'd say let's keep going along the beach. Riché and the others have probably made it further into the island at this point. We might be able to catch them if we're not going through the tall grass."

Cobra nodded. He took one last look around this area and then ran back toward Roselin. Hooks had now caught up to them. He was breathing heavily. "I'm not running any more on that beach. That sand is too hard on this wooden leg."

"Fine," said Roselin. "You check out this area. We're going along the beach toward the mountain."

"You call that a mountain? Ha! We've got hills bigger than that in the home country," Hooks said, objecting.

"Call it whatever you want, but either way it'll give us a better view."

"Well, why don't fighter boy come with me?" he said, motioning toward Lin. "Just in case we run into some trouble."

Roselin nodded. "Yes, it may be a good idea to split up. We can cover more ground that way."

"Let's move then," Cobra said, as he had already started to run down the beach.

"Cobra, wait up," Roselin said. She looked back at Hooks and shrugged, wondering if there was anything else she should tell him.

"Don't get into trouble without us," Hooks said with a chuckle in his voice.

Roselin quickly caught up to Cobra. They were running on the very edge of the sand where it met the grass of the forest. This provided a more stable footing for moving quickly. As they ran, they were diligently looking to their right to see if they could notice or hear anything in the forest. Cobra stopped completely at one point after seeing a bush move. A bird flew from it, and they continued on.

Except for the birds, the island seemed uninhabited of wildlife. There was a stillness to it that brought an eerie silence to everything. It was like they could feel anxiety in the air. Most likely these feelings of anxiety were a result of them anticipating a scuffle when they encountered Riché and his men. They were preparing themselves mentally for the clash that would occur.

Even though Cobra was used to the occasional skirmish, Roselin was not. Most of the time her adventures were lived through the lives of sailors who would share the stories of the seas. Much of her life was spent navigating the demands of running her restaurant. That provided her with enough challenges in and of itself. Nevertheless, she was happy to help Cobra with this task. She had grown fond of him and, after their talk at the restaurant, she wanted to see him rewarded for his hardships. She felt it was the least she could do for him.

Eventually, Cobra and Roselin made it to the base of the small mountain. They could see a faint trail ascending the side. They quickly followed it. Twenty yards ahead, they saw a wooden sign. Approaching it, they could see another trail moving to the right, back down to the interior of the island.

They both stopped at the sign and saw that it was in a foreign language. "Can you read it? What does it say?" Cobra asked urgently.

Roselin knew this language because it was a common tongue she had encountered on her island. The dialect was different, and she struggled a little. "It… it… it says that there's riches down the mountain. There's also a warning with it, but I can't tell what it's saying."

Cobra looked up the hill. "And what about up there? Does it say anything about going up the mountain?"

Roselin shook her head. "It's hard. It's something about pursuing it with your heart. Better than gold… I think, but I don't know for sure. It says that it's better."

Cobra was instantly struck back with remembering the treasure and how it offered something magical that would change his life. This was what he wanted. He felt conflicted between pursuing it and saving Marc-Claude. His desires felt pulled in two different directions.

Roselin could see he was struggling and offered to resolve his dilemma. "Cobra, you go up top and I'll follow this trail back down. You can get a better view from up there anyway."

"Thank you," he said, knowing that she was helping him satisfy his conflict. He turned and started running up the side of the hill. He called back, "Don't do anything dangerous, Roselin."

She watched him run up the hill, worried about him, but hoping his heart would be satisfied with what he found.

※

Riché, Marc-Claude, Maud, and the two crewmen progressed further on the island toward the opposite side of the mountain. The gold coins were now found with more frequency. Eventually they stopped picking them up, realizing they were getting closer to the treasure. In Riché's mind this little adventure was already taking more time than he had anticipated, and he was ready to get off this island and take Marc-Claude back to Von Dechauer. A few times he even questioned himself as to why he let Marc-Claude talk him into looking for this treasure. He kept telling himself that the bonus of finding this treasure would be worth it. They progressed on.

The group was walking through thick vegetation again. In fact, the vegetation was growing thicker with every step. Marc-Claude took his time stepping through the high grass. He was still consciously trying to slow down the group. He was hoping to think of something to buy himself some time. His gait was unsteady with his hands tied behind his back. He particularly needed his hands for balance when climbing over different fallen objects.

Marc-Claude wondered if he could use this instability for his advantage. His foot got caught under a root, and he felt himself slip. This time he figured he wouldn't try to steady himself. He just went down on the wet grass. He intentionally groaned loudly as his body fell.

"Get up! We need to keep moving!" Riché yelled at him.

Marc-Claude turned his body to better face Riché. "I can't. My hands are tied, and I can't make it easily through this cursed jungle." He paused to clear his throat. "You know, I could move a lot faster if you untied me."

Riché gritted his teeth, upset because he knew that Marc-Claude was right. They could move at a faster pace if Marc-Claude's hands were freed. Riché pulled his sword and walked over to where Marc-Claude was lying. He paused just a moment, wondering if this was a good idea, but then he thought that with two crewmen with him, Marc-Claude had little chance of escape.

He was about to cut the ropes when he figured he ought to first warn his prisoner. Abruptly he stomped on Marc-Claude before pressing his foot against the center of his back. He then reached forward with his sword and lightly stabbed Marc-Claude in the back of his shoulder.

"Aww!" Marc-Claude screamed, burying his face into the grass.

"No! Stop!" Maud yelled.

After ten seconds he pulled the sword back. Marc-Claude breathed heavily in relief. Riché looked to his men, "Pick him up!"

The two men obeyed, coming close and putting him back on his feet. Marc-Claude's head slumped while the crewmen held his arms. Riché grabbed his chin and held it up for him to make eye contact. He put his face close to Marc-Claude's and spoke angrily. "Don't even think about escaping. If so, I will bring more pain on you than you can imagine."

Marc-Claude didn't respond, but simply nodded. His shoulder hurt, but it wouldn't stop him from trying to escape. He just knew that he would have to be sure he could escape if he tried. The crewmen released him, and he fell to the ground.

"Let's move," Riché called out.

Slowly Marc-Claude arose and continued with the group. He reached up to readjust his bandana. He felt the soreness in his shoulder, but thankfully the pain wasn't strong enough to immobilize it. For now, he would just need to bide his time until an opportune moment presented itself. Hopefully when it did come to fruition, he could bring Maud with him as well.

The group could see the greenery of this wooded area clearing up a few feet ahead. The beach was coming into view in front of them. Moving to the edge of the wooded area, a large red and green vine was on the ground, separating them from the clearing of the beach. It was a peculiar sight. One of the crewmen was the first to reach it. He bent down and looked closely. He noticed it was actually four vines that were interwoven. This cluster of vines was large, coming up to the height of his knees.

The crewman kicked it with his foot. The vines moved slightly. He looked back at the others and shrugged, thinking it was nothing to be concerned about. But as he turned to look back at the vines, he felt something wrap around his legs. He quickly looked down and saw two vines had become untwined and wrapped around his calf muscles. The vines immediately pressed his legs together and threw him to the ground. He dropped the sword he was holding as he was pulled to the left, closer to the mountain. The man was screaming as he was taken.

"Come on!" Riché commanded as he quickly moved in the direction the man was pulled. Holding out his sword, the other crewman forced Marc-Claude and Maud to follow. This area was clear of trees and bushes but none of them hardly noticed as they were anxious to find out what happened.

It didn't take them long before they found the answers to their questions. "What the devil!" Riché called out when he saw what was in front of him.

On the edge of the woods against the rocky side of the mountain was a large Venus flytrap that was about eight feet in height with a dozen or so vines acting as appendages. The creature's mouth was opening up as it pulled the crewman to itself. The creature's color was an odd mixture of dark red and black. It stood out from the greenery of the forest from which they had just come. A handful of the creature's vines and roots were sprawled throughout the area, drawing from the nutrients of the land.

"What is this despicable creation?" Riché exclaimed, pulling his sword.

"Let's get out of here!" the now lone crewman cried fearfully.

Before they fully realized what was occurring, two more vines wrapped around Maud's legs and started pulling her toward the creature. "Maud!" Marc-Claude yelled. He jumped on Maud and tried to hold her down. He only slowed the progression as the vines kept dragging her.

At this point the mouth of the creature was closed. The men's attention had turned to Maud, and they missed the moment when Riché's crewman entered into the mouth of the creature.

Slowly the mouth of the plant opened back up and its teeth dripped with a green slime. There was no denying that this creature was still hungry. "Help us, please!" Marc-Claude called out toward the others.

The crewman ran toward Maud and Marc-Claude. He laid on top of them to further slow the progression. With one hand he held on and with the other he took his sword and began hacking away at the vines pulling them.

"Hurry!" Marc-Claude yelled as they were now eight feet away from the mouth.

Riché had his sword pulled as he moved closer to the creature. A vine tried to push him away, but he combated it with his sword. The vine moved swiftly, and it was difficult for Riché to get a firm hit on it. He knew time was of the essence, and he would need to get to the body of the plant soon. He couldn't let Marc-Claude be eaten. Holding out his left arm, he let the vine wrap around his left wrist. He felt the tension began to pull. This gave him an easy target. He swiped hard with his sword and cut most of the way through the vine. He then pulled hard and tore the rest of the vine away.

Now free, Riché ran toward the body of the creature and stabbed the side of it. The plant screamed out a slithery growl. It opened its mouth further and out came some sort of black appendage. He didn't know if was a tongue or another vine, but either way he wanted to kill it. Riché tried to swipe at it, but it grabbed ahold of his sword, trying to take it away. Reacting frantically now, he pulled a dagger and stuck it into the side of the appendage. He did this again, trying to get his sword released from its grip.

The creature was still pulling Maud and Marc-Claude in closer. They were now only about three feet away from its mouth. The crewman was able to cut through one of the vines, but it was in vain as another then wrapped itself around Maud's foot and continued to pull. Now seeing how close they were to the mouth, he decided to flee. He rolled off them and ran to the side.

"No!" Marc-Claude yelled. The creature lowered its mouth completely on the ground and opened wide. They were pulled within inches. On instinct Marc-Claude put his feet on the sides of the creature's mouth, stopping the inward pull. He looked into the foul interior of the creature. He couldn't let them be eaten. Straining as hard as he could, he kept his legs in place. "Riché, help us!"

"I need my sword," he yelled back. He had now reverted to stabbing the body of the creature with his dagger, while still trying to pull the sword away from the creature's appendage.

Marc-Claude glanced over and saw Riché trying to retrieve his sword that was being pulled into the mouth. Knowing he couldn't hold his feet in this position much longer, he did the only thing he knew to do. He quickly took ahold of Riché's sword. "Let go!" he yelled to Riché. In a fraction of a second, Marc-Claude held tight to the sword and tucked his legs in. He was pulled into the creature alongside Maud. His arm scrapped against one of the teeth, but he didn't notice at the moment.

The creature shut its mouth, enclosing them into the darkness. Maud screamed out incomprehensibly. She was pressed up against the crewman who had been previously swallowed.

Marc-Claude felt the tension on the sword release. Motivated by fear, he moved as fast as he could. He pushed the sword against the interior wall of the plant. He could tell it went all the way through to the other side. He then pressed down, making a hole in the side of the creature as it descended. A little light came in from the outside. It was a struggle moving the sword downward, but soon Riché saw it protruding. He was able to lift his foot and press it further. The blade slid down through the wall of the creature and onto the bottom root that was planted in the ground. A large slit was in the plant. Riché grabbed the sides of the wall to tear it open. The crewman who was close by came to help, and together they were able to open the plant wider to create a larger opening.

Once opened, Riché reached inside and grabbed ahold of Marc-Claude. The creature began to weaken and slow from the damage done to it. Riché pulled Marc-Claude, who was holding tightly onto Maud. With one hand Marc-Claude grabbed the outside of the plant and helped pull. It was only a few seconds later before the two of them came out of the creature. Riché fell backwards as they slid out of the creature. They landed on top of him, covered in a green sticky substance. Riché quickly pushed them off.

Marc-Claude stumbled to his feet before moving back to the creature. The sword was still protruding at the bottom. He reached into the hole and pulled the weapon out by the handle and laid it aside. As best as he could, he widened the opening and then stuck his arm in again, trying to feel for the crewman. He looked back at the others. "Help me. We got to get him out."

Riché's other crewman came over and reached inside with Marc-Claude. Quickly finding him, they grabbed ahold of the man and dragged him from the plant. He let out a gasp as he hit the ground. His eyes were closed, and he was shaking. There was a wound on his forehead that was bleeding, and like the others, he was covered in the green sticky substance. He looked pale. Marc-Claude rolled him onto his side, hoping this would help him breathe.

The creature had completely ceased moving at this point. Riché was brushing himself off. He walked toward Marc-Claude. "Leave him. We need to keep moving."

Marc-Claude turned. "I want to make sure he'll be fine, mate."

"We don't have time." Riché then looked to the side and saw that Maud had now recovered. In typical Maud fashion she had now moved onto something else. She was examining one of the creature's large black roots. She was fascinated.

Riché noticed that this root from the plant was coming from an area to their right, around the corner of the rock wall of the mountain. He took a few steps, wondering if he could see more. Initially he didn't see anything else of interest with the root, but he did see something else of much more value. A devious smile formed on his face as he saw a handful of gold pieces lying about twenty yards ahead. It was obvious that more treasure was just around the corner.

He looked back and yelled at the others. "Let's go now."

"But your crewman," Marc-Claude pleaded.

"We'll come back for him, but we're moving now!"

Chapter 18

Riché led them around the rock wall of the mountain, and there they found what they were looking for. A bountiful amount of treasure lay before them. Gold, jewels, and various coins among overflowing treasure chests sat on the outside and at the entrance of a twelve-foot-wide cave. Looking into it, they could see it slightly descended in elevation. But peeking inside, they could see more and more treasure lying against the sides and floor of the cave. It was beyond what any of them had imagined. In every sense of the word, it was mesmerizing.

Instantly Riché ran to it and scooped up a handful. He moved it around in his palms, feeling the weight of the gold. Slowly he looked back at the others. He couldn't believe the fortune that had come upon him. Images of power and fame flashed in his mind. He knew from that moment on, his life would never be the same. He was definitely not going to be doing the bidding of Von Dechauer anymore. He thought of his father. No longer would he work for him either. He would carve his own name and make his father submit to his wealth. In this current daydream, he was already thinking this wealth would make him one of the most powerful men that had ever lived.

The crewman held out a sword toward Marc-Claude as he moved him to the entrance of the cave and sat him down a few feet inside, beside a treasure chest. Marc-Claude was awestruck by the treasure as well. His desire for the wealth came back strongly. He dreamt of what this treasure would mean for him. The fame he acquired from fleeing Von Dechauer would be a trifle compared to the recognition he would receive if he was able to secure a portion of this wealth. The flashes and images of power filled his mind as well.

As Riché stepped further into the cave, he continued to move his hands through piles of treasure, seeing if there was anything more to find in the midst of the gold. There were a few steel weapons and goblets and plates among the coins. He was setting aside anything he thought would be of specific interest, particularly that which he wanted to take with him on the first shipment. He spoke out quickly. "We're not going back to Von Decahuer. All three of you will work for me permanently. I will be the most powerful merchant and explorer this world has ever seen. Through this wealth, we will build an empire."

The treasure extended as far as they could see into the cave. None of them had torches or the capability to make fire, so there was no way of initially knowing how far back the treasure went into the cave. It brought a greater sense of mystery to this discovery. Marc-Claude particularly wondered what kind of treasure could be found the further one ventured into the cave. He thought maybe the most luxurious of items were placed toward the back of the cave.

Maud was still examining the root of the plant that had extended from this cave all the way around the corner to the edge of the woods. Riché and the crewman didn't pay her much mind as she inspected the black root. She pushed away some of the gold that was lying on top of it. It quickly became apparent that the root stretched further into the depths of the cave. "Listen, fellows, I don't like the looks of this. I'm thinking this gold might be cursed."

"Quiet!" Riché shouted back. His voice echoed in the cave. He continued again daydreaming about the treasure that lay before him.

Marc-Claude realized that the guard was only casually watching him. He then looked over at Maud. Her last statement troubled him. He whispered to her. "Maud... Maud." He got her attention. "What do you mean by cursed? Do you think this is dragon's gold?"

"I don't know," she whispered back. "I ain't never seen anything like this. I wouldn't touch any of it."

Marc-Claude continued to look around at the treasure that lay before him. It glimmered and shone and appeared too good to be true. Yet still, his heart was drawn to it. He wondered how much he should listen to Maud's warning. He also wondered about Riché's statement about not returning to Von Dechauer. Though he didn't know if Riché would follow through with this statement, at least he could use it to buy himself some time.

Looking down at the treasure, Marc-Claude moved his hand through the gold that was lying beside him. Strangely, the more he touched it, the more he felt drawn to it. A temptation grew within him.

"Don't think about taking any for yourself," the crewman said as he saw Marc-Claude looking at the treasure.

Marc-Claude simply smiled in return. He then glanced down at the gold again and noticed just a piece of a green jewel that lay buried. Quickly, he moved the gold aside and pulled out an emerald that fit in the palm of his hand. Slowly with his other hand he felt the hard stone. It was beautiful and, in his heart of hearts, exactly what he wanted to see. He began to tremble slightly. He held it up to the opening of the cave and the light of the outside shone through it. He desired its beauty. His hand started to tremble. Memories flooded his mind.

"Put that down!" the crewman called out. He quickly strode over and knocked it out of his hand. The jewel bounced a few feet away. "Don't touch anything!"

Marc-Claude didn't respond to the man. He just sat staring at the jewel. He shook his head, trying to break his concentration. "Something's not right," he said under his breath. No longer did he desire this treasure.

Cobra was on the pinnacle of the hill. He was moving toward a cliff that overlooked the east. If he was being honest with himself, he would have told himself that he was now looking for what was hidden up on this large hill, as opposed to saving Marc-Claude. The trail he was following was growing more and more faint the more he ascended.

He moved to the edge of the cliff, overlooking the world below. There was a clear view of the ocean. Looking up, the clouds blocked the sun, and the black birds flew overhead. Stepping even closer to the edge, he peered below and onto the beach. He couldn't see anything of significance that would help him find Marc-Claude.

Cobra walked back toward the west side of the cliff, trying to see if there was anything more that could be seen on this side of the island. The grass was tall and thick. He high-stepped and blazed his own trail as he slowly fought through the foliage. Sweat was running down his forehead from the energy he was exhibiting.

He was getting closer to the edge when he saw the faint impression of a trail. It was moving him back toward the woods. He turned with it and followed it as best as he could. His pace quickened as he wondered if this was leading him somewhere important.

He entered the woods again and found himself surrounded by trees and thick vegetation again. For a moment he thought he had lost the trail, but he found it a few feet away. A tree had fallen, and he jumped over it, now moving as fast as he could. The question raced in his mind, 'would he find what his heart desired?'

It wasn't long into the woods when he saw a clearing among the trees. This area stood out as it was obviously a place that at one time had been intentionally cleared. Reaching the edge of the area, he paused to examine it, looking from side to side. It was about thirty feet in length and about the same in width. Weeds and other small greenery were on the ground of the area, but it was obvious that this place once bore significance.

To his left, he looked and saw what appeared to be a grave. He noticed what he assumed to be a headstone over slightly raised land. He walked over to the headstone and cleared away some of the tall weeds that were in front of it. The writing was faded, but one word could clearly be seen, *Sophia.* There were a few statements written under it, but the weathering of the headstone made it difficult to read. He could only make out a few words. It was evident that this was the final resting place of the lost Princess Sophia.

Glancing to his right, Cobra saw something curious that caught his attention. Slowly he walked closer. It was some type of pedestal with a box or item on top. Vines had grown up and around it, so he wasn't able to clearly see what was on the pedestal. Stepping in front of the structure, he reached out to touch it. He paused and pulled back his hand, knowing this was where everything had been leading him. A flood of thoughts and emotions entered his mind. He'd been looking for this for the past six months, and his desire had only grown the more he thought about it.

Cobra was struck with fear too. The fear of disappointment came onto him. What if he opened this box and this whole hunt turned up to be a disappointment? What if this journey was a dead end, and he was left with nothing? Would his life suddenly become meaningless? The questions grew and felt paralyzing for a moment. He rubbed his forehead as he struggled with these thoughts.

Knowing these questions would forever haunt him, he bit his lip and reached forward to the structure in front of him. He began pulling away at the vines and leaves that were intertwined on it. It wasn't long before he discovered that it was, in fact, a small treasure chest. For another moment he stood looking at it, wondering what he would find inside. Slowly he reached down and clicked the latch on the front. He found it opened without difficulty.

Inside he saw two books stacked on top of one another. One book was written professionally, like it was penned by a scribe, while the other looked personal as if it was a journal. Glancing briefly at this 'journal' he could see it was written by Sophia, the one who hid the treasure. It was her memoir. He opened the first page and read her title, *The Journey into the East, and the Hiding of the Treasure.* This intrigued him greatly, but not as much as the other book that accompanied it.

Putting down the memoir, he picked up the book written by a scribe. He knew that whatever this book was, it would be the one that changed his life. Maybe it would be a book of spells, or possibly hidden secrets that were beyond this world. It would change him from the man he was today to something he'd always dreamt he could be.

Glancing at the cover, he could see the title written in an unknown language, but under it appeared to be a translation, *"The Book of Wisdom."* It caught him off-guard. He opened the cover carefully, trying not to damage the book. The language was an unused language from years gone by. Even the characters were unfamiliar to him. Yet within the pages were additional pages stuck between them. On these pages was a common language, one he could he read. Comparing these additional pages to the text, it was obvious to see this was a translation.

He began reading from the first page. It was the purpose of the book. *"To know wisdom and instruction; to perceive the words of understanding; to receive the instruction of wisdom, justice, judgement, and equity; to impart shrewdness to the morally naïve; to the youth knowledge and discretion, let the wise hear and increase in learning, and the one who understands obtain guidance, to understand a proverb and a saying, the words of the wise and their riddles."*

Cobra's knees hit the ground as he read these words. He had heard of this book and knew it was the famed Book of Wisdom written by a ruler named Solomon. The story was well known to him as he had learned it in school and read about it elsewhere. A man named Solomon was granted a gift, anything he wanted, from the Mighty Righteous King. Solomon could have asked the King for whatever his heart desired, and it would have been granted. Many thought Solomon would ask for great riches, for the Righteous King owned wealth beyond this world. But instead, he asked for wisdom to rule the people that he governed. The Righteous King was pleased with this request and granted it to him. Solomon in his wisdom then was able to pen many wise sayings and proverbs for his people. And now, Cobra was looking at this ancient, famed Book of Wisdom.

Deep inside, Cobra felt convicted of his own pride, anger, and lust for power. He had read other writings inspired by the Righteous King, and he knew that wisdom, justice, and mercy were what his heart should be pursuing. Somewhere along the journey, he had gotten off course. He had wanted to quickly change who he was through sorcery or wealth, but these were not what the Righteous King would want. In this book, the way was laid out for him. Wisdom and instruction should be what he pursued. He would not be a fool and despise them.

He flipped through the book, looking at the ancient text while also scanning the various portions of translation. There were essays, warnings, and poems, along with many simple proverbs. He flipped back and forth through the pages. Bursts of excitement filled his heart, yet he was quick to calm himself as the book and the translation pages were very old and he didn't want to damage them.

As he was flipping through the Book of Wisdom, one of the proverbs stood out to him. *"The one who trusts in riches will fall, but the righteous will flourish like a green leaf."* The word 'riches' particularly stood out to him. He thought this was ironic in light of the promises of this island.

After another minute of flipping through the book, Cobra shut it and closed his eyes. His mind felt cluttered, and he needed to focus. As he sat there, he again thought of the Righteous King as this book was inspired by his wisdom. Cobra believed in him. He loved him and his words. He feared breaking the King's commandments, disappointing him. He cleared his mind and purposed to once again follow the Righteous King and his writings with his whole heart.

When his mind felt clear again, Cobra opened up the book again and began to read more from the opening lines of introduction. He craved the wisdom found therein. Reading carefully over the next few lines he found a warning...

"*My son, if sinners entice you, do not consent. If they say, 'Come with us, let us lie in wait to shed blood; let us lurk secretly for the innocent without cause; let us swallow them alive like the grave, and whole like those who go down to the Pit; We shall find all kinds of precious possessions, we shall fill our houses with spoil; cast in your lot among us, let us all have one purse'* – *My Son, do not walk in the way with them. Keep your foot from their path; for their feet run to evil, and they make haste to shed blood.*"

Cobra paused and read that warning again. Particularly he read the line again about the evil ones finding "*all kinds of precious possessions.*" It reminded him of where he was and what was being pursued. Reading the evil plan mentioned here made him wonder if this was also a warning for this island. Strangely a thought crossed his mind, "*Would the evil and riches of this island, swallow them up in a pit... in a grave?*" He wondered if these lines could be warning him.

Suddenly, Cobra felt worried for Marc-Claude. He shut the book and grabbed the other one. He began running out of the clearing and out of the wooded area, thinking about what the best way down the small mountain would be. His hope was that his best friend Marc-Claude was far away from this supposed treasure.

Chapter 19

Riché continued to look through the treasure, setting aside all the different pieces he thought were of the greatest value. The more he looked, the farther and farther he went into the cave. Minute by minute his dreams were growing with visions of grandeur and power. His crewman continued to stand by the cave's entrance. His sword was pulled as he watched Marc-Claude and Maud.

The two prisoners sat on opposite sides of the cave. Maud had stopped exploring and just sat with her arms crossed. It was clear she had a lot on her mind. At one time Marc-Claude tried to go to her side, but he was quickly reprimanded. He would simply have to wait and keep biding his time.

Their attention was suddenly diverted when they heard the black birds starting to fly closer to the cave. A few even landed near the entrance and seemed to look inside. Riché didn't pay them much mind compared to the others, as the treasure was still his focus. Maud's eyes grew larger as she particularly thought this was bizarre. Up close it was easy to see that this was not a species of birds she'd ever seen before. Their look was that of a vulture, but their color and size was that of a crow. The sheer ugliness of them made them look particularly menacing.

"Riché!" the crewman called out. "I don't like the looks of those birds."

Riché only gave them a passing glance. "Just chase them away."

A half dozen got closer to the entrance. The crewman became more nervous. He picked up a handful of coins and threw them in their direction. "Get out of here!" he shouted. A few of them flew away, while the others looked at him in a curious manner.

While this was occurring, Marc-Claude noticed something else very peculiar. At the top of the entrance to the cave was a spearhead without a handle stuck in the roof. It was large for a spearhead, and it was made of translucent diamonds. Being distracted by the treasure, everyone hadn't noticed it before now. There was a gleam and shine to it, even with no direct light from the sun.

Marc-Claude wondered about this piece of treasure more than anything else at the moment. He knew that there was something about this item that was fundamentally different from anything else here. He wondered if this was the opportunity he was looking for, especially with the crewman distracted.

He took off his bandana and wrapped it around his hand, knowing that if he tried to grab for this it would probably be sharp and cut his hand. He put his hands on the ground in an effort to spring up and grab the item. It was about seven and a half feet off the ground. He knew he could make it with a quick spring. He held his breath, and slowly counted down in his mind ... *3 ... 2 ...*

Before he was about to jump, Maud whispered, "Psst!"

Marc-Claude looked at her, "What?" he said under his breath.

She could tell he was looking at the spearhead. She mouthed the words and shook her head. "Don't do it," she said, looking worried.

It was apparent from the look on her face that Maud knew something more about this spearhead. He figured she must have deciphered more as she sat there taking in her surroundings. He longed to speak with her about it, but that was not an option.

Thinking about her warnings, Marc-Claude debated with himself the plan of grabbing the spearhead. In actuality, Maud's warning tempted him more. Being a man who always loved adventure, this was one he knew he couldn't leave without knowing what would happen. And at the very least, maybe he thought he could use this as a weapon to help him escape.

He looked around one more time and could see the crewman was still distracted with the birds. It was now or never. Marc-Claude quickly sprang to his feet, grabbed the spearhead, and pulled it from the roof of the cave. Two things surprised him in that moment. One was how sharp it was. His bandana shielded his hand slightly, but all his fingers were cut in the process. The other thing that surprised him was how little effort it took to remove the spearhead from the stone. It was like it was simply sitting there, not placed in very deep. He quickly sat back down and crossed his arms, concealing the spearhead.

The crewman took notice. "Hey! What were you doing?"

"Nothing, mate," Marc-Claude responded.

The crewman angrily walked over to him. "What did you do?" Marc-Claude didn't respond. "Answer me!" he shouted again.

Suddenly Maud got up to run out of the cave but tripped on some of the treasure. This frustrated the guard even more. "Hey, get back here."

"What's going on?" Riché shouted from deeper in the cave.

It was then that Marc-Claude noticed a strong wind starting to blow into the entrance. All the birds flew away, squawking as they left. Another gust of wind then blew into the cave, just about knocking over crewman.

"Get out of here!" Maud shouted.

Marc-Claude got up to run, but the crewman stopped him, holding out his sword. "No, sit back down!"

Another stronger gust of wind blew into the cave. It was so strong some of the treasure items flew into the cave. An empty chest got caught in the wind and hit the crewman in the back of the legs. "Aww!" he yelled, falling to the ground and dropping his sword.

The wind immediately became constant and grew stronger and stronger. "Run!" Riché screamed.

Marc-Claude got up and tried to leave. The wind was rapidly growing so strong that coins, gold, and other various jewels were now blowing into the cave in a constant stream. Marc-Claude grabbed ahold of Maud and tried to pull her to her feet. He wasn't able to get very far outside the cave before the wind increased enough to where he couldn't move. Eventually it knocked him to the ground. With one arm he was holding onto Maud, and with the other he still held the spearhead. Acting on instinct, he looked to his right and saw the large black root. Quickly he stuck the spearhead into the root and pushed it in, thus securing it from the wind and making a handhold for himself. He held on as tight as he could as the wind would have pulled him into the cave.

Unfortunately, the crewman was never able to regain his stability. Gold and various items of treasure hit his face and his body as he was in the direct path of the wind. He tried to fight it as best as he could, but found it useless. Eventually another treasure chest hit him in the torso, and he lost any bit of balance. He rolled along with the wind into the depths of the cave where the ground opened up into a pit. Any light of the sun faded away. He saw a dark red light before he passed out and was gone.

Riché had managed to make it to the entryway of the cave and had grabbed onto a large rock before the wind pushed him into the cave. He was on the left side of the entrance. His hat had blown off in the process.

Marc-Claude struggled as held tightly to Maud. The wind was blowing with hurricane strength. If it got much stronger, there would be no chance of them resisting. Branches, sticks, leaves, and other items from the outside were starting to fly past them into the depths of the cave.

It was at that time that Marc-Claude heard a faint yell through the storm. "Marc-Claude!" He looked up and saw Hooks and Lin about fifty yards away coming toward them. Even though he was in the middle of this storm, for a moment he was relieved to see them alive.

They continued to move closer. It was apparent that the wind wasn't as strong from where they stood. The wind was obviously connected to this cave and working to pull them inside. It was not coming from the outside, but from within.

"Hang on!" Lin shouted. The two men braced themselves as they inched closer. They crouched lower as they came nearer and moved to the side of the rock wall. When they got within twenty yards, the intensity of the wind became too much. They were both knocked down and began sliding toward the entrance.

"Ahh!" Hooks yelled out as he felt himself moving toward the mouth of the cave. The scene looked ominous and out of every place in this world, this cave was the last place he wanted to be. Quickly he dug his left hook into the ground. Lin grabbed ahold of his leg. They stopped.

"Help!" Marc-Claude called out. "We can't hold on much longer!" His muscles ached, and his ears hurt as the piercing force of the wind kept moving at full strength.

Slowly Hooks loosened his grip with his hook enough where they inched closer to Marc-Claude. His hook would slide through the ground until he would dig it further back in, stopping their slide into the cave. From Lin's perspective, it was a frightening experience because he couldn't know for sure if Hooks had firm control or not.

Maud continued to scream out. "You can't let us go in there, Marc-Claude! Even if it kills us, don't let go!"

With all his might, Marc-Claude moved his arm to gain a better grip. Maud also adjusted hers, grabbing more securely onto his waist.

Eventually Hooks and Lin made it closer to where Marc-Claude could reach them with his free hand. Hooks was against the ground facedown. Both of his hooks were dug into the ground. Lin held onto his legs. Marc-Claude knew he had to switch his grip onto Lin. The vine was starting to tear more, thus lessening his grasp. He reached one arm around Lin's legs. When that arm was secure, he quickly let go of the vine and grabbed ahold with his other arm. He found this grip more stable as Hooks was even just a few feet further away from the mouth of the cave and the force of the wind.

Strong rumblings then began that felt like a small earthquake. "What is that?" Marc-Claude called out. Looking closer, he saw the two sides of the cave starting to close in, thus shutting off the entrance. This only made the wind stronger, pulling in more debris, treasure, sand, and anything else that wasn't secure.

It was at that time that Marc-Claude noticed Roselin had arrived onto the scene. She was holding onto a root she had cut free from the Venus fly trap and now she was slowly making her way toward the mouth of the cave. With this root she could work toward the group at a better angle than the root running along the base of the rock wall. As she continued to move closer, Roselin felt extremely anxious, but she didn't think twice about whether to try this or not. Her friends needed help.

Hooks looked up from the ground and saw her coming his way. "Get out of here! We're going to die!"

"Then we die together," she said under her breath. With every inch she felt the force of airstream become stronger.

Reaching the others, while still holding onto the root, she lay on her side on Hooks' back, thus preventing him from slipping even further. Her elbow was pressed against the back of Hooks' head in such a way that his face was buried into the ground. He screamed out and yelled insults, but no one could hear him.

Riché was still in the mouth of the cave, holding tightly to a rock implanted in the ground. The wind was strong, but he was lying in a spot where the ground dipped slightly. The full strength of the wind was not bearing down on him yet, but that was changing as the whole structure of the cave was slowly shifting. He had to keep readjusting his body. His only plan at this point was to hang on and hopefully find a way to climb out of this airstream.

∽∽

Cobra was coming down the mountain as quickly as he could. The two books were in his hands. It was easy to tell where he should go as he could see branches from trees blown in a strange fashion. He wasn't concerned about the danger. His only thought was whether or not he had a chance to save his friends. Cobra didn't think twice about what he was doing.

He came down to the top of the rock wall, near the dead Venus fly trap. He paused for just a moment to make sure it wasn't a threat. He set his books down beside a rock, shielding them from the wind. Quickly, he then jumped nine feet down onto the ground. He saw the crewman lying beside the plant. He was stirring slightly, still covered in the green substance of the plant.

The ground continued to shake. It was a subtle movement from where Cobra stood, but yet it was a reminder of the danger he thought his friends were in. He ran a few feet around the corner and saw the others hanging onto the root as the cave was pulling them in. He had arrived not long after Roselin had climbed on top of Hooks' back. Looking at the cave, he could see what the others had seen- the walls were slowly moving in. A faint red light glowed from somewhere deep inside the cave.

Without a moment to lose, he crouched down and began moving down the root. Like the others, he struggled with the wind, but his body mass made him slightly more stable.

As the cave continued to close, the width of the airstream became thinner but more potent. Roselin found herself beginning to slip ever so slightly down the root and off Hooks' back. This had a consequential effect all the way down the chain. Marc-Claude and Maud particularly were struggling and losing their grip. Lin seemed to feel the worst of it out of everyone. With Marc-Claude and Maud pulling on his waist and his arms holding onto Hooks, he felt as if he was being stretched thin. He called out to the others, "Not much longer, don't let go!"

For a brief moment Lin's words were encouraging, but then the wind picked up and they felt their bodies ever so slightly rising off the ground as the gust of wind began flowing under them in spurts. This frightened them all to the point where they couldn't even yell, they were in so much fear.

It was then that Hooks felt one of the worst feelings at that moment. His right arm began slipping out of the brace attached to his hook. He turned his head to the side and yelled out, "I'm slipping! I'm slipping." Just then a stronger gust of wind shot through with a constant stream and lifted them off the ground a few inches. Hooks' arm detached from the hook.

He gasped, but in that moment, Cobra suddenly arrived and grabbed his arm. "I gotcha, little fellow." Instantly, he laid on top of Hooks and Lin. He held tightly to Roselin. Marc-Claude and Maud quickly took ahold of his large body and held on with all their might. They all had their best grips as Cobra's body mass proved to be the needed anchor. Hope arose within them that they would possibly make it through this trial.

A few gold coins flew toward them and hit Cobra in the face. One piece particularly hit him in a soft spot on his cheek. "Aww!" he cried out, knowing that would leave a bruise. He shook off the pain and looked back to the mouth of the cave. He could see Riché holding on for dear life as the mouth of the cave inched closer to closing.

What Cobra found curious was that it looked like Riché was debating with himself. The young sailor didn't look worried as much as conflicted. Cobra saw his eyes watching as the coins flew past him. He began to realize what Riché was thinking. The temptation of the riches was too great for the young man. It was pulling him into this grave. The words of wisdom ran through Cobra's mind. *'He who trusts in his riches will fall.'*

Cobra yelled out, "No, don't do it! Stop!" His yelling was in vain as his voice couldn't be heard over the wind. And besides that, Riché already knew what he was going to do.

The young explorer knew that the treasure would be trapped in this cave when it shut. He wasn't thinking clearly, and his mind was telling him he couldn't live without it. He closed his eyes and let go of any handhold he had. His body then slid into the airstream and into the depths of the cave. He was eventually taken into the pit. He was seen no more.

Cobra had to look away as he feeling sorry for Riché. The young man had so much potential in his life, but now it was thrown away. Gone in an instant. The temptation of the gold and the riches led him into the depths of this trap. All of these thoughts brought great sadness to him.

The cave continued to close inch by inch, and the airstream became stronger. Though less than five minutes had passed, it felt like hours to Marc-Claude and the group. The strain on their bodies was agonizing, and the random pieces of treasure and debris hitting them made their struggle even more unbearable.

As the entrance of the cave was now less than two feet, it appeared to be closing faster. Strong gusts of wind struck their bodies, lifting them off the ground. At this point, even Cobra was being slightly picked up. Roselin wondered if they could somehow pivot outside the direct flow of air as it was thinner at this point. But even that plan seemed impossible, and their best option was simply to hang on.

The entry was now only a few inches wide. The pull was so strong. Marc-Claude could not hang on any longer. He and Maud both slipped off Cobra and tumbled toward the cave. They screamed briefly and closed their eyes. Their backs hit what now looked like an ordinary rock wall. The entry was completely closed... and the wind stopped.

Chapter 20

Roselin, Cobra, Hooks, and Lin laid on the ground trying to catch their breath. Their muscles ached, and they felt dizzy. Ironically, the clouds had cleared, and the sun had begun to shine. Cobra rolled his body off Hooks and Lin. The two men groaned from relief. Slowly, Roselin picked herself up off the ground but quickly had to catch herself as she was unsteady. She brushed her hair aside, clearing it from her eyes.

Cobra rose to his feet. He was stumbling as he tried to walk toward Marc-Claude and Maud. Maud was now on her feet, while Marc-Claude was still on the ground. As Cobra reached them, he spoke to both of them. "Are you hurt?"

"Well, I'm fine." Maud said, sounding upbeat. "I landed against Marc-Claude as we hit the wall of the cave. Or I guess it's not a cave anymore."

Cobra bent down and turned his companion on his side. "Marc-Claude, are you ok?"

"Uhh..." he groaned. He was disheveled and what little hair he had on top of his head was unkempt.

Cobra smiled as he knew his friend well enough to know that groan meant he was basically fine. "You didn't break anything did you?"

"No," he said with his eyes closed. "By... by... by any chance is there any more treasure left?"

Cobra looked around. "Uh, there's a few coins lying around, but it's mostly gone."

"Good. This would be the one time I wouldn't want any of it."

"I never thought I'd hear you say that," Cobra said, proud of his best friend. He was happy to hear that this treasure hadn't tamed his heart, like it had to Riché.

By this time Roselin, Lin, and Hooks were upright and approaching them. They all looked as if they had been through a war. Hooks was fiddling with his hook, putting it back into place. "What was that madness that about killed us?" he asked.

Maud spoke up. "Well, my nephew here was trying to rescue us, but he didn't realize that was shutting the mouth of the cave."

"How did you shut the mouth of a cave?" Roselin wondered.

"Now that's an interesting question." Maud paused, chuckling a bit before continuing. "There was a magical weapon at the top of the cave entrance, opening the door to a grave or another world. I don't know, but anyway, he took that off and it began to close in on us."

"And pull us in too?" Marc-Claude added in a tired voice.

Maud slapped her knee as she spoke. "Oh yeah. I had a feeling something like that would happen. But, good ole' nephew here, pulled it anyway, and good thing too. He saved us from that Riché kid. That boy would have slowly followed that enchanted treasure all the way into the depths of that cave and pulled us in with it."

"Wait!" said Hooks. "Are you saying that treasure was enchanted?"

"Oh yeah. Oh, yeah." Maud continued to get more animated the more she talked. "Most of it was. There were a lot of other things too, scattered around. Some of those things were just an illusion, which means they were fake."

Hooks rolled his eyes. "I know what an illusion is, Maud."

Maud pointed at the root. "Marc-Claude put that weapon in that root."

Lin went over to the cut in the root. Kneeling down he reached into the slit and felt for the spearhead. It wasn't long before he pulled out the diamond weapon. He held it up showing it off to the group. Some of the others took a moment to inspect this weapon that had caused so much commotion. As a whole they were mesmerized by the beauty and exquisiteness of it.

Roselin then turned to Cobra. "Was there anything on top of the mountain? Any treasure?"

"There was."

Instantly Marc-Claude perked up, ignoring his pain. "What did you find, Cobra? Should we all journey to the top?"

Cobra shook his head and smiled. "No, that won't be necessary. I was able to bring it down myself. If you will pardon me a moment, I'll go get it." He turned and left, leaving the others in suspense. Marc-Claude, particularly, was left in wonder. He began getting excited, thinking that whatever Cobra had found was of immense power or value. A smile formed on his face.

It wasn't long before Cobra returned with the books in hand. Marc-Claude was a little confused. Without thinking he said what was on his mind. "Cobra, is this perhaps a book of maps, possibly leading us to more treasure on the island?"

"Not at all. I found the memoirs of the Lady Sophia," he said proudly. "But also, with that something even better."

Marc-Claude leaned forward, feeling the suspense. "Yes, and what else?" The others were curious as well.

"I found the ancient Book of Wisdom written by Solomon himself under the direction of the Righteous King." He then held up the book for all to see.

Maud's eyes grew wide. "Oh, my!" Roselin, Lin, and Hooks were equally shocked. They had heard of this book and the legends about it.

Roselin slowly stepped forward and reached out her hand to touch it. Her hand was trembling as she felt the cover of the book. "It can't be," she said under her breath.

Marc-Claude cleared his throat. "Well, that sounds like a nice book, but was there anything gold or shiny with it?" There was pleading in his voice. The others ignored him as they looked at the books Cobra had brought. They read random proverbial sayings found throughout the Book of Wisdom, pausing to laugh or reflect on what they read. Marc-Claude just laid back down, trying to recoup.

Roselin took a moment to read some of the content found in the memoir. She read of struggles and conflicts within Sophia's mind. She read of a desire to follow the book of wisdom, but also being tempted by the wealth she possessed. It became apparent there was more to her than what legend foretold.

A black bird flew past her line of sight. Roselin quickly looked up from the book. She glanced around the area and snapped back to reality that this enchanted island had come close to capturing them. She looked back at the closed door of the cave before addressing the others. "Let's go back to the boat. I want to get far away from this spot."

"I agree," Hooks added. "I've had enough of this accursed place."

"But I don't think my nephew here is ready to walk," Maud said, sounding concerned.

"Hold this," Cobra handed his book over to Maud. He then walked over to Marc-Claude, who was drifting to sleep at this point. Without being fazed, Cobra reached down and picked up his good friend and threw him over his shoulder.

Marc-Claude tried to stop him, speaking out with great fatigue in his voice. "I can walk. I can walk."

Cobra patted him on the back as he held him. "Oh, don't worry about it. You just rest." He began walking away. "After helping me find the Book of Wisdom, there's no way I will ever be able to repay you."

"Uhh..." Marc-Claude groaned.

✌︎

The group took their time walking back to the ship. Lin and Roselin started off carrying the injured crewman who had been inside the plant. His arms were around their shoulders as he took small steps. Eventually his strength returned, and he was able to walk by himself. The same came true for Marc-Claude. As they got closer to the boat, Marc-Claude slid himself off Cobra's shoulders and began walking back. Cobra protested, but Marc-Claude insisted. Hooks spent his time looking for more random gold coins and jewels along the beach. He didn't have much success as only a dozen items were found.

As the group arrived back at the boat, Marc-Claude couldn't help but smile at seeing the sight of the large vessel. Corleone and Gabriella were looking over the side of the boat waving at them as they arrived. Marc-Claude looked over at Cobra, "So how long did you have to wait before their boat came for you?"

He shrugged. "It's hard to say. Maybe two hours. Probably felt longer than it was." Marc-Claude chuckled at the irony of it all.

A ramp was lowered, and the group walked out into the shallow water and then onto the boat. The crew began clapping as they welcomed them all back. The faces of everyone displayed jubilation, seeing Cobra and the others had successfully rescued Marc-Claude and Maud. Leah and Rachel were also among them. They were extremely happy to see everyone had made it back safe and sound.

Gabriella stepped forward, "We're so thrilled to have you back, Marc-Claude."

"Listen I can't... I mean...," Marc-Claude stuttered, feeling humbled for all Gabriella and Corleone had done for them. "Thanks for coming for all of us," he eventually was able to say. She simply smiled in return.

Many cheers and much gratitude were shown as the group made themselves at home on the boat. An assortment of bread, cheese, and fruit along with fresh wine was brought before the guests. Marc-Claude particularly didn't hold back, instantly helping himself. The others quickly joined in. Riché's crewman was taken to the holding cell with the other prisoners while the guests were getting comfortable.

After everyone had gathered their food, Corleone signaled to get everyone's attention for an announcement. As with everything Corleone did, he spoke with majesty and prestige in his voice. "And now, I want to hear what happened to all of you, and how you broke free from the young explorer."

Everyone looked to Marc-Claude and Cobra. Marc-Claude took a deep breath and looked over to his close companion. "Do you want to go first?"

"Sure!" Cobra said with much excitement. A part of him was still overflowing with joy from finding the Book of Wisdom. Cobra started off telling a detailed account of all that had happened after he had left their boat. Hooks added a few points in correction. Cobra particularly gave great interest and detail to the part of the story where he found the books of Sophia.

Marc-Claude then told his account of being pushed through the island by Riché and then their battle with the vicious plant. Maud would add in points of interest, saying such things as "I've never seen anything like that," "It was incredible," or "Marc-Claude's so clever." A couple of times she included a random fact about a distant relative.

The crew listened to every word intently, enjoying the account being told. Occasionally they asked questions for clarification. Marc-Claude didn't mind any of this as it fed his ego.

As Marc-Claude's account came to a close, Corleone had one final question. "So, at the mysterious cave, you weren't able to find any substantial treasure?"

"Sadly, no, mate. Simply some type of trap or strange magic."

"Yes," Roselin added. "I don't think we would want anything we found there anyway."

"Very true, very true," Corleone said. He then turned and motioned to his crew. "But I do wonder if you would be interested in this treasure chest not far from where we anchored. It looks ordinary, some of it is currency from the Empire."

"Wait... What?" Marc-Claude said, instantly filled with excitement.

A large chest was then brought out, carried by four men. They struggled as they brought it into the presence of the group. Marc-Claude was speechless as the chest was set before him. It was close to four feet in length and sat two feet in height. His eyes grew wide as he wondered about the treasure that was inside. He reached out to open the lid. "May I?" he said to Corleone.

"Proceed," he replied, holding out his hand. "As far as I'm concerned, it's all yours."

Slowly Marc-Claude lifted the lid and found exactly what he was hoping for. Inside he saw real gold coins, along with diamonds, and a few pieces of jewelry. Though it was only half full, he knew this was more than enough to make him wealthy. He ran his fingers through the coins and held some in his hands. He pulled a handful of the coins out to show the others standing around. "Aha! Glorious treasure for us!" The crewmen were particularly enamored by it.

A disenchanted look formed on Roselin's face. "No thank you! I don't want anything to do with this island." A similar expression was on Lin's face as well.

"Fine, more for me, mate." Marc-Claude then picked up two handfuls of it, thinking through all he could do with this wealth. He thought too about how his fame and admiration would increase among other seafarers. It was almost too good to be true.

At that moment Corleone's three kids came up and looked inside the treasure chest. They had watched when the chest was brought onto the ship, and they had wondered what was inside. Like all kids they were amused by it, yet their minds went to what it would be used for. "Father, this is wonderful," said their daughter. "This treasure can be used to help repair the orphanage."

"Oh, this is going to be great," said their older son. "Maybe we can help fix the wall on the south side, so mice won't spoil the food in the pantry."

"Yes, yes! What a wonderful find," the daughter said with a joyous expression.

"No, I'm sorry, children," Gabriella interrupted. "But this treasure belongs to Marc-Claude. He's been looking for this treasure for a long time and has endured many hardships to find it. It rightfully belongs to him."

"But... but, the orphans need this treasure," the oldest boy said.

"We could even buy them an abundance of vegetables, milk, and other things for them to eat," said their daughter.

Their younger boy then started crying. "I want to help the children!" he cried out.

"There, there, young lad," Corleone said. "We will just have to keep exploring, hoping for the best, and trusting in the guidance of the Righteous King. Everything will be fine."

Marc-Claude's spirit dropped as he could hear the younger boy weeping in the background. He loosened his grip on the coins, and they slid out of his hands. He took a deep breath and closed his eyes. Trying as hard as he could, he attempted to block out everything around him and think about this treasure. But for him there was one thing that he couldn't silence—his conscience. Moving as tepidly as he could, Marc-Claude stood to his feet and faced the crowd. His shoulders were slumped, and he looked dejected.

The crowd went silent. "Marc-Claude, do you have something to say?" Corleone said.

Maud spoke up. "He don't look so good. Kind of sickly."

Marc-Claude cleared his throat, silencing the crowd. "What I want to say is..." he trailed off in a mumble.

"Hey! Speak up!" Hooks shouted.

"I'll tell you something," Maud added. "My sister's family has always had trouble with mumbling. I think she got it from her husband. That's Marc-Claude's grandfather. He's a nice fellow, but I warned my sister that he would be mumbling his whole life. And another thing..."

"As I was saying!" Marc-Claude interrupted. He bit his lip, trying to muster up the courage again. Finally, he reasoned with himself just to say it and get it over with. "Corleone, Gabriella, you can have this treasure... for the orphans."

The crowd was silent for just a moment, shocked at what they had just heard. "Marc-Claude, are you sure?"

Gabriella said. "You worked so hard to come here. You can't mean this?"

He brushed his hand to the side. "No, no... I... I mean it. It's yours."

Suddenly everyone broke out in celebration. Much clapping and many cheers rang out from the vessel. Cobra came over and threw his arm around his best friend. "I always knew you would do it. I knew you would. I knew you would!"

The crowd continued to celebrate before Corleone stopped them. "May we pause and just say thank you... to Marc-Claude, the generous!" More cheers and celebration erupted. Many in the crowd came over and patted him on the shoulder in celebration.

In the midst of it all, Marc-Claude turned and looked at the open treasure chest. All of the coins and jewels seemed to sparkle even more now that they were out of his grasp. In the end, he knew he would be happy with his decision, but for this brief moment, he felt like crying.

Roselin, Hooks, Lin, Maud, Leah, and Rachel came over and joined Cobra with their arms around him. "Great job, old boy... great job," one of them said. The celebration continued, and Marc-Claude found himself unable to suppress his smile.

Epilogue

"So, there I was, stuck inside the jellyfish. I had no weapons besides my hooks. I was fighting vigorously, doing whatever I could do to not be stung by the cursed creature, and better yet, not being lost forever in the belly of a jellyfish. You guys would have never gotten me out." The others laughed.

Corleone's crew, along with Marc-Claude and company, sat by a torch fire at Roselin's restaurant, listening to Hooks' account. Roselin had some of the most exquisite food and drink brought out to them. Together, they all laughed and recounted the adventure they had just been through. Some exaggeration was given by Hooks, but the others were quick to correct his details. Overall, they were simply enjoying their evening as friends.

In the morning Corleone, Gabriella, and their crew would be gone. They wanted to check in with their village and particularly, the orphanage. They were anxious to share with others the exciting news about the treasure Marc-Claude had given them. There would maybe even be enough wealth to build a brand-new, larger orphanage, and provide food for at least a year. The future was bright for them.

Corleone and Gabriella did give the others a little of the gold treasure. Roselin and Cobra particularly tried to refuse, but they insisted. It wouldn't make them wealthy, but for Marc-Claude and Cobra it was enough that they could buy a new boat, which is what they needed more than anything at this point. Thankfully, Roselin knew of a man who would sell them one.

In an act of mercy, Corleone had let all of Riché's men go free. He took their weapons off their ship and had one of his crewmen guide them out to sea. Once they were closer to island of Seul, he let them go free. Cobra, Roselin, and Lin agreed this was the right plan and one of the crewmen even offered a heartfelt apology as well. Hooks seemed reluctant to this act of mercy, but once he heard the contrition in the men's voices, he felt satisfied knowing his side won in the end. The men would simply head back to the Northern Empire, recover from their injuries, and start a new life for themselves.

Leah and Rachel were planning on departing in the morning as well. The owner of the theater they worked for had been searching for them since they went missing. Word had been sent that they were safe and sound at Roselin's restaurant. Upon hearing the news, he redirected his ship directly toward their location. Rachel and Cobra promised to keep in touch. In fact, the two girls offered the whole crew free entry into one of their plays. It would be a long journey, but definitely something they would want to include in their future travels.

The stories and jokes continued. Laughter was in no short supply. Someone watching from the outside would have assumed these individuals had known each other for years. It was truly the time of leisure this group needed.

Marc-Claude took a sip of his drink and glanced out onto the beach. There he saw Cobra, sitting by himself, reading under a nearby torch. This wasn't unusual. He had been reading ever since they left the island. In fact, he had already memorized a lot of the proverbs found in the Book of Wisdom. But for right now Marc-Claude didn't want him to miss this time of enjoying an evening with friends. He sat his drink down and left the group. As he got closer to Cobra, he could see the Book of Wisdom sitting beside him, and in his hands was the open journal of Sophia.

"Interesting reading, mate?" Marc-Claude said as he walked up.

"Yeah," he said slowly. "You wouldn't believe the adventure and the struggle she had in bringing the treasure to the island."

"Huh... well why out of all the islands of the world did she choose that one?"

Cobra sighed. "You can read her thoughts. She wanted a place where she could offer the Book of Wisdom, but also have a punishment if people chose the riches instead. She'd learned of this island and the power it had through legends. It seemed like the best place to carry out her plans. That evil cave could capture people, while also having a place on a mountain for the Book of Wisdom."

Marc-Claude found this interesting but was a little bit at a loss for words. "Whoa, mate... that sounds... I don't know, dastardly."

"She was a very conflicted woman. I think the illusion of more riches by the cave tricked her."

"Naturally, mate. Her mind slowly got focused on the enchanted gold and jewels."

Cobra shook his head. "It's like she had the writings of wisdom but didn't always use them or seek the wisdom in it."

"Kind of like finding a treasure, but never spending it or using it."

"Well, I would say that wisdom is the true treasure. As it says in the book, '*How much better to get wisdom than gold, to get insight rather than silver.*'"

Marc-Claude chuckled as he sat down beside his friend. "You got to admit, mate, a little gold is still very nice."

Cobra shrugged. "It's ok, but I think wisdom's going to be my lifelong pursuit. I'm going to seek it with all my heart."

Now, Marc-Claude laughed deeply. "It sounds like you're going to quit the seas and become a philosopher."

"Oh, you'll see, Marc-Claude. I'm going to read this whole book and memorize a lot of it too."

"I'm sure you will." Marc-Claude stood back up and brushed himself off. "But first, why don't you come over and join us. We've got friends who are over there enjoying themselves. I'd hate for you to miss out on the fish."

Cobra got excited suddenly. "You ought to hear what this book says about friends." He cleared his throat and tried to speak properly. "*'There is a friend who sticks closer than a brother.'* That's like you and me, Marc-Claude. Friends till the end. Closer than brothers."

Marc-Claude rolled his eyes and smiled. "Thank you, Cobra. That was very nice. Now will you please come join us?"

"Alright. You don't have to get so upset."

The two men walked back to the group as Hooks was starting to tell another story. The firelight of the torches still shone bright against the dark night as the group casually ate and relaxed. There didn't seem to be an end to the telling of stories or jokes. More fish had been brought out, along with plenty to drink.

Upon seeing the two men arrive back at the group, Maud was the first to speak up, "So, Marc-Claude, a few of us were talking about where to go to next."

He was taken aback. "Umm…" His eyebrows were raised as he held up his index finger. "Wait, what do you mean by that?"

"We were just wondering where we're going after this."

Hooks spoke up, "Yeah, what do you say, Captain?"

"Yes, please, Marc-Claude. I have nowhere to go," Lin added.

Marc-Claude turned toward Roselin. She held up her hands in a defensive position. "Don't look at me. I have to stay here and run this place. You can come back whenever you'd like, but I'm not leaving."

Cobra put his arm around his best friend and smiled as big as he could. "Yes, so where do you think we'll go next?"

Marc-Claude turned to look at the moon reflecting off the water. There was a grand world out there on the seas. And now, he may have gained a permanent crew. There was no limit to where he could explore. He smiled as many more adventures were already playing through his mind.

The Journey of a Lifetime

1

Several years ago...

Marc-Claude stood on a cliff edge. It was early in the morning and the sun was rising over the ocean on the horizon. He'd followed a trail up this far and he was about to enter into a thick forest area. He took off his bandana and wiped the sweat from his forehead. For a man who was not yet thirty, he was in good shape, but still the hike had been steep.

He tied the bandana back around his head and looked toward the sea. He could see his boat docked down below. It would be well hidden on this side of the island. By far most people came from the west and would dock on that side. Marc-Claude wanted it that way since he didn't want his boat to be seen by any other vessels.

Looking closely at his boat, he could see the brown-haired woman on board sitting by the railing of the boat looking up at him. With a smile on her face, she waved at him. Marc-Claude smiled and waved briefly back. He couldn't help but worry, hoping she would be okay in the hot sun. The boat wasn't particularly large and there was only a small cabin from which she could get some shade, but unfortunately the cabin was often stuffy and hot.

Nevertheless, Marc-Claude quickly brushed aside any of these worries. Adrienne was one of the most self-reliant women he'd ever met. She would make do with whatever situation came her way. And if by some chance she did have a miserable experience, she wouldn't complain or be disgruntled. She was that kind of person.

"See you soon, Adrienne," Marc-Claude whispered as he then turned and went into the wooded area. There was no path on this side of the forest, so he would need to weave through the trees and step through the tall grass as best as he could. He knew approximately where he was going, but hoped a little luck was on his side with finding his destination.

After Marc-Claude had gone about a hundred yards he took out the dilapidated map again and looked it over. From what he could decipher it looked like he was going in the right direction. The destination was a cave in the middle of this forest. Supposedly it was an abandoned dragon's cave, most likely filled with gold and other odd treasures. He had gotten word about this area from an old pirate on the seas. The pirate, knowing he was too old for an adventure, sold Marc-Claude his map. After acquiring this map, he quickly got his ship ready, picked up Adrienne, and set sail.

Rumors were spreading that others were looking for this treasure as well. Others with many more resources than he himself had. As he began to think about this, he found himself quickening his pace. In no way did he want to be seen by others.

Thinking again of Adrienne, for many years now Marc-Claude had wanted to take her on a sea journey. She never asked, but Marc-Claude knew her well enough to know that this was her heart's desire. He wanted to wait for a trip that would be good for her. She usually stayed close to home and didn't venture out to the seas. When this treasure hunt came up, she first refused, not wanting to be a burden to Marc-Claude, but after his insisting she happily said yes, and there was no looking back. She was having a grand time on this journey of a lifetime. Marc-Claude took her to a few random eateries and even introduced her to other friends and seafarers that came their way. For a girl of the city, this was an adventure she'd never forget. She soaked up every experience and enjoyed every moment.

All of the joy coming from Adrienne brought a newfound joy to Marc-Claude as well. It motivated him and reminded him to take pleasure not just in the treasure but also in the journey. This was the kind of encouragement he needed as he was one who was often obsessing with treasure. Adrienne was good for him, helping to put his focus in the right areas.

As he passed through a few more trees, he came to a small hill in the forest. This was a good sign. Moving through the trees he reached the other side of the hill and found what he was looking for, the cave. "Ah, yes, Marc-Claude! You've done it again," he said to himself. He took out his map again, double checking just to make sure this couldn't be the wrong cave. "Oh, what a clever man I am," he whispered.

Confirming that this was the right location, he put the map in his pocket and walked into the large cave. The entryway was thin. He actually had to turn himself sideways and duck slightly to make it through. He groaned a little as his back scraped against a jagged rock. It was simply a small price to pay for the treasure he would find inside.

Making it through the entryway, he could see the cave opened up to a large room. The roof of the cave was probably fifteen feet in height, close to thirty feet wide, and fifty feet deep. It was odd how big it was compared to what it looked like from the outside. A light was coming from a large hole above. This made it easy to see around the cave. It looked as if there were a few crevasses, possibly leading to other areas of the cave. A small pool of water was in a corner. Some species of bugs were flying around the stagnant water. He'd prefer to stay away from that side.

Marc-Claude stepped further into the cave. At first he didn't see anything, but peeking around a rock that jutted out, he saw what he was looking for. It was his heart's desire... treasure! It wasn't much, simply one treasure chest with a few items sitting beside it, but nonetheless, it was still treasure.

The happy seafarer stepped closer to his prize. The items sitting close by were odd pieces of jewelry or random pieces of metal. Much of the jewelry looked to be broken. It could probably be melted down to something more valuable, but in its current state it wasn't worth much. He looked closely at the lid of the chest and saw that any locking mechanism was broken. Marc-Claude then didn't hesitate to reach down and open it up. The lid snapped off the back, falling to the ground. Looking into the chest, he could see that it was less than a quarter full of treasure, of which was mostly gold coins. He rubbed his chin as he examined it over. He shrugged, knowing that this hunt didn't turn out to be as prosperous as the rumors, but still he was thankful to have some reward from this treasure hunt.

    Marc-Claude grabbed the edges of the chest to see how heavy it was, wondering if he could carry it back to the boat by himself. When he grabbed on to the left side of the chest, he found the wood extremely soft. His fingers actually went through the wood. He chuckled in slight disappointment, knowing that this chest would not make it back to the boat.

    Looking back into the chest, he could see that he had shuffled around the coins inside trying to pick it up. What intrigued him was that he could see something green in the midst of the gold. He reached down and grabbed the item from among the coins. His eyes grew wide as he held it in his hand. It was a large emerald cut in an oval shape, slightly smaller than his palm. "Oh my, oh my. You sure are a beauty," he said, feeling mesmerized.

    Marc-Claude stood to his feet and rubbed the jewel with his other hand. He stepped more into the light. The jewel looked even more stunning with the light reflecting through it. He held it up higher toward the light. It appeared flawless, without any slight nicks or indentions. Two simultaneous thoughts came at once- he wondered where this jewel had come from, and, also, how much it was worth. A lot of the people he sold items to wouldn't be able to afford something like this. This would possibly have to go to a person of royalty or a collector. Either way, he knew there would be someone who would want this luxurious jewel.

Suddenly he was snapped out of this daydream by the sound of voices coming toward the cave. He knew he didn't want to be seen in this area. It may cost him his life. Quickly he ran toward the chest and grabbed a handful of coins and stuffed them into his pocket. He then looked around and spotted a crevasse in the cave. Wasting no time, he went toward it and found that it was actually a small tunnel in midst of this cave. Squeezing himself in, he saw that it quickly ascended. He maneuvered his body upward through the tunnel, trying to get some distance between him and the opening.

Eventually, Marc-Claude made it to another opening. He found himself near the top of the cave, looking down onto the floor. There was nowhere else he could go but the same way he came. He was stuck for now. Carefully he peeked toward the entryway of the cave, waiting to see who would emerge.

He didn't have to wait long before he saw a band of pirates squeeze through the opening. There were a half-dozen of them total. They were an odd-looking bunch with large mustaches and neatly combed hair. He looked carefully just to see if he knew any of them, or, at the very least, if he could figure out who they were. So far nothing came to mind. He could also hear faint words from them. It wasn't a language he was familiar with.

The pirates looked around the area, examining it just as Marc-Claude had done a few minutes before. At one point he thought one pirate was looking right at him, but soon enough he looked away to another area. They continued to speak to one another in their language. It almost sounded to Marc-Claude as if they were arguing, typical for pirates.

Just like Marc-Claude, eventually they found the treasure chest. A couple of the pirates pushed each other out of the way, fighting among themselves as to who was going to look through the treasure first. This led to more of them fighting among themselves. This seemed to go on for a few minutes. Watching them closely, Marc-Claude was starting to become annoyed with these men. He rolled his eyes in frustration, watching the bickering accelerate.

After a full fifteen minutes the man who looked like the oldest of the bunch stepped forward as the one who would look through it first. He bent down and started running his hands through the gold, taking inventory of it all. A few of the other pirates were obviously still upset and appeared to be saying nasty things about the one looking through the treasure. At this point Marc-Claude began to chuckle, thinking this whole thing was ridiculous.

The room then fell into silence as the men accepted the fate that this particular pirate should be the first one to look through the treasure. This bored Marc-Claude even further and being bored was one thing that Marc-Claude greatly hated. He would have to do something to keep himself entertained. Taking a gold coin from his pocket, he looked at it closely. He knew it was somewhat valuable, but his idea would definitely be worth the price. Gently he kissed the gold coin before throwing it at the senior pirate below.

The coin hit the pirate in the back of the head. Instantly he stood up in anger and looked back at the other pirates. "Os epoisai ekeina?"

They looked confused. "Tis ei se legeis?"

"Su ginoskeis tis ego eimi legeis?" the senior said in anger.

A small skirmish began to ensue as the pirate tried to figure out who threw something at the back of his head. Now, Marc-Claude found this truly entertaining. A few minutes passed and the men calmed back down, but Marc-Claude was determined not to go back into boredom. He simply threw a piece of gold at another pirate that was not paying attention. This began the same argument and another small skirmish ensued.

Marc-Claude continued this pattern two or three more times. Eventually lines were drawn among the pirates, and they pulled their swords. They faced each other as it looked like they had banded together in groups of two. It appeared that their plan was that each group would look through the treasure and take portions of it for their pair. One would look through the gold, while the other would watch out for shenanigans. With them carefully watching each other like this, Marc-Claude knew he would have to give up on his game. Nevertheless, he was thankful for the fun he'd had while it lasted.

Eventually, the pirates left, cleaning out most of the treasure. They were still arguing slightly as they squeezed through the opening. When Marc-Claude thought the coast was clear, he climbed back down out of his tunnel. His clothes were a little muddy, but he didn't care. He laughed to himself as he spoke quietly. "Thank you, mates, that was a jolly time indeed."

Marc-Claude pulled the emerald out of his pocket, looking at it again in the light. He was thankful that it had stayed well-secured with him as he was maneuvering through the tunnel. "You sure are a beauty," he said with a smile. He tucked it back into his pocket and left the cave.

2

Marc-Claude arrived back at the boat in the latter part of the afternoon. He found Adrienne in the same spot where he left her. She was sitting in a chair by the edge of the boat. The only difference was that her arms were tucked under her head as she was fast asleep on the railing. A butterfly was resting close beside her, as if it was protecting her. Thankfully Adrienne's light brown skin would protect her from any deep sunburn that might occur. Marc-Claude smiled, seeing her look so peaceful, not worrying about anything in the world. He envied her as he found her demeanor truly a modern marvel.

He stepped up and sat on the edge of the railing next to where her head laid. The feel of his presence awakened her. Her eyes blinked and she sat up. "Welcome back," she said with a smile. "I'm not sure how long I was out for." She began wiping her eyes as she gained her bearings. The butterfly flew away.

"Hope I wasn't gone too long for you," he said softly.

"Oh no. It's fine. I think just all of the traveling and new sights the last few days have made me tired. Everything's catching up with me now."

"Well, in that case, sorry to wake you," he said laughing slightly. The two fell into silence for a moment as he gave her time to awake fully. Marc-Claude could be impatient at times, but when he was with Adrienne it felt like the world could wait. He looked out toward the ocean. A few seagulls were diving for fish as the sun still shone bright. The ocean water lapping against the island's shore further made for pleasant resonances. It was picturesque, and Marc-Claude was content to sit here looking out into the ocean.

A few more minutes passed before she spoke up. "Did you find the cave?"

He looked at her with raised eyebrows. "I sure did," he said slowly.

She was smiling big. "Well... did you find any treasure?" asking facetiously.

"Oh, most definitely. It was a hike, but I found the cave... with a treasure chest inside."

"Much gold?"

"Some, not a lot," he said with a shrug. He then reached into his pocket. "But I did find this." With that Marc-Claude pulled out the green emerald.

Adrienne put her hand over her mouth, awestruck with the beauty of it. "Wow! Marc-Claude, that's beautiful. Was it just with the treasure in the cave?"

"Oh yes. Buried in the midst of the gold." He held it out for her to take it. "If you look closely, you can see how pure it is. Not a single flaw or anything."

She gently took it from him and looked it over. She even held it up in the light. It dazzled even more with the rays of the sun reflecting through it. "It's wonderful," she said quietly.

"Isn't it though? I'm hoping to get a large bounty for it from a collector."

She shook her head. "I... I can't even imagine how much something like this would sell for."

Marc-Claude laughed one more time as he stood to his feet. "Hopefully a lot of money. I'll take a collection of jewels as well."

He began walking away, hoping to get things in order to set sail. Adrienne called out to him. "Do you want it back?"

Stopping in his tracks, he looked back at her. "Why don't you hold on to it for me? You always do a good job with taking care of things, sis."

"Thanks Marc-Claude. I couldn't have asked for a better brother."

"Love you so much," she said under her breath. Since they were young Marc-Claude had always kept an eye out for taking care of his younger sister. He was the third out of five kids, and she was the fourth. Their younger sister Clara was more self-reliant and seemed to always be looking for ways to help others. Even though Adrienne was two years older than her, Clara tended to take care of her older sister as they grew up.

As for Marc-Claude and Adrienne, they seemed to have a special connection. She took a special interest in his sea voyages and would often inundate him with questions whenever she saw him. Being one who always enjoyed talking about himself, he loved these questions and inquiries into his life. And over time with him telling her these stories, he grew to not only see her as a sister but also as a friend. Her desire for a trip like this began to grow, and for years this trip had been in the works. They had discussed it many times, but Marc-Claude simply needed to wait for the right time and place. So far, it had been everything Adrienne had dreamt of.

Marc-Claude took a few minutes to change his clothes and put back on his large captain's hat. At this time in his life, when he was out to sea, he wanted to look the part of a captain. He then returned to the deck, feeling renewed and ready for another voyage.

The anchor was pulled on board and Marc-Claude took his place at the helm. It wasn't much longer before the boat was to set sail on seas again. On the side of the vessel were written the words *'The Life-Time Journey.'* For short, Marc-Claude would refer to it as 'The Journey.' The boat was his most prized possession. From the time he was a youth he'd had the desire to purchase a vessel like this one. Growing up in the Northern Empire, he took odd jobs working wherever he could to save his money. He also took to gambling and found himself quite good at it. Today he enjoyed games and the fun of winning, but when he was younger it was of practical value. He wanted to win more in order to buy this boat.

The vessel was his pride and joy. He took great care of it and cleaned it as often as he could. It had become a part of his identity over the last few years. Seafarers from regions around the Northern Empire and to the west began to recognize him. He valued this recognition, and it further motivated him to keep buying, selling, and exploring wherever he could. Occasionally he would come across maps or different relics that would lead to hidden treasures or artifacts of years gone by. Through all of this he was able to further build a name for himself among those on the seas.

Adrienne looked up at him at the helm, steering his ship. She couldn't help but smile as she admired her brother. The sun was shining on him as he looked ready to conquer the world. She sighed before speaking loudly, "Marc-Claude, you remind me of a king, ruling from his throne. Ready for any challenge."

He laughed slightly. "Ha. Yes, I like that imagery. A mighty king on his throne, ruling over his dominion." He paused to hold out his arms wide. "King Marc-Claude, reigning over the seas! Conquering all!" The feelings of supremacy grew stronger. "Nothing can stop me. Ha-ha! I'm unstoppable!" Ironically, at that moment the butterfly was flying close to his face and landed on the side of his mouth. A piece of its wing got in his mouth. "Plah!" he yelled out as he began spitting and wiping his mouth. The butterfly appeared to fly away unharmed. "What was that?" he said, slightly angry.

Adrienne was laughing hysterically. From her perspective, she saw it all transpire as the butterfly flew close to his face and landed on the edge of his mouth. She could tell he hadn't been paying attention to it, and now it was a truly humorous yet ironic situation.

As Marc-Claude came to his senses, he saw his sister laughing. The joy on her face helped to dispel any anger he felt toward the small creature. "Well, I guess there's one thing that can stop me."

She chuckled one last time. "Oh, brother, you sure do keep things exciting."

Marc-Claude didn't respond, but simply grabbed ahold of the wheel and adjusted the direction of the boat. Seeing his sister laugh was priceless to him. Possibly the only thing he loved more than gold.

A few moments passed before Adrienne spoke up again. "Well, captain, where to now?"

"Hmm... since we're not far, I figure we'll head to a southwest region of the Empire. There's a town called Ardentes that's fairly isolated, governs itself. I might inquire and see what the emerald is worth. I also hear they have some fine music and institutions of learning in this area. I'd love to see if the rumors are true, and if there's anyone here who could help us."

"Oh yes, I've heard of this area.... Sounds like an adventure."

Marc-Claude smiled again. "I'm sure it will be."

⚜

Later in the day Marc-Claude and Adrienne sat together as they watched the sun set over the ocean. The land of the Empire was not yet in sight in the east. Nevertheless, their eyes were turned to the west as they had a clear view of the reflection of the sun on the water. A vast array of colors was seen on the horizon. The two of them had been out to sea for five nights now and this was by far the most beautiful sunset of all. Marc-Claude sat straddling the railing with a bottle in one hand. His bandana was over his head as his captain hat rested on the deck. Occasionally he would glance over at Adrienne who was looking peacefully into the sunset. Her hands were folded under her head. A pleasant look was on her face as she soaked in every instant of this event. Seeing his sister enjoying this sunset was worth the years of planning and waiting. No matter what they found on this trip, this was the true treasure.

A few minutes passed and Adrienne took the green emerald from her lap. She had been holding it all afternoon and evening. Now she held it up in front of her eyes and looked as the colors of the sun reflected through this emerald. It gave her just a little bit more simple amusement.

As she brought the emerald down from her eye, a pair of swans flew across their sight of the sunset. Adrienne now laughed quietly at the beauty of it all.

"It's quite a sight, isn't it, Sis." Marc-Claude said, before taking a drink from his bottle.

"Gorgeous... you told me the seas had beautiful sunsets, but your description fell short of what we're experiencing now."

"Aye." He nodded ever so slightly. "It's like the treasure you always have at the end of the day, no matter how your expedition went. This prize will be waiting for you."

Adrienne smiled even bigger. She loved when Marc-Claude got poetic like this. Every so often he would write a song to a tune he knew. She couldn't figure out why, but he seemed to be embarrassed by this. He would try to keep his writing a secret, though all the family knew that deep down inside himself Marc-Claude had an affinity for writing songs.

The two of them fell into silence again, and both of them began to daydream. The sun was lower now with only a fifth of it able to be seen on the horizon. They watched it get lower before their very eyes. Adrienne particularly wanted to soak in every moment. She hoped to remember this for the rest of her life.

When the sun was just about out of sight, she spoke out quietly. "I wonder what God thinks of all this?"

He laughed slightly. "I don't know, Sis."

"Well, if he's the Maker, do you think he enjoys the sunset as much as we are at this moment? Or do you think rather he takes pleasure in the fact that we're delighting in his creation?"

Marc-Claude shrugged and took another drink of the bottle. "I think you're overthinking it. Just enjoy it."

She glanced over at Marc-Claude and spoke facetiously. "Maybe this is how I'm enjoying it. Have you ever heard the saying, 'The unexamined life is not worth living'? I think that applies to all of life."

"Yes, I've heard that... but even sunsets?"

She paused to think for a few seconds before continuing. "Yes, hmm... sort of. Think about it like this, what is your life in light of this sunset? Do you feel small? Or important? Or does it make you think about purpose, and that the meaning of life goes beyond what we often burden ourselves with?"

He wasn't sure what to say. Adrienne had a naturally philosophical mind and was always interested in the deeper meanings of life. At all times it seemed like she was searching to understand and learn from the grander moments of life. There was something beautiful and infectious about it. When hearing her speak about these things, it seemed easy to conclude that there was a profound wonder of life beyond the temporal burdens.

Nevertheless, for Marc-Claude, as a usual occurrence, a bit of humor came to mind. "Adrienne, the sunset does help me to think more about one of my favorite things."

"And what's that?"

"Gold! And lots of it!"

Adrienne laughed as she shook her head at the irony of his comment. Marc-Claude joined in as well as they watched the final bit of the sun descend over the horizon.

3

Marc-Claude was at the wheel navigating his ship toward the southwest region of the Empire. The water was slightly more turbulent as a strong wind was stirring up the seas. The moon was shining bright, helping to light the way. They were making good time as the wind was in their favor. The seas were still clear as they hadn't seen another boat all day.

Once they arrived in the Empire, Marc-Claude would check to see if an inn was close by. If not, they could stay on the boat. Marc-Claude wouldn't mind this option, but with his sister he would always want to make sure she was comfortable and there was nothing of inconvenience to her. He had saved up plenty of money for this trip. Expenses wouldn't need to be spared.

Adrienne still sat in her same spot against the railing. She hadn't said much since the sunset and her demeanor had changed. She would drift off to sleep and then awake for a while. Marc-Claude was worried about her. She was no longer smiling but looked to be deep in thought. If the waves hadn't been so rough, then he would have stopped and checked on her. He knew though if he stopped even for a moment, the boat would drift off course.

Marc-Claude tried to distract his mind from worrying. He thought about some of the news of the seas and rumors of treasure that were circulating. Once he was out on his own again, he had hoped to pursue one of these destinations. But now thinking of these rumors and far off lands, a part of him wondered if he really wanted to explore a far-off area. After spending this time with his sister, he couldn't imagine leaving her for months at a time. He wanted her regularly in his life, much like when they were younger. This trip was changing him, and he knew he would never be the same after it.

Suddenly he heard a thud against the deck of the ship. He looked down at Adrienne and saw that the emerald had slipped out of her hand onto the deck. He wondered if she had fallen into a deeper sleep. "Adrienne!" he called out. "Adrienne!" She turned to look at him, and he could tell her posture didn't look normal. Abruptly her body started to go limp, and she fell out of her seat onto the deck.

"No... no!" Marc-Claude yelled. Immediately he left the wheel and ran toward her.

"Adrienne, Adrienne! Speak to me!" he pleaded. He gently lifted her head. She was breathing fine, but she was obviously becoming unconscious. "Please, Adrienne, please!"

She let out a deep breath and with her eyes closed, spoke with a tired voice. "I'm fine, Marc-Claude. I'll be okay."

He brushed the hair out of her eyes. She looked so peaceful with her head resting in his lap like this, but he knew she was anything but fine. He looked out to sea, wondering how far they had to go till they arrived at the Empire.

4

In a small shop in the southwest region of the Empire, the lights were dim as a large man inked the outline of a dragon tattoo on the arm of a pirate. A small candle was close by helping to lead the way for the artist to work. He'd been doing this work for six years now and had gotten quite good at his artistry. Patrons were beginning to come from farther and farther away in order to utilize his craftmanship. He could now honor just about any request that crossed his path. Word of his skills was spreading fast.

Unfortunately for the artist, word was also spreading about the illegal activity that went on in this shop. The artist would harbor stolen materials for various criminals. The items ranged from paintings to weapons and various chemicals, along with metals, and gems, stolen from the mines of Grimdolon. A few officials from the Empire had come by a week ago inquiring about his shop. Thankfully, these items were hidden at the time. Nevertheless, he knew they would be back. He hoped he would be ready for them.

The artist's name was Curtis, but few knew his real name. He went by the alias of Cobra and that is how everyone knew him. Now in his late twenties, the name of Curtis was long forgotten. He was a tall, large man, whose hair was greatly thinning on top. It wouldn't be long before he shaved it all off. A lot of his weight was muscle mass. Mostly of the time he wore a sleeveless shirt, showing off his biceps. Even though he was somewhat soft inside, his presence was intimidating enough to keep people from taking advantage of him.

As far as his family, he basically felt like an orphan. His mother was in her seventies, and his father was nowhere to be seen. Cobra had been raised by his mother and grew up in a stable household. Rules and morals were taught to him, but his mother was also quite lax in regard to structure and general discipline. He often got into trouble, but his mother's simple admonitions kept him from crossing certain lines in his life of mischief.

"What's taking so long?" the pirate said.

Cobra said nothing, barely hearing the man. The idea of the authorities learning about his secret operations was highly on his mind. This last week he had found it difficult to focus on the tasks that were in front of him.

The pirate continued, "I was told you were the best. But you don't seem like you know a thing about what you're doing."

"Just let me work," Cobra said under his breath.

Another few minutes passed, and the pirate noticed that Cobra was shaking more. "I don't know why I'm even paying for this. You stupid..."

Upon hearing this, Cobra pulled back from the man and just looked at him in disgust. The pirate snarled back at him.

Quickly Cobra reached forward and grabbed him by the neck and squeezed. The pirate grabbed Cobra's hands as his eyes got wide. The two men looked into each other's eyes. There was absolute terror in the pirate's face.

Cobra spoke calmly, "Let me finish the drawing."

Processing what the artist just said, the pirate nodded as best as he could. Slowly Cobra removed his hands from his neck. The pirate began to cough as he was bent over. Cobra let him take his time in regaining his composure. The pirate was afraid to complain any longer.

Time passed slowly as Cobra continued to work on his artwork. He felt a lot less pressure, knowing that the pirate would no longer be grumbling about the amount of time this took. He worked and worked, sparing no detail in working on this particular tattoo. This was a rarity for him these days. In his downtime Cobra would sketch out different designs that he thought would be fun to try. He had done some elaborate designs in the past, particularly on seafarers and pirates. When these individuals would then travel the world, Cobra's art would often be displayed as the pirates specifically would be anxious to show off their new body art.

Unfortunately for Cobra, with the newfound popularity of his shop came less time to work more slowly on individual tattoos. He was rushed at times and was often left with an unsatisfied feeling about the job he did. He was just running through the customers, not like the old days when he took pride in each individual design. This unsettling feeling, mixed with his anxiety over the illegal activity, brought a miserable period in his life. He felt trapped in this life he had built.

Suddenly the door flew open to the shop. It was a young man, a teenager, who often brought word among the community. "Cobra, you got to get out of here. They're coming."

"Who's comin'?" He immediately stopped his work.

"Some of the Duke's men. They're going to arrest you." The young man spoke urgently. There was no denying he believed this was a great threat.

"How much time do I have?"

"Not much... you need to leave now!"

Cobra quickly got up and grabbed a few personal items. He stuffed them in a cloth bag and made his way to the exit.

"No," the young man said. "Go out the back. They might see you if you go through the front."

He turned and made his way toward the back of his shop. "Hey, what about my tattoo?" the pirate yelled. Cobra ignored him as he left the main room of the shop. He entered his personal quarters where he kept some of his stolen materials. He grabbed a small bag of gold coins before exiting into the dark of night.

Cobra entered a dark alley and moved down the passageway. He heard voices coming his way. He quickly ducked between two shops, crouching low and letting the voices pass. He had no desire to hear if these were the actual ones that were after him. They passed by and he continued on his way.

The mountains blocked him to the east and the sea was toward the west. Cobra imagined the Duke's men came from over the mountains, and he didn't want any chance of coming in contact with them. He decided to take his chance going toward the sea. Maybe he could find a boat to steal or maybe hitch a ride with a mariner who was at port. Either way he knew that he didn't want to be an enemy of the Empire. A long sentence would await him if he was caught.

A small, wooded area stood between him and the sea. Taking no caution, Cobra ran through the area. He moved through the trees as best as he could. The darkness made this journey extremely difficult, but he didn't have time to think through if there were any better options. He simply had to flee.

Cobra tripped on a log and fell face forward onto a bush. Thorns cut the sides of his arms. He tried to stand up, but his boot couldn't gain traction, and he fell again. As quickly as he could, he gained a better footing and pulled himself to his feet. He continued on his way.

After running for eight minutes, the ocean was coming into view through the trees. He wondered if he should move even farther away from his shop. Looking to his left, he ran southward. As he hurried, he tried to scan the beach and see if he could spot a boat near the shore. So far, he saw nothing. This was unusual as there was typically at least one vessel no matter what time of the day it was. This was disappointing, but it only provoked him to just run faster. Eventually if he kept running, he knew he would find something.

He began to think again of going to prison. The thought sickened him. His mother tried to raise him better than this. This would be a grave disappointment to her. Especially with the amount of stolen material he had in the shop, he knew that he would spend years upon years in prison. This could not be an option. Cobra would need to do all he could to get away.

As he ran through the woods, he began to speak out quietly. "Help me... help me, please." He didn't know who or what he was crying out to, this only came instinctively. He needed help and was hoping that maybe some sort of deity out there would be listening. At the moment it was the only thing he could trust in.

Looking out at the sea, Cobra saw a boat arriving at the shore. It was about a hundred yards away. This looked to be his only chance as this was still the only boat in sight. Throwing caution to the wind, he ran toward the boat as quickly as he could. This vessel may have soldiers or merchants on board, but either way he would risk it and find out soon enough.

Running out of the woods, he approached the vessel and quickly climbed onto the boat. Even still he hadn't stop to assess who may be on board. He simply jumped on. Landing on the deck, he ducked low, hoping none of the Empirical forces had seen him. He tried to catch his breath as this was the first time he stopped since leaving his shop.

He was startled as he heard someone crying out. "Adrienne... Adrienne! Wake up." Cobra looked over to see a man holding a woman on his lap. As best as he could tell, it looked like the woman was unconscious.

Instantly his curiosity was piqued. Maybe he could work this to his advantage to offer help in exchange for this boat. Or at least, maybe he would use this dire situation to make them move to a new location where they could receive better 'help.' Cobra looked around, checking his surrounding once again to make sure all was clear. He moved toward the two individuals, trying his best to look intimidating.

As he got closer, the man on his knees turned and looked up at him. He was a little startled seeing this individual, "What are you doing on my boat, mate?"

"I... uh... well... uh..."

Suddenly, the young lady groaned, and her eyes slowly opened. "Adrienne! Are you there?" The young lady was now moving slightly, and her eyes were open, even though they looked tired. The man holding her pulled her closer.

"What's wrong with her?" Cobra asked.

The man rocked her back and forth. Not hesitating, he spoke freely to this stranger. "She has a disease. It affects her nerves. She hasn't had an episode like this in a long time, years in fact. She needs a specific medicine called Limusfin. It's rare, made from a chemical found in the mines of Grimdolon."

Cobra's eyes brightened. "I got some of dis, back in my shop. You're welcome to go get it."

"No... we can't, mate," the man said, shaking his head. "This is my sister. She can't walk. A few years ago, the disease took the usage of her legs. You got to go get it for us."

"But..." Cobra was stunned. He felt lost between two worlds. He couldn't say anything else as his mind tried to rationalize and figure everything out.

The man continued. "Please. My name is Marc-Claude. I'd go if I could, but I can't carry her, and I don't want to leave her. I need your help."

Cobra nodded. The compassion his mother had taught him in life was starting to come through and all of his own personal worries seemed to fade away. Though he knew this would put him in real danger, he knew he had to help this woman. He would not be able to live with himself if he let this young lady die without offering his help.

Adrienne groaned again and shut her eyes.

"No...no!" Marc-Claude called out.

Instantly Cobra bent down and picked her up. "Come on, there is no time. I'll take her right to it."

Marc-Claude jumped to his feet, not hesitating. "Forever grateful, mate. Let's go."

༺༻

The journey back to his shop was a lot slower, but Cobra moved as fast as he could as he went through the woods. Adrienne had moments of waking up and then falling back to unconsciousness. This worried Marc-Claude as she had never had an episode this bad before. In fact, her disease had very little effects as of late. This was one reason why they thought it would be a good time to make this voyage. With all the good moments they had experienced on this trip, the disease had been far from their minds.

Cobra easily maneuvered through the wooded area. He had little trouble carrying Adrienne's small frame. He said little and didn't think about the consequences of what he was doing. The health of this woman was the only thing that now mattered. Along the way Marc-Claude had talked a little about who she was and her struggle with the disease. This only added to Cobra's concern for her.

They left the woods. "Follow me," Cobra said, moving them toward the alley from which he had come not long ago. Marc-Claude didn't question Cobra. He could only hope he was telling the truth. It was Adrienne's only hope at this point.

The three arrived at the back of Cobra's shop and entered into the back room. Thankfully there were no men in this room. Cobra gently set Adrienne down in a chair. "Watch her," Cobra said to Marc-Claude. He stood beside her and steadied her as Cobra went to look for the medicine on his shelf.

He looked up and down his shelves and noticed there was a problem. The shelves had been ransacked and many of the items were gone. Marc-Claude noticed he was frantically looking. "What's wrong?"

"It's... it's not here. A lot of my things have been taken."

"What! ... Do you know where it could be?"

He was searching frantically as he talked. "I didn't tell you this, but the law is after me. That's why I came to your ship. I wanted to escape and not come back here, but... but..."

"But what?" Marc-Claude was getting upset.

"The lady needed help, and I couldn't leave her." He looked at her closely and saw that her energy was fading again. "I'm sorry. I don't know where it is, but I know it was just here..."

"Stop right there!" Suddenly bursting into the room were two Empirical soldiers dressed in armor and holding bows and arrows pointed toward them.

Cobra froze, fearing he was caught and concerned that he wouldn't be able to help this young lady.

5

Marc-Claude and Cobra looked at the two men with arrows pointed toward them. Even Adrienne perked up a little, hearing the threat from the soldiers. She steadied herself on the chair.

"We don't have time for this," Marc-Claude said. He pulled a small knife from his belt. He stood up and stepped toward them. "You men are going to have to leave."

The men took a step back but didn't lower their arrows. "We're here by order of the Grand Duke himself. We serve the Emperor."

Marc-Claude wasn't backing down. Nothing was going to stop him. He was calm, but spoke forcibly. "I assume you boys took the medicine from this shop. Medicine we will be needing, and I'm going to do whatever it takes to get it."

Cobra saw the look in his eyes, and he knew he wasn't bluffing. This was not going to end well. Marc-Claude kept moving forward with his knife in hand. The men pulled back their arrows further. Cobra knew he had to intervene. "Stop!"

Marc-Claude halted. Cobra stepped toward them. His hands were up in a defensive position. "Please, this girl needs help. I need some of the medicine that was in this room."

No one said anything, but one of the men pointed his arrow toward Cobra. "Move back!" one shouted to Cobra. They didn't want him getting anywhere close to them. Seeing the size of his frame, they knew he could do great damage in a fight.

Marc-Claude lowered his knife. "He's telling the truth. It's my sister here. She's sick. He has a disease and needs the medicine called limusfin."

"Limusfin?" one of the guards said.

"Yes, that's correct."

"Is she paralyzed?" the guard said quietly with a sense of concern.

"She is," Marc-Claude responded solemnly.

The guard began shaking slightly. The others didn't know it, but he was holding back tears. He was in his fifties and had a gentle look about him. A few moments passed and no one said anything. Eventually the soldier lowered his bow. "I know this disease. My son had it. It took his life a few years ago."

Marc-Claude threw down his knife, showing clearly that he didn't want to fight. "Will you help us?"

"Yes. We loaded many of the materials in the back of a carriage. We can see…"

"What are you doing?" the other guard shouted. "Put your bow back up! These are criminals, trying to trick you."

This soldier took his eyes off Cobra. Barely having time to think, Cobra knew this was his time to strike. He quickly jumped toward the soldier and tackled him. The bow dropped out of his hands as he fell to the ground. Cobra landed on top of him. The soldier yelled out with a gasp of pain. He didn't even try to fight back as Cobra was much heavier, and there was no way he would be able to beat him in a fight.

"I'm sorry," the other soldier said to his comrade. It was clear he was going to be doing what he could to help this young lady, even if it meant risking his job.

Marc-Claude walked to the door and into the shop. "Where is the carriage with the medicine? We don't have much time."

"Right this way." The soldier led them through the shop and out the entry door. The carriage was out front. The soldier quickly got to work unlocking the back. "We must hurry. A whole troop left not long ago, looking for the fugitive. We stayed behind to gather the stolen supplies from the shop. I'm not sure when they'll be back."

The doors opened, and Marc-Claude could see the vast amount of supplies and weapons stashed within the carriage. He wasted no time in climbing in the back and looking through the supplies. If it was another time, he would have enjoyed searching through this inventory and possibly helping himself to some. But this time was different.

His sister's health was the only thing his mind was preoccupied with.

The soldier looked around the carriage and listened carefully. He was nervous thinking about the others returning. "You must hurry."

Marc-Claude was looking frantically through a wooden crate. Thankfully it wasn't long before he pulled out a small bottle. "Got it!" he exclaimed. He quickly stood and jumped from the carriage.

At this point Cobra came from the shop carrying Adrienne in his arms. She was conscious.

"Where's the other soldier?" Marc-Claude asked.

"I tied him up," Cobra said calmly. "He shouldn't be gettin' loose either."

Marc-Claude turned to the soldier with them. "We greatly appreciate your help, mate. But are you going to be in some sort of trouble when the others come back?"

"Ahh," he said, brushing his hand aside. "Happy to help with the young lady. Hopefully I can convince my partner to keep it quiet. We'll see."

Marc-Claude smiled slightly. "Much appreciated, my friend."

The soldier and Cobra caught each other's eye. The situation became awkward. It was like the soldier didn't know what to say to him in that moment. Cobra put on his tough look again. He tried to speak angrily. "I hope you know, I won't be coming back."

The soldier nodded and shrugged casually. "I figured as much." He rubbed the back of his neck as he looked off to the side. "But... uh... thank you for helping these folks. After what I went through with my son, I wouldn't want anyone else going through that."

Cobra said nothing in response, but on the inside, he was grateful to know this man was letting him go.

Marc-Claude interrupted. "Come, Cobra, take her to the woods. We'll give her the medicine and then get her to the ship."

Cobra didn't object but was happy to follow Marc-Claude if it meant helping this young lady... and escaping the Empire.

※

The three of them left the area of Cobra's shop and went a few hundred yards into the woods nearby. They took time to administer the medicine to Adrienne. Almost instantly it seemed to have an effect. Her mind was clearer, and she felt better. This encouraged Marc-Claude and made him feel motivated to get back to the boat. His plan was to get her back home as fast as he could. She lived with one of their brothers in the southeastern portion of the Empire. Marc-Claude planned to go south around Mendolon and Grimdolon, and then turn north toward the southern region of the Empire.

Overall, he had come to terms that Adrienne's health was failing. Sadly, her days were numbered, and a funeral would be in the near future. For the past six months Adrienne's health had seemed to be stable, and Marc-Claude had hoped there was no threat of the disease taking effect on this trip. Unfortunately for them the disease struck, and she was bearing the effects of this dreaded sickness.

The disease had no official name. It was rare but well-known. Some called it the slow killer; others called it the fade of despair. Most commonly Marc-Claude heard the term, "the spinal death." This was rooted in the idea that it first affected one's spine, placing an actual sickness within it. The disease would eventually cause paralysis of the legs and affect other nerves in the end. There were other effects along the way, including the random loss of consciousness and a weak immune system. Adrienne had been affected since she was young. At first the effects were mild, but six years ago the symptoms started to noticeably get worse. All the family had been notified and were aware that time was short.

They arrived back at the boat. In Marc-Claude's inner chambers there were two beds. Adrienne was placed comfortably on one of them. Marc-Claude and Cobra quickly got to work on getting the boat set to sail. Cobra proved to be a great help with all the work. He had spent a little time on the seas and was familiar with the ins and outs of navigating a boat.

Marc-Claude took his place at the wheel and the boat drifted through the dark of night, out to sea. The sea was rough and fought against them, but they were able to persevere and get the boat going in the right direction. As they were moving along, Cobra went to check on Adrienne one last time. While he was carrying her from the boat to the shop and then back again, Marc-Claude had told him much about Adrienne and her general kindness and love. Through all of this Cobra had naturally grown in his affection and concern for her. A part of him felt like she was his responsibility as well.

Cobra climbed the steps toward the helm. Marc-Claude saw him approaching, and he knew he had checked on her recently. "How is she?" he asked, not taking his eyes off the sea.

"Yeah, she's fine, sleeping. I think the medicine's still working."

"Good. Maybe we can give her a little more after she wakes up." Cobra said nothing, but simply took a seat beside Marc-Claude.

Neither of the men spoke for close to an hour. The sea drifted along, and Marc-Claude steered the boat, fighting with the winds. Cobra's mind glided between thinking about his shop to thinking what would come next for him. He always knew this day would come, but now that it was here, he felt lost. He had no plans. All that mattered was the moment.

Marc-Claude looked down and saw Cobra sitting, thinking to himself. He decided to break the silence. "Sounds like you'd gotten yourself into some deep trouble, mate."

"Yeah, I knew it would come someday," he said dejectedly.

"So... you were in the business of harboring stolen materials?"

Cobra shrugged. "Well, sort of. That was my tattoo shop. I had a good business going, but I got to where I would keep things for friends. They would pay me, and others then wanted to do the same. My shop is kind of blocked by the mountains, so a lot of the authorities don't come looking around. I should have said no a long time ago, but things got out of control. It ruined my business in the end."

Marc-Claude chuckled. "Well, I guess it wasn't the smartest plan after all."

"What's that supposed to mean?" Cobra said, instantly getting angry, triggered by the word 'smartest.'

This surprised Marc-Claude. "Whoa, calm yourself, mate, I was just making conversation."

Cobra felt instantly ashamed for letting his anger get the best of him. "Yeah, sorry. I'm grateful for you letting me tag along. I had to get away from them people."

"So, what is your plan anyway?" Marc-Claude said, changing the subject.

He buried his head in his lap. "I got no plans. I was hoping..."

Marc-Claude interrupted. "Hey, I can't hear you, speak up. Hold your head up."

He lifted his head. "Sorry, I don't know what to do. I was trying to escape when you came along."

"Were you thinking about stealing my boat?" Marc-Claude said with a smile. Cobra didn't know what to say, but simply blushed. Marc-Claude continued with a chuckle in his voice. "That's all right, mate. No bother. Just right now, I'm greatly thankful you came along. With the help you gave to my sister, I don't know how to repay you."

Cobra smiled and stood to his feet. He was grateful to be accepted so suddenly. This wasn't always the case for him. "Well, maybe I could just sail with you for a while as I figure everything out."

"Sure, stay as long as you like."

"Many thanks."

≈≈

As the sun was coming up over the horizon, Marc-Claude let Cobra take the wheel as he wanted to see Adrienne himself. Cobra had checked on her a number of times through the night. Usually he had found her asleep. But this last time she was stirring, and Cobra said she was asking for Marc-Claude. He wasted no time in descending the steps and, as quietly as he could, entering her room.

Instinctively he removed his bandana. He tended to do this at times when he felt sincere. He brushed his dark hair to the side, trying to get it somewhat in order.

"Hello, Marc-Claude," Adrienne said quietly, seeing him enter. She was lying in bed. Even though the room was a bit warm, she was covered with a blanket. Her head was resting comfortably on a pillow.

"How are you feeling, sis?"

"I've been better. The medicine did help me sleep through the night." She shifted her body.

"Anything you need? Anything I could get you?"

She thought for a moment. "Maybe a few musicians to help calm my nerves would be great," she said, jesting.

"I'll get right on that."

Marc-Claude brought a chair close. Adrienne pulled one of her hands out from under the covers. As he sat down, he reached out with both of his hands and held hers. He leaned in close to her. "What do you think is happening with the illness?"

She looked at him sincerely. Tears started to form in her eyes as she thought about what she was going to say. She spoke in complete honesty. "I think this is the beginning of the end."

Her brother nodded in return, knowing this was probably the case. He took a deep breath before speaking again. "I hate that we couldn't have gone longer, or even done another voyage."

"It would have been fun," she paused to smile. "But I'm thankful for this time we had together. This trip has been more joyous than I could have even imagined."

"Me too... me too." In that moment any sadness he felt was drowned out by the recollection of the good memories they had had together.

"I hope I wasn't too much of a burden."

A dismissing look formed on his face. "No... no, don't be absurd. This trip wouldn't have been the same without you. I usually go alone. It was nice having you as a companion."

She smiled even bigger. "Before you know it, you'll have a whole crew."

"Don't count on it."

She chuckled. "Oh, one day you'll be sitting on a beach somewhere with a whole slew of characters."

A dismissing look formed on his face. "You make it sound like I'm going to be commandeering a group of scallywags and strange individuals."

"And you as their captain!"

All Marc-Claude could do was laugh at the suggestion.

The room quickly fell into silence as the two of them took in the moment. The boat rocked as it moved through the ocean. Marc-Claude laid his head on her shoulder. She patted his head gently as he rested.

Marc-Claude began to think of some of the memories growing up in the eastern region of the Empire. They had a good childhood. Their parents were well loved by their kids. They provided a stable home for them, and even though they weren't wealthy, they were never in great need or want. Marc-Claude and Adrienne spent much time playing adventures and games together. They fought on occasion, but for the most part they were inseparable as they were often out on a new adventure in their minds. Marc-Claude tended to get in trouble from time to time, but even then, he knew their parents didn't love them any less. Through it all they were a family and that would never change. They would face everything together.

"Marc-Claude," she said, breaking the silence.

"Yes?" he said curiously.

"Before I'm gone, there's something I want to tell you."

Quickly he put his head up. "No, Adrienne, don't talk like that. We still have time before the end. You are..."

"I know... I know," she said interrupting. "But, while we have this moment, there's something I just wanted to warn you of."

He was taken aback as this was completely not what he was expecting her to say. "Oh, go on."

She breathed deeply before looking straight into Marc-Claude's eyes. "Be careful in your pursuit of gold. I fear it will entrap you."

His eyes grew wide. "Ah, absurdity," he brushed his hand aside and smiled. "My little sister is the only one who can entrap my heart."

She smirked. "Oh, Marc-Claude, you're too kind, but in honesty, I'm worried about you. I'm glad you enjoy these journeys, but I just never want the love of gold, or money, to lure your heart in... take you in deep with desire... and lead you down a pit you can't escape."

"A pit... hmm... sounds like an adventure," he said, trying to make a joke.

"I'm serious. The love of money can lead you to all kinds of evil." She moved her body to face him more and sat up a little. There was an urgency on her face. "Please, just promise me that you'll be careful and not let this desire capture you, entrap you."

Marc-Claude shook his head, wondering where this sense of urgency came from. He tried to think of some way to object, but he looked back at the resolve on her face and knew there would be no way of talking her out of it. "I... I..." Marc-Claude stumbled over his words as he felt like a different part of him was taking over. It was hard to describe, but it was like an inner conscious was speaking, a greater part of himself. "I promise that... um... that riches won't trap me... like a pit. My heart will stay clear."

Adrienne took a deep breath, thankful to hear what he had said. She laid back down, feeling relieved. A weight had been lifted off of her. Marc-Claude could feel that his promise brought relief to her. He felt very odd about this, but he was thankful to see that her mind seemed at ease.

"Just rest now, just rest," he said softly to his sister. She closed her eyes and gradually drifted off to sleep.

6

The next three weeks passed quickly. Marc-Claude and Adrienne made it back to her home in the eastern part of the Empire. Cobra stayed with them through it all. Adrienne was taken to her oldest brother's home where she tried to recover. The other members of their family were contacted. Her parents and her younger sister had moved south a few years ago to the Forest of Saison and were initially difficult to notify of Adrienne's situation. Thankfully, Adrienne's oldest brother had a messenger that knew of their location and would occasionally travel in secret to meet with them. It took a while, but eventually all of their family members gathered, and they were able to meet with Adrienne before she passed away.

Her passing was free of pain. The family had plenty of limusfin to help lower the pain and lessen the symptoms. Each of her siblings and parents felt as if they were able to have ample time with her before she passed. It was bittersweet. They would greatly miss her and the inspiration she gave, yet they knew she was in more pain than she had let on. Now she was no longer suffering.

Adrienne's request was to be out on the sea when she died. Specifically, she wanted to be on Marc-Claude's boat, 'The Life-Time Journey.' Of course, this request was honored. She was on the boat for a day and half before quietly slipping away in an early morning hour as the sun was rising.

Marc-Claude knew of a small island thirty miles east of the Empire. It wasn't on any map he'd ever seen as the island was only eighty yards in length with a few trees scattered on it. The family agreed it would be the perfect place to bury their sweet Adrienne.

Currently, a few dozen family and friends stood around her grave, taking time to remember her. Before she passed, she asked if Marc-Claude could say a few words at her memorial. For anyone else in the world he'd probably would've said no, but for Adrienne he didn't think twice. Standing in the middle of the island in the midst of everyone he took a minute to gather himself. His father had already given an inspirational message about life and eternity and in a way, nothing else needed to be said, but Marc-Claude would honor his sister's wishes. Many were worried about him doing this speech as he could often be unpredictable.

"Are you sure you can do this?" Cobra whispered to him as he was about to walk in front of everyone.

"We'll see," he responded.

His mother walked over to him. "Now's the time," she said quietly.

Timidly, Marc-Claude walked to the front of the group. All eyes were focused in on him. He cleared his throat before getting started. "So, ... um... we are gathered here on this lovely day to..." He was interrupted by the subtle sound of thunder in the distance. "Oh," Marc-Claude said, surprised. The crowd chuckled at the irony of it. Marc-Claude began laughing as well. This made others laugh in return. It was a helpful moment that lessened any tension in the air.

Eventually when things calmed, Marc-Claude relaxed and decided to speak more from the heart. A smile formed on his face as he began. "What can I say about Adrienne? I know we all loved her and were immensely grateful for the joy she brought to our lives." Many in the crowd nodded. "And, oh, I wish you could have seen her on this trip. She enjoyed the seas and felt alive on the water. It was an adventure for her, and she loved hearing about my exploits. Like a few weeks ago, I found this treasure chest before a group of pirates could. I hid away and threw coins at them. It was great. They didn't know where they were coming from... and, oh I'm so clever ... eventually they started fighting among themselves and..."

Marc-Claude stopped as he looked at everyone's faces. Seeing their puzzled looks, he knew he'd gotten off track. "Sorry," he said under his breath.

He continued speaking from the heart. "What I meant to say is that Adrienne made everything better. Whether it was retelling an adventure or simply enjoying our time on the sea. Wherever we were and whatever we were doing, she brought it to life and helped me to see that life wasn't about our triumphs as much as it was about the people in it. She lived life to the fullest and helped others to do the same."

His mind went blank for a moment. Silence fell over the crowd. Marc-Claude looked around and saw some had tears in their eyes. He quickly regathered his thoughts and kept going. "So, that is one of the best lessons we can take from her life. Like Adrienne, we can make this world a better place. We can help touch everything we come in contact with and make it better. Just like how she made this world a better place." Marc-Claude was a little surprised about the words coming out of his mouth. He'd never spoken at a funeral before. He was amazed at how the words flowed.

He felt pleased with himself, but he knew he had to wrap it up before he got off track again. "And... uh... I just want to say, 'Long-live the memory of Adrienne, our beloved sister... daughter... and friend.'"

There was a moment of silence before Marc-Claude's dad started slowly clapping. Others in the crowd joined in. Marc-Claude's mom was standing close by, and she threw her arms around him. "That was wonderful, oh, so good, my boy."

One of Marc-Claude's brothers walked up and slapped him on the back. "Wow, that was really surprising. You actually gave a good speech, and everyone understood it. It was pleasant and kind too. Crazy!"

"Um... thanks," Marc-Claude said, not sure how to take that compliment.

Cobra was off to the side crying. The brief memories he had with Adrienne really touched him, and now his emotions were getting the best of him.

The family and friends took their time saying goodbye and enjoying each other's company. They had come on six different boats, and many hadn't seen each other for years. Lots of hugs and stories were exchanged. Particularly many shared stories of Adrienne and how she was an inspiration to them. More tears were shed along the way.

After a while Marc-Claude's youngest sister Clara walked up. "That was a good speech you gave, Marc-Claude."

"Thank you, sis. How are you holding up?"

"I'm fine. Glad she's not suffering any longer."

"Yeah," he responded. He knew Clara was telling the truth. She was a strong individual that rarely let her guard down emotionally. Others would often characterize her as resilient.

She turned around briefly and looked behind her before turning back. "I met your friend Cobra. Had a good talk with him."

"Oh yeah? What do you think?"

She nodded and gave a half smile. "I like him. It sounds like he's got nowhere to go and no plans for the future."

"Yes... he's gotten himself in some trouble lately."

Clara leaned in. "Well, you should like him then."

Marc-Claude laughed. "I think he's a good mate. Not real bright, but I'm thankful for his help with getting Adrienne her medicine."

"I guess you can use him for a crewman on 'The Journey.'

Marc-Claude got quiet suddenly and looked off to his side. A look of nervousness formed on his face. Clara could tell something was on his mind. "Marc-Claude? What's bothering you?"

He looked back at his sister. There was a hint of sadness in his voice as he spoke. "I don't think I can keep it."

"Your boat?" she said, speaking a little too loud. "But that's your boat! Even I remember how hard you worked for it. No, you can't get rid of it."

"I've got to. Too many memories. I'll think of her every time I board and set sail. I fear those memories will become too painful over time."

Clara shook her head. "Don't you want to remember her?"

"Of course I want to remember her. I'll never forget her, but I can't hang on to the past either. I don't want my mind to always go to the day she died. There was so much more to her life that I want to remember as well. Selling the boat will actually help me remember her more fully."

"Are you sure? Could I talk you out of it?"

"No, it's what I've got to do. I think it's the only way I can heal. I got to let her go."

Clara knew there was nothing else to say. Besides that, she thought maybe Marc-Claude was right. He wouldn't be able to heal properly if he was constantly recounting memories of her death. Thinking about it more, she became proud of her brother for thinking through this situation very maturely. That wasn't something he always did.

The crowd was startled as rain started to fall heavily on them. Many scattered and ran back to their boats.

◈

The next day Marc-Claude and Cobra were again out to sea. This time it was just the two of them. Their goodbyes with the others had been abrupt because of the storm. Marc-Claude wasn't sure when he'd see his family again, but hopefully one day he would make it over to the Forest of Saison specifically to see where his parents and younger sister now lived. It was on his list of places he'd like to explore. Talk of mystery surrounded it.

The day was beautiful, and the skies were clear. Cobra was busy fixing a loose board on the deck. When he learned Marc-Claude was selling the ship, he took it upon himself to make sure it was in top shape. He cleaned the deck, replaced some of the nails, and fixed anything that was broken or in need of repair. Marc-Claude was pleased with his work. Though he was used to traveling alone, he could see how it would be beneficial to keep him on board for an expedition or two.

Marc-Claude contemplated where he could sell his boat. He would need to quickly buy another one, so maybe someone would take a straight trade for a different vessel. Maybe even downsizing and getting a little bit of extra money wouldn't be a bad thing either. There were a number of possibilities that went through his mind, but either way, there was no doubt that selling this vessel was the right course of action.

Cobra came up the steps toward the helm. "I think I fixed that last board."

"Oh, yeah, thanks. I didn't even realize it was loose."

He walked behind Marc-Claude and put his tools away. He then walked back toward him. "So, what's the plan? I think I heard ya speak to your sister about it."

"Yes," Marc-Claude said under his breath, not feeling like talking but knowing that he needed to communicate his plans. "As you know we're going to first sell this boat or trade it in. Whatever seems like the best plan at the time. Then I want to check out this cave I heard about in a southern land."

"Do you think there's treasure in it?"

"I don't know, but it's worth exploring."

"Hmm..." Cobra scratched the back of his head. "And what do you think you'll do after that?"

Marc-Claude looked over at him with a half-smile. "I don't know. We'll see where the wind takes us."

Slowly, Cobra smiled back in return. He was thankful Marc-Claude said nothing about when he would need to leave. There was nowhere for him to go, so he was beyond grateful that Marc-Claude allowed him to be aboard the ship. He figured he wouldn't ask anything about him needing to leave. He didn't want to approach the topic or even put the thought in Marc-Claude's mind.

But with Cobra, something else was on his mind. A question he couldn't shake. "Marc-Claude, there is something I want to know."

"Okay, go ahead."

"When Adrienne was with us, you know how I'd go to check on her? You remember that?"

Marc-Claude rolled his eyes. "Of course, I remember that. You have been with me for the last three weeks."

"Sometimes, I'd go in there and I'd see she was holding onto a green emerald."

"Yeah. That's right."

He rubbed the back of his head. "I'm just curious where that came from."

Marc-Claude bit his lip as he thought about the memory of it. A part of him was saddened thinking about that jewel. "I got it from a treasure chest in a cave. It was actually the day before we met you. Right away she took a liking to it and said it would remind her of this journey. I told her she could have it."

"That was nice of you. It was probably worth a lot of money."

"Don't remind me."

Cobra blushed, feeling slightly embarrassed asking him these questions, but he still had another on his mind. He looked out to sea and asked his last question. "Well, what are you going to do with it, now that Adrienne's gone?"

Marc-Claude waited a moment or two before answering. The memories flashed through his mind. It was more painful thinking back on that day of her burial than it was being there in person. He began to miss her. Looking back at Cobra, he spoke directly. "I buried it with her, mate. I couldn't ever look on that jewel again without thinking of her. When I found that jewel, it felt like my heart's desire. But then seeing her with it and seeing her enjoying its beauty, I knew that it would be forever hers. I'll never look on it again and it'll stay with her always."

Cobra found this interesting and sentimental. There were more questions he wanted to ask, but he thought twice. It may be difficult for Marc-Claude to relive them. And besides that, if he was with Marc-Claude for a little longer, then there would be plenty of time to talk with him more about his sister.

He started to walk down the stairs. "Uh, Marc-Claude, I'm going to go down to the deck and check some of the rails and make sure it's good to sell. If you think of something else that needs to be done, please just tell me."

"Many thanks, mate," he said, not taking his eyes off the sea.

Cobra continued to walk down the steps. Reaching the deck, Marc-Claude thought he might give him one important reminder. "Hey, Cobra!"

"What is it?"

"You may want to put on a hat. You're going to get a terrible sunburn out here on the top of your head."

"Oh, I don't think so. I should be fine."

"Just don't want you getting burned, mate."

Marc-Claude looked back out to sea as the boat glided through the water. Out on the horizon there were nothing but blue skies and endless oceans yet to be explored.

About the Author

Tony Myers is a fiction author. He enjoys finding creative ways to illustrate and communicate truth. He and his wife, Charity, currently live in Waterloo, IA with their four kids. Visit his website at www.tonymyers.net.

Also, check out these other titles from Tony Myers. Available at most online book distributors.

Singleton

"This book has a twist you never saw coming. It has characters that you become emotionally attached to. The ending is just an absolute display of high morals."

    - B&N reviewer

Stealing the Magic

"Myers delivers a page-turning mystery that grips the reader with its relatable characters and compelling plot. A taut, satisfying story for young suspense lovers and seasoned readers alike."

    - Pamela Crane, literary judge and author of the award-winning *A Secondhand Life*

The Valley and The Shadow

"My wife and I bought two of these books, and we read them in less than 24hrs - we couldn't put them down. Tony did a great job of taking a very tough topic and helped provide hope for those in need. Highly recommend this book to those who are going through a valley in their own life right now."

    - David Wilson

The Beauty of a Beast

"Nothing captivates an audience of all ages like knights, princesses, dragons, beasts, and courage. The Beauty of a Beast proves that true. It is one of those books with a very familiar plot line, but an extreme twist at the end. While reading it, I was on the edge of my seat. Tony Myers does a fantastic job of capturing his audience's attention and not letting it go till the end of the book. Each character comes alive with every paragraph as their world becomes as real as ours. This clean, mind-blowing, nail-biting, easy-to-read book will have you eagerly turning each page and then anxiously anticipating the next book!"

- Aaron Moore

Made in the USA
Monee, IL
13 March 2023